For my family, who have indulged my imagination, and have
accommodated my numerous schemes for too many years to count.

Lulio

A novel by B.H. Cameron

Hinchinbrooke

Chapter 1

John Portillo greeted the day with the shrill sound of his clock radio in a shroud of pitch-dark blackness. Morning did not kiss him gently on the cheek and say hello – it grabbed him like a drill sergeant, assaulting his senses as it has six days a week for twenty years. In the city that never sleeps, he was lucky to even get the occasional cat nap.

The first frost which arrived with the fall leaves soaked deep into his marrow with a fiery ache. Struggling to pull his arm out from under the pillows supporting his wife's head, he let the motion of his roll to the side pull his limb along. Until he had achieved the necessary momentum to rise to a sitting position, he floundered in the snarl of sheets like the hapless sea creatures he would see washed up on the Jersey shores as a kid. *They always said the plumbing was the first thing to go, but they were wrong. Dignity is the first thing you lose, even before the hair on your scalp suddenly relocates to your nose and ears.*

His wife had become so used to this routine that she did not bother to stir. Nothing between the hours of eleven and seven – save for the rusted civil defense siren at the end of the street sounding off – would have elicited so much as a dismissive yawn and a roll over to the other side. He envied her but did not begrudge her this. He knew he was a pain in the ass to live with – she had told him only so much on more than one. She had given up enough as it was. So had he, but the shared sacrifices were made mostly of his volition. She was merely the pliant and loyal sidekick. Why bother to take away this one meager creature comfort?

Slowly, he rose to his feet, and began what was his variation of the daily ritual - a quick shower, a shave - every other day – followed by turning on the coffee maker for his still sleeping wife.

No time to wait for it to run through.

The late fall air was particularly crisp, and it felt heavy on his lungs. His cough produced a rattle of phlegm in his chest that he could not rid himself of, although, as the day wore on, it always would seem to pass.

He would grab some eggs and toast from an all-night diner along the way to the L train at Nostrand Avenue. A little place run by a Greek named George, or Gus, or Peter – he could never keep it straight. He would get his coffee, cream, and no sugar, followed by two poached eggs, some thick bacon, and toast, lightly browned with generous slabs of butter. He could not stand margarine – not the taste so much, but the idea of it. More specifically, it was the idea of people telling him that he should switch to it.

Once he had finished his meal, and had downed another cup of coffee, he would get on the next available train that would take him from his little corner of Brooklyn, over to the Jamaica station, then onto the ride straight into Manhattan – Kew Gardens, Forest Hills, Woodside, and finally, Penn Station. Once there, he would jump onto either the Number 2 or the Number 3 over to Wall Street. The odd time that he was running late, he would have been tempted to flag a taxi, but with the construction on Broadway at Fulton going on like it was, it would easily take twice as long, and cost far more.

About two or three blocks north of the station, on the edges of Tribeca, he operates a simple newsstand that he had inherited from his father, and his father before him. It was a small shack by the standards of his downtown competitors, but big enough to accommodate a counter and a few crowded racks for newspapers, magazines, snack foods and chewing gums. The traditional hunter green exterior was faded to a dull tone, like the worn slate of a children's chalkboard. Beyond some minor conveniences that he had added since he took over, it had changed little over the years, save for the more risqué publications that no longer needed to be sheathed in a brown paper wrapping.

He had arrived within minutes of the newspaper vans dropping off their day's editions – the Times, The Sun, the Journal, and a dozen more that would all be snapped up well before noon. Although he was slightly off the beaten path, the stand was still close enough to Wall Street and the action that there was a healthy enough clientele. Besides, as his father, and grandfather, had reasoned, the small dip in traffic was more than compensated for by the lower rents and licensing fees.

Within the five boroughs, and beyond, there are thousands of John Portillos. Whether you are inclined to call them the salt of the earth, the backbone of the nation, or the silent majority, they exist, and they ungrudgingly provide the grease that keeps the machinery of society going. That, however, is not the purpose of this tale. As honorable and worthy as it may be, Portillo's story is one that will have to wait until another day. Our attentions, instead, drift toward the well-dressed man who climbs out of the back of a large black Cadillac that pulled up to his newspaper stand.

Well-coiffed and impeccably groomed, the man wore a tan colored camel hair coat that all but concealed a black, pinstriped suit. Both the brushed cotton shirt and the silk tie were a fine shade of muted pink, so much the style of the self-proclaimed 'Masters of the Universe' that made their living in and around the New York Stock Exchange.

"Good morning, and what a lovely morning it is," the man exclaimed, as he puffed out his chest like a rooster pacing the yard among the scratching hens.

"It's cold," answered Portillo, matter-of-factly. He rubbed his hands briskly, more to illustrate his point than to warm them up. He was not fond of such people. They were, in his experience, rich and obnoxious, and would not recognize hard work if it fell across the hood of their sports car and pounded its fist against the windshield. On the other hand, they were his bread and butter, and without their business, he would not have a business himself. What made him feel better was the fact that he was taking money, albeit small amounts, from people he judged to be picking the pockets of the public writ large. Every issue of the Journal, and the casual "keep the change" aside felt like he was sticking it to the man. Whether or not you could interpret it as such was irrelevant – on those long and bitterly cold days, he took whatever inspiration you could.

"It's bound to warm up soon," countered the man, in a voice that Portillo thought to be a little too cheery for this time of day.

He shook his head in a gentle disagreement. "For you, maybe, when you get back in your car, but I'm gonna be freezin' my balls out here for a few more hours." *These guys were all the same – my life is good, so it must be good for everybody else.*

The stranger smiled kindly, but Portillo could not help but see a degree of pity and condescension behind it. "I'll take a Journal," he said.

Portillo had not finished setting up his stacks yet, so he took a pair of scissors to cut a bundle of papers to get at one. "Fresh as they come," he said as he handed it to him. "Mind the ink. It rubs off the first three of four in each bundle."

"Thanks," said the man politely. "Well, I can't start my day without my news fix. But what am I saying? You must be on top of everything going on in the world with a place like this."

Portillo shrugged. In fact, he never touched any of the papers, except to set them up and parcel them out to his customers. Like his father and grandfather before him, he read only books – fiction or not, it did not matter. His father had explained long ago that keeping up with the constant flood of changing news would drive you mad. You would end up knowing the price of everything and the value of nothing at all.

For him, the news need only tell you what was done, where it was done, and who did it. As a people watcher – through inclination as much as through circumstance – he had wanted to understand why things happened. Literature examined the entire panoply of human emotion, and human absurdity. It gave the depth and context that made more sense than whatever expert of the day was picked for their insights. His books were his Rosetta Stone for a world that became more and more incomprehensible by the day.

It may have made him less susceptible to the mental vertigo of the global news cycle, but it did have some drawbacks. It was expected that a purveyor of news and information would have some sense of goings-on – at the very least, be able to come up with some pithy comment. As Portillo never engaged in such talk, there was an assumption that he lacked both the capacity and curiosity to be engaged. It was not uncommon for people to infer that he lacked some cognitive agility because he did not know who got voted off what reality television show, even though he might be holding a copy of Joyce's "Ulysses" or Cervantes "Don Quixote" in plain view.

He looked at the man, who casually opened the paper, giving a brief scan of the pages. "You know," he added, without any hint of curiosity. "I don't see many of your kind down here."

"My kind?" asked the man. "Whaddya mean by 'my kind'?"

"Oh no, not that," laughed Portillo, pointing at his customer's attire. "I mean camel hair coat, big car. You guys usually send someone down to get them for ya."

The man laughed a little. "Maybe I want to remember my roots, and how hard I had to work to get this coat and that car," he said, only realizing after the words had passed his lips that his comments were too trite, too clever by half.

Portillo shook his head dismissively, as he bent over to cut the strings on the other newspaper bundles. Setting the bar for these guys was a bit like adjusting a limbo bar after each successful round, and this guy did not appear to be a stranger to crawling on his belly.

"Hard work? Yeah, like that'll do it. Look, I work 12-hour days, 5 or 6 days a week, whether it's nice or shitty outside, and I own my own stand. I've been doin' this job for almost fifteen years, and I took over from my old man who did it for thirty. If anybody outta my neighborhood's gonna make it big, it would be me – and I ain't holdin' my breath for it."

The man grinned. "It's not how hard you work," he said. "The secret's how smart you work…In the end, you gotta believe in yourself. Doesn't matter what people say, or what life throws at you. It's all about confidence to see and seize opportunity."

Portillo had done his best to ignore the overtones. He had a low enough toleration at the best of times – close to zero, in fact. Besides, it was too early and too cold to be treated to some trite and naïve Horatio Alger, up by the bootstraps, story of perseverance and inspiration. In his experience, these tales were less an instruction on how to succeed than simply a sanitized re-telling of how someone made their money. He was not sure if it was to provide some feel-good message to the masses, or to cover up the secret to getting the good life, lest every working stiff on the street try to home in on their territory. Maybe it was a little of both.

"Buddy," he said, "you are so full of shit. I think you are one of these college punks comin' down here to yank my chain. I work hard, and I work honest. I do right by my family and my church. There isn't a goddamn thing you can tell me about bein' successful."

The man smiled thoughtfully and lowered his head for a moment. He knew that he was coming close to crossing the line.

"You're a decent guy," he began. "Kind of remind me of my father, so I'm going to tell you how I got here – no lies, no bullshit. Everybody's story is different, but I grew up in Queens and now I live in Manhattan. If you wanna know how I did it, I got the time to tell you."

These guys were all grade 'A' egotists, and egotists liked nothing more than talking about themselves. If you did not come out and offer them a platform to pontificate, they would find some verbal sleight of hand that gave them the chance. Regardless, it was turning out to be a slow morning, and the old saying about giving a fool enough rope seemed *a propos*. When a big shot feels the need to justify themselves before a relative nobody, it can only mean that he has a guilty conscience. His book may have been more intellectually edifying but listening to this fellow might prove to be far more entertaining.

Not wanting to feed the beast by appearing too interested, Portillo shrugged with some feigned indifference. "Well, I ain't goin' anywhere, and there's nothin' on the radio, so suit yourself," he said, as he offered up a stool and a cup of coffee from his thermos.

Chapter 2

Raimundo Lulio de Vega came into the world kicking and screaming. His mother, having a relatively short labor, was grateful for her baby's eagerness to come into the world. His father, sensing an innate feistiness and energy in his infant son, was extremely pleased and proud. They both had the sense that this child would be different – not necessarily unique, but that there was something of a sense of predetermination that followed them home from the hospital.

Predetermination. That concept sat well with Ray's father, as it applied equally to every situation where the boy was concerned. It explained the initial hope and promise, as much as the eventual disappointment and disillusionment. He still argued that things went off track when he agreed that his son would be named after his wife's youngest brother. She, being a devout and pious woman, had reasoned that it was fated that the combination of the names coincided with a great Saint of the Church and of the Spanish people, and that the Lord surely had a plan in place for the child. He, on the other hand, being more familiar with the exploits of his brother-in-law than a medieval priest, had felt a deep sense of foreboding for precisely the same reason.

Max Lulio was a first-generation New Yorker. His parents had left their home outside San Juan, like so many of their compatriots, after the War. The only problem with life in Puerto Rico was that one could scarcely afford to live it well. Many, like Max's parents, had decided that since the Constitution extended "Life, liberty, and the pursuit of happiness" to them as well, they would pursue it all the way to the eastern seaboard. As he remembered, life in those days was brutally simple. It boiled down to three things – hard work, fear of God, and respect for the law. Anything beyond that was the concern of others, and a needless distraction for a young family struggling to gain a foothold in a new land and a big city.

Max had his moments of weakness, however, like any pubescent lad amid the temptations of rock and roll, and teenage infatuations. Nevertheless, he had been clever enough to turn some of his inclinations to his advantage. A love of hot rods brought him to apprentice in a garage, which, in turn, secured him a decent position as a mechanic with the transit authority, and all the benefits that a union job afforded. He was also shrewd enough to know when to make a change. Just when his back and legs were getting stiff, and when a mechanic had to be more of a computer technician than anything else, Max made his way into a second career of driving the buses that he had serviced all these years.

Pragmatism had marked the elder Lulio's life so much so that it had become a religion and a calling. And, like every zealot, it was not enough to live by a strict code. One had to take the gospel forward to the unwashed masses - to proselytize to those who had ears to hear, as well as the patience to endure.

The discussions between him and his brother-in-law, Raimundo, for example, were the stuff of legend. His wife Roberta's youngest brother was the apple of his parents' eyes, and the bane of Max's existence. He had taken over what had been a reasonably profitable family grocery and had slowly but surely run it into the ground. After leaving New York, and tramping around the South West, he had settled down to a sales position of some sort in Tempe. That, of course, had been ten years ago, by the date of the last Christmas card that had found its way to the Lulio home. While Roberta, or Bertie as she was known, sincerely thought that the pain of their parents' death prevented him from making contact, Max asserted it was more likely to have been the pain associated with his own death, speculating that his brother-in-law's forwarding address was most likely in a concrete supporting beam in one of Las Vegas' newer casinos.

It was not that he hated Raimundo. He loved Bertie and respected her parents, so his natural inclination was to try to like him. Whether or not his definition of trying had risen to the exacting standards of his wife's *familia* was, every now and then, the subject of a debate in the Lulio household. Nevertheless, in his mind, he had given his brother-in-law every conceivable consideration. Max disliked the flashy style of dress, what he saw as insincere pretentions, and the almost oblivious attitude he had to how his choices impacted his own family. Max saw a selfish and self-involved schemer who left nothing but a stack of bills and shattered dreams in his wake.

One could only speculate as to why Max's relationship with his son would be cursed by Bertie's insistence on naming him Raimundo. Max, of course, wondered with an equal amount of mental effort, why his wife had made such a demand, and made it unconditional. He would never say it aloud, but the decision had put him on the defensive from day one. People grew into their names, he would argue. It was only a matter of when, and not if.

Bertie, of course, was quick to counter that she knew of a great many men named Max who were not grumpy and obstinate to a fault. Indeed, she would point out, that she had an Uncle Max who happened to be a jovial and out-going gentleman. She would then follow up with asking when he intended to grow into his name. This line of logic, however, did nothing to help matters between the senior and junior Mister Lulios.

Ray did not turn out exactly like his ne'er do well uncle, but neither was he completely free of the character traits his namesake was so known for. It was the worst of both worlds for Max, as he was similar enough to get on his nerves, but different enough that no one else would notice. People often allow for the fact that youth and indiscretion go hand in hand. Even if Max could call his son on some act or perceived failure, most observers would have been prepared to give Ray the benefit of the doubt, and instead, chide him for being 'too hard' on the poor boy.

One did have to give Max his due, for he did try, albeit in his own way. He attempted to share his passions, baseball, and classic cars, with his son. There were the dozens of matinee games at Shea Stadium, and even more trips to a local garage owned by one of Max's friends. For a man schooled in the old ways, these activities were as close as he was going to come to baring his soul. He interpreted his actions as a sort of gift – an emotional inheritance that he could bequeath to Ray. For him, it was the latter-day equivalent of passing on legends and folk tales to the younger tribe members gathered around the campfire. He was not a businessman, or a scholar. He was a grease monkey, and the most intimate thing he could give his son was his tools, and a passion for using them.

Unfortunately, these were not some ecumenical cultural talismans. They were the clear and obvious predilections of a single man. This was an attempt to begat a man in his own image, after the fact. What Max did not understand was that despite his passions, there was nothing sacred about the subjective. Like so many others, before and after, he would become disillusioned when the man he was helping his son become was not the spitting image of himself.

Ray learned quickly that feigning interest was the best policy. Go along to get along. And, over the years, Max began to believe that he might have gotten through to his son. It was not until Ray had well entered puberty when Max knew what his son really thought. He overheard his son talking to his friends about these trips, which he sarcastically referred to as 'pop-flys and fly-wheels.' That is why Max had refused to admit he gave up on Ray. In his mind, Ray had given up on him first.

Nevertheless, Max did not abandon his son. He still worked hard to provide a roof over his head and food on the table. Even if he did not necessarily do it for some familial emotion, he did it out of a sense of duty. Having his son living on the streets and scrounging for a living was more a reflection on him as a father, than it would have been on Ray. That, of course, was beyond the fallout that such a move would have on his marriage. If Ray were the first to be shown the door, Max was confident that his wife would make him the second.

And so, the relationship between the two Lulios resembled some Cold War standoff. Both were equally unhappy with the status quo, and would have done something about it, if it were not for the fact that either one could inflict damage on the other. Mutual assured destruction ruled the household, making them a nuclear family in every sense.

Ray did not know what he wanted in life, only what he did not want. He did not know what kind of man he wanted to be, but he knew that he did not want to be like his father. He knew he wanted success in life, but he did not know doing what. His only two criteria were that they involve some degree of fame and fortune, and that they conform to the path of least resistance. That was his defense when people accused him of being lazy and wanting something for nothing. He would counter that he expected to work for success – he was not naïve – but he did not want to work too hard to get it.

Max, having been weaned on motor oil, demanded to know how someone could win a race by riding the brakes, or not pushing the gas pedal to the floor. As persuasive as Ray could be in most instances, he never was able to explain away this paradox to his father's full and complete satisfaction.

He knew that hard work was not going to win the day. If that were the case, he would argue, why are day laborers not the wealthiest people in the neighborhood? Effort was important, but not as important as his father would assert. In this respect, Ray attempted to appease his father by observing that while Max worked twice as hard as his superiors, he would have been lucky to have earned half their salary. It was none too subtle a bit of sophistry that had some marginal success.

But what was the answer? Ray believed he had stumbled upon it. Newspapers and television stories were replete with the tales of billionaire investors who transcended the old, stuffy, Waspish stereotypes and lived life to the fullest. Just as Washington was called Hollywood for ugly people, Wall Street offered the lifestyle of a rock star for those too tone deaf to play a chord. Buy low, sell high, and buy a place in the Hamptons. Move cash from one pile to another and, voila, you had a yacht. Keep an eye on the pension funds of some union or association, and eventually you had enough for a wine tour of Provence.

But they were orgasmic moments of fantasy, over just as they were getting good. Self-awareness, or self-doubt, crept in and made Ray scramble for a fig leaf. The higher the payout, the greater the demands were. Maybe Max was right. Why would anybody just grab some guy off the street and give him a job that paid millions? Through high school, and now well into a business program at junior college, Ray struggled to come up with the answer to this challenge – his proverbial eureka moment. This was easier said than done. Instructors instructed, and inspiration was not mentioned anywhere in their collective bargaining agreement. Ray often wondered if interest and enthusiasm should not have been included as well.

Inspiration, however, is like love, or a missing set of car keys, in that it never shows itself until one stops looking for it. And so it was with Ray, and his eventual realization that, like his teachers, he was destined to just go through the motions. Then, like a gift from the heavens, came Robin St. John Roberts and his simple, yet powerful, message of hope.

It was there, among the endless collection of ads for sex chats and miracle absorbent dish rags, that he found this diamond in the rough.

"See beyond the ordinary – be beyond the ordinary." It was so succinct, and yet so completely profound.

This elegant and charismatic man, impeccably dressed, weaved purposely back and forth across an elaborate stage before an audience of thousands. His English accented voice kept up a staccato like pace, with a punctuated emphasis on words like 'empowerment', 'belief' and 'opportunity.' The presence of the man did not ask for polite consideration. It demanded attention and respect. His mannerisms were slightly exaggerated, but not grossly so. His animated physicality flowed so well that it was difficult to tell whether it was natural or slightly choreographed.

Snippets of this concert were dispersed intermittently with first person testimonials of men and women who had dreamed of, and achieved, lives less ordinary, courtesy of this great man and his message of liberation. All the while, along the bottom of the television screen, was printed a toll-free number, along with the logos of all the major credit cards. For nearly an hour, Ray remained fixated on this program, and the unrelenting rapid-fire barrage of profound observations and exhortations to action.

Through it all, Ray felt as though, by some magic, this man had been able to tap into his subconscious, extract every whim and desire, every passion and point of principle, and articulate these divinations in a way that he could never do – not to his father, not to anyone else. Roberts was right. All the criticism he had endured all this time – all the indifference – was just 'negative imprinting,' designed to undermine his self-image. After all, it was true what he said about it being easier to tear others down than to raise oneself up.

Ray had his eureka moment. *Of course! That's it! Dad is just jealous of my potential! The bitterness he is projecting simply masks the pain he feels for his own lost dreams. I have a chance at a life that he could only aspire to obtain. Instead of resenting him, I must embrace him – show him love and compassion. He needs to know that he has value in this world too.*

This epiphany made the whole father and son dynamic in the Lulio home make sense to him. It fit a pattern. It had a context. And the following evening, over dinner, Ray saw his big chance to finally put right this situation, to bridge this wide and deep emotional chasm between them.

"Dad," he began, "I saw something on TV last night that changed my life, and I want to share it with you."

Max scarcely looked up from his plate of food, not bothering to drop his fork. "You better not have run up the phone bill again. Those tarts charge after the first minute. Besides, you think any woman who looks like those on television would be sittin' at home talking to the likes of you?"

"I'm not talkin' about that," protested Ray. "This is serious. I saw something that is going to set my path to the future."

"How much?" asked his father, without missing a beat. *Did it not always come down to money – his money?*

"Max!" interjected Bertie. "Don't shoot him down like that! He's trying to get his life straightened out."

Mister Lulio stared silently at his son for a moment, his right eyebrow raised in a knowing look as he waited for a response to his question. *All right, son - here's your chance to prove the old man wrong.*

"Two hundred and fifty dollars…," Ray said quietly, sensing that he was walking into a trap of sorts.

"A-ha! And there it is!" Max shouted, pleased at his obvious vindication. "I knew there was a catch!"

"I'll pay you back. I promise," Ray said rather meekly.

"You don't even pay room and board – how are you going to pay me back for this?" argued Max. He was on a roll now. The moral high ground was his, and there was no reason to give it up yet. "Forget it. If you want that stuff so bad, you'll get off your ass and earn the money to buy it yourself!"

Max left the room, leaving his wife to make peace with Ray. It did not help. He felt like a condemned man refused an eleventh-hour reprieve. No future beyond that of a minimum wage slave, working like a mule until your back gives out. *How can you say you loved your son, but still wish that kind of life on him?*

"Ma, he just doesn't get it," protested Ray. "I thought a father was supposed to want better for his kids? I'm just trying to improve my life, that's all."

Bertie leaned in toward him, and extending her reach, she clasped his hands in hers. "Your father is a stubborn mule, and has more bad moods than good, but he's not a mean or cruel man – you know that. He's never missed a day of work where he wasn't truly sick, and he's never laid a hand on either one of us. You've never missed a meal or been without anything you really needed. And remember that he is paying for your tuition to go to college."

She squeezed his hands ever so slightly. "Remember that," she repeated.

After helping her wash up, Ray went down the hall to the closed door of his parents' room. It was quiet inside, but he knew his father was in there – reading a book, taking a nap, or just staring out the window. He was old school, and 'decompressing' meant stewing over what made you angry until it dulled your brain and made you just want to sleep. Ray was tempted to knock, and apologize, but he knew that in the attempt to explain himself, he would only stoke the furnace even hotter than it already was.

Thinking the better of it, he turned around and, heading to the living room and the front closet, he donned his wool overcoat, and headed out for a walk. Despite the differences in the two men, both needed peace and solitude to work through their feelings. Ray thought it best not to mention it, and Max tired of the pleasure of his victory.

Within a couple of weeks of that unpleasant evening, a large package, addressed to Ray, was delivered by courier, to the Lulio household. Bertie had signed for it and left it on the dining room table until the men came home.

"What is it?" asked Max, half out of curiosity, and the other half out of dread.

"I dunno," replied Ray, as he set the box on the dining room table and began to open it. He was no less surprised by the delivery than his father.

Inside was the entire Robin St. John Roberts DVD and workbook collection – the package that Ray had wanted to buy.

"So," said Max, with a self-satisfied tone. "You said you needed the money to buy that crap? I guess if you want something bad enough, you'll find a way to pay for it."

Bertie came in to see what was going on – her husband gloating over having taught their son a lesson in hard work and sacrifice, while Ray was busy ignoring him as he dove through the shipping box like a four year-old on Christmas Day.

Max smiled and walked out of the room. It was time. Stay long enough to hammer your point home, but not long enough to get drawn into whatever it was his son was eagerly rifling through. It would only serve to upset him over what he considered to be Ray's flighty and profligate nature.

Amid his glee, Ray raised his eyes ever so slightly, ensuring that his father had, indeed, left the room, then turned to his mother and whispered, "Thank you."

Missus Lulio smiled gently and said, "You're welcome." After a moment of introspection, however, her facial expression dimmed a bit. "You know, Ray, your father's not completely wrong."

"Whaddya mean?" he asked, more with surprise than with any sense of betrayal or disappointment. "Don't you believe in me? You bought this for me, didn't you?"

"Of course, I believe in you," she assured him. "And I understand that these things take time, but…"

With that, she leaned in and placed a gentle hand on his shoulder.

"…but," she continued, "at some point in time, you have to make good on all this talk, or at least try…Even if you fail, you still have to try."

Ray smiled knowingly. "Well," he replied, "I was saving this for later, but a recruiter came by the campus today. I was talking with him at the booth, and then he invited me to go for a coffee. Anyway, long story short - I have an interview next week."

"Really?" she exclaimed, finding such news to be an immediate validation. "Where? Doing what?"

"The man's name is Rob Bortelli," said Ray as he dug a business card out of his shirt pocket. "See, he works at Tuckner Wass, on Wall Street, Ma."

Missus Lulio was duly impressed, although Ray felt that she would have fussed had he said it was a sales job at a 'Big and Tall' clothing store. "I've heard of them," she said as she studied the embossed lettering on the card. "They have commercials on TV about saving money and investing. They are a pretty big place, aren't they?"

"Yeah, they are," he answered. "One of the biggest investment firms in the world. New York, London, Tokyo…they're all over the place. I was surprised that they were even looking around our school. Usually they don't hire anyone who didn't go to some Ivy League university and get an MBA. I think it's some kinda outreach into different communities."

"You don't think it's some public relations stunt?" asked Missus Lulio, clearly worried that her son might be led like an innocent to the slaughter.

Ray shrugged. "Ma, I don't care. I might not get the job, but even if I do, it's a job, and it pays well. I don't care why they hire me, so long as they do."

The notion had crossed his mind more than once that afternoon, that a venerable Wall Street investment bank was going 'slumming' to show that they were good corporate citizens. They could give him a meaningless job with no responsibilities, and low end pay, just so they could have a photo and story for next year's report to the shareholders. But the fellow who he had met with – Bortelli – had seemed genuine enough. He was a quiet and respectful guy who made Ray feel as though his chance of a position, and that said position was legitimate, were equally valid.

"Ma, I know I don't show it, but sometimes I have doubts," he explained. "Some of the stuff that people say to me – it really sticks, and a lot of it hurts…I guess what I am trying to say is that if I don't believe in myself, they won't believe in me either. I need to believe that, deep down, I deserve this job, and that getting it is a fulfillment of my destiny. If I let any doubt or negativity creep into my head, it won't happen.

"That's why I appreciate these DVD's more than you'll ever know. I need to get rid of all the negative thoughts and my fear, and that's exactly what this guy has done for so many others. Self-confidence is what it's about.

"I've got a week to get myself prepared for this interview, and this will help more than you know…I love you, Ma."

With that, Ray leaned in and gave his mother a warm hug, which she willingly reciprocated.

"Well," she observed, "Your father will be in our room gloating for an hour or two, so you have time to get started."

Self-confidence. That was easier said than done. And yet, what choice did he have? He had the interview lined up with Tuckner Wass and getting that was a stroke of luck. Luck or work – which was best? His father seemed to think he knew the answer to that question, but did he really?

Chapter 3

The week went by too quickly for Ray's liking. The interview was, without question, the greatest opportunity that he could ever have hoped for and preparing for it was a challenge commensurate with its import. Every moment not spent in class, or studying for his exams, was dedicated to making himself ready for this moment. He watched the Roberts DVD's with religious fervor, absorbing every possible bit of advice for mental reinforcement, every suggestion at beating back the naysayers and the critics. He had downloaded every bit of information he could from the Tuckner Wass website, from the corporate history to the biographies of the senior management, to the various operations of the company. He studied the positions and figures to the point where he could recite them with as much alacrity as his father could recall Tom Seaver's earned run average with the Mets in 1969.

Some people work their fingers to the bone for years and end up with nothing. Others spend more time playing golf and get a thousand times more. *So, it can't be work. And yet, rich people get cancer, divorces, and all the other crap that poor people do, so it's not all luck either. What happens when you don't have luck or work on your side?*

He muttered to himself as he walked toward Tuckner Wass Plaza. *I guess, in the end all I got is me.*

Numerous times in his life, he had walked these streets, never giving any consideration to who owned them, or what was done inside. The massive building now loomed large, like the Emerald City in the Land of Oz. He now had to go inside and have an audience with the Wizard. He craned his neck upward and pondered whether he was ready. He knew he had the heart for the job, but did he have the courage? Did he have the brain? He shrugged off the doubts and went inside.

The trading offices were on the tenth floor of the tower. He boarded the elevator with a mass of butterflies churning in his stomach. Stopping and starting, people coming on and getting off. The process only piqued his nervous tension. All he could think of was wishing for something to take his mind off the interview. He got his wish when the elevator doors opened.

Clad with a Bluetooth set, her hands were quickly pushing telephone keys like a virtuoso pianist. "Good morning, Tuckner Wass. Can you hold please…Good morning, Tuckner Wass, please hold…Good morning, Tuckner Wass, how can I help you? … I'm sorry, Mr. Raphaelson is in a meeting this morning…No, I'm not sure when he'll be back. Let me put you through to his assistant…"

Ray walked over and stood at the reception desk, staring at this woman who, for some reason, had captured his attention. She was beautiful, yes, but not stunning. She was just a naturally beautiful woman. Shoulder length hair, dark brown that produced natural strands of gold when the light hit it from a certain angle. Dark eyes, but beautifully big. Other women would use loads of eyeliner and mascara to produce the same effect. She wore a sheer blouse with a camisole that just caressed the cleft of her bosom, which he had judged to be reasonably impressive.

"Can I help you, sir?" she asked, in a way that seemed to imply that she knew exactly where his eyes had been hanging just a little too long.

"Uh…yes. I have an appointment to see Rob Bortelli. My name's Ray Lulio."

She pressed a few more buttons, and then said into the headset "Mister Bortelli, a Mister Lulio is here to see you…All right."

She got up from the desk, removed her headset, and turned to her desk mate.

"I'll be a minute. I've got to take this fellow to see Bortelli," she said.

Ray followed the receptionist into a large auditorium sized room, covered with desks, chairs, phones and computer terminals. There were at least a hundred men and women in a variety of poses

– sitting, standing, whispering, yelling, or a combination of any that varied from second to second. Along the back wall was a large electronic board that flashed a jumble of letters and numbers dressed in plus and minus signs.

Off to the side were a collection of offices, and it was at the third one that the woman stopped, knocking on the partially opened door.

"Mister Bortelli, I have Mister Lulio here," she announced.

"Thanks, Connie...Come on in, Ray. Glad you could make it," said Bortelli, as he walked forward to shake his hand. "You didn't have any problems getting here?"

"No, sir, not at all...I really appreciate this, Mister Bortelli," said Ray, glancing over to notice another man in the room.

"Come on, I told you to call me Rob...Look, I want to introduce you to our CEO, Hal Raphaelson."

The man walked forward and, with a firm grasp, grabbed Ray's hand and almost shook it off.

"Lulio...You Mexican?" he asked, in one of those ways reminiscent of an old man who conveniently forgot every social advance in the last thirty years, not realizing he had committed some faux pas.

"Uhhh...my father was born in Puerto Rico?" said Ray quizzically. *What the hell kind of interview was this?*

"Ahh," answered Raphaelson. "Anyway, Rob tells me you want to be a Tuckner Wass trader."

"Yes, sir, I have been researching your company, and I really..."

"...and you want to be part of a world-class team...yeah, yeah, yeah. Got to stop you there," interrupted Raphaelson. "Every little snot-nosed Wharton grad comes in here after they memorize our company history on Google. I got at least fifty of them lined up for this afternoon. Why should we take you instead of them?"

Ray stood dumbfounded by Raphaelson's blunt candor. *Was this a joke?* Bortelli seemed to be a straight-forward kind of guy, but was this some sort of set-up? Maybe it was to see how he would bear up under pressure?

"Uhh, I didn't go to Wharton. I went to East Brooklyn Community College," he said, almost apologetically.

"You think I give a shit about that?!" answered Raphaelson,

not letting up for a moment. "I got enough Wharton, Harvard and Stern guys like Bortelli here kissing my ass! I don't need an ass kisser – I need an ass kicker! Are you an ass kicker, Ray?!"

"I do what I have to," he replied, not sure where this was going.

Raphaelson walked up to just a couple of inches from Ray, almost nose to nose, and said in a muted voice "What I want to know is whether you have the huevos…Just how big are your huevos, Mister Ray Lulio?!"

Ray looked into Raphaelson's eyes like someone who had just been slapped across the face. *What the hell kind of question was that - and what kind of job interview was this?! Even drunk uncles at Christmas dinner did not act like this!* Surely this was some sort of hazing ritual, and not an expression of corporate policy. Not sure what to do, Ray concluded that the only way to answer a ridiculous question was to give an equally ridiculous answer.

"They're big enough," murmured Ray, totally taken aback by the sudden invasion of his personal space. Raphaelson smiled slyly and stepped back.

"I said 'how big are your huevos'?" he intoned in a growl.

"They're big," answered Ray, in a more determined voice. *You're not going to give me a job. You're just yanking my chain. Fine, then, I'll play your stupid little game. After all, can't lose what I never had to begin with!*

"How big are they?!" yelled Raphaelson.

"They're huge! They're fucking bowling balls!" Ray barked back, almost beside himself.

For a moment, there was silence. Then Raphaelson began to laugh. He patted Ray on the back, then turned to Bortelli, nodded, and said "Fix this sonofabitch up with a job on the sales desk…Welcome aboard, kid!" Then he was gone.

Ray turned to Bortelli, confused. "Did I just get hired?" he asked, with a look of disbelief.

"Yep," said Bortelli, nodding his head as though he could read what Ray was thinking.

"So…that was some sort of test, or something?"

"Yeah," sighed Bortelli, as he went behind his desk and took a seat. "A test of my patience and my loyalty…No, that's Hal, in all his glory.

"Look, Ray, you can start Monday, but a word to the wise. Hal's like those lights you hang up on your back porch for moths. You fly close enough to cover your butt, but any closer, and zap. Sales might not be as glamorous as trading, but he tends to leave it to me."

With that, he reached over and pressed the button on his intercom. "Hi, Connie, it's Rob. I'll need you to take Mister Lulio to HR so he can get processed…Thanks."

Within a couple of minutes, the receptionist who had acted as his guide reappeared at the door. "Sales isn't as sexy as trading, but you have to walk before you run. In the meantime, I'll give you every chance to learn the trade" said Bortelli, as he gestured toward her. "Connie will get you set up for Monday morning."

"Thanks, Rob… for everything," replied Ray, as he reached across the desk to shake his hand. "I promise I won't let you down," he said as he turned to follow his guide out the door.

Connie headed down the corridor at a brisk pace, forcing Ray to step lively as he followed in tow.

"So, what's your last name, Connie?" he asked.

"Gondela," she answered, in an almost mechanical tone.

"It is very nice to meet you, Connie Gondela…"

"I don't date traders," she interrupted, all the while not breaking her pace.

"Excuse me?"

"I don't date salesman or traders."

"I was just asking…"

"Well, you can stop asking. I saw you looking at my boobs…Look, I've been here five years, and most of the guys in the trading room have hit on me twice – first when they're hired, and second when they get a bonus big enough to buy a sports car to overcompensate for you-know-what."

Ray stopped dead in his tracks, forcing Connie to stop as well, and turn around.

"Lady," he began, "I don't know about any of that. All I know is that I was trying to be polite, just like my mother taught me to do, and all you wanna do is bust my balls. As for looking at your you-know-whats, well, I'm a guy – to be honest, we'd stare at a pair regardless of what they're attached to."

Connie looked at him with a slight frown. "I'm sorry…," she

began.

"Ray...After all that, you can at least call me Ray," he remarked.

"Okay... Ray," she continued. "It's been a rough morning, and this place is a madhouse at the best of times. It's really nothing personal."

Ray laughed. "No problem," he said. "Hey, get to know me and you'll find a whole new set of reasons to hate my guts!"

Connie smiled, and held out her hand. "So, we're square?" she asked.

"Never any question," he replied, gently shaking her hand. "You'll let me buy you a coffee, though? Just friends?"

"Come on," she said with a smile, turning and resuming her path. "You have a date with Gladys in HR before you get anywhere near me."

Ray followed her into another set of offices where all the pedantic minutiae of modern corporate tenure was dealt with – payroll, health insurance, 401(K) enrolment, and so on. After the better part of an hour, he felt as though he had signed and initialed enough paperwork to have bought a house, lease a car, relinquish his first born, and donate a kidney in one fell swoop. Once he had signed the final dotted line, and flexed out the cramp in his right hand, Connie returned to lead him to the next stop on his journey. There, she handed him a colored sales package.

"And here is your orientation," she said. "When you get home, watch the DVD and read the materials, okay?"

"Okay," he shrugged, as he took the folder from her.

"It's important that you do both together," she cautioned. "Don't read the materials before or after the DVD. You need to do it together."

"Why?" he asked with a smirk. "Will it cause some disruption in the space-time continuum if I don't?"

"Caroline's has an open mike night. We don't," she intoned without the slightest hint of a smile. "Be an ass on your own time – not on ours."

Ray smiled weakly as he followed Connie to the long battery of desks that comprised the sales unit. She gestured to an empty desk between two large, rather animated men who were bouncing back and forth between numerous phone calls, while their noses were almost pressed up against their computer display screens.

"You'll be sitting there Monday," she said matter-of-factly. "And don't expect any time to get up to speed. The learning curve here is a two-hundred-foot cliff."

The cacophony of ringing telephones and testosterone infused yelling was an assault on his senses the likes of which he had never experienced. No walls to hide behind, it was all out in the open, like some perverse gladiatorial exhibition of old, where the crowd declared the fate of the competitors with green and red arrows rather than thumbs extended or lowered. What had he gotten himself into? He saw the Harvard MBA's, the grizzled old veterans of the pits who could rip your beating heart from your chest, and quants who could have easily snagged a Nobel in Mathematics had they not answered the call of almighty mammon. He was not even a minnow in this pond, but perhaps the greenish slime that the minnows fed on.

Regardless of what he felt inside, he could not let it all intimidate him. *Two arms, two legs. That is all they are. Pants go on, one leg at a time. Still wipe their asses when they take a shit. Human – just human. Slightly different models, but built on the very same chassis, his father would say. Same engine burning fuel the same way. Intake, compression, combustion, exhaust…Suck, squeeze, bang, blow…Suck, squeeze, bang, blow…*

"What did you say?" asked Connie.

"Uh…nothing," muttered Ray.

Her expression softened a little. "Anyway, I know this is probably a lot to absorb. It might help if you got to meet everyone outside this place. We usually all end up at Shaughnessy's on West 57th. Come any time after eight."

"What about this DVD?" he asked.

"Well, I suggest that you go home and make some popcorn. You've got a movie to watch," she smiled.

Chapter 4

That afternoon, when Ray finally returned home, the house was quiet. His father was still at work, while his mother was likely down at the parish hall, helping with any number of committees she had volunteered for. It was perfectly peaceful and quiet. He placed the DVD in the player and proceeded to study the production as carefully as he could.

It began with the typical corporate video song and dance about the company's illustrious founders, Morris Tuckner and Herbert Wass – two cousins who made their way from the pogroms of Eastern Europe to the pier at Ellis Island – and how they built a titan of modern American finance with little more than hard work, old world values, and shrewd insights. The journey, of course, was guided by animated versions of the founders who leapt off portraits hanging in the company's corporate lobby. This tour, however, did not quite conform to the information he had come across when he entered the firm's name into Google. No mention of bankrolling Papa Doc Duvalier in Haiti, or Nicaragua's Somoza family. Ray mused to himself how they would have animated those scenes.

Over the course of the next hour, he followed the film closely, looking for any information on arbitrage, on quants, or IPO's. There was nothing, except more animation, more talk of the glorious past, and the bright future. It was what you would show shareholders to get them to forget what it was that they wanted to ask you. It was like the films that they showed on sex during health class in high school - forty-five minutes of bad animation and cheesy acting, only to find out the real story from Marky Faustino behind the gymnasium when you were sneaking some of his father's Marlboros.

Guessing that the only reason that the firm insisted that he watch the DVD was to justify the expense of making it, he switched it off with ten minutes to spare. After all, it was not like some Oracle was going to appear in the closing credits and tell him everything he needed to know the following week.

After a quick bite, a shower, and a shave to lose his '5 o'clock shadow', he headed out the door and back into the city to the place where Connie had told him they would be. He thought about her as he rode ever nearer to the downtown core, where the train left the light of day and descended to just below the flesh of Manhattan. She was cute, but she had an edge, like most of the girls he knew from the neighborhood.

He reasoned that an offence was the best defense and bitchiness was just a cover for insecurity. Not that she was bitchy, he told himself. At least, she was not completely that way. Maybe it was being in an office around all those people, and she just had her game face on. Those places were notorious for the adrenaline and testosterone that flowed through the hallways. Maybe she had no choice but to be that way – even when she was answering phones yards away from the trading floor. He had spent so much time trying to get a take on Connie that he almost missed his stop.

He had found Shaughnessy's easily enough. The pub was a hive of activity, with people using the establishment as some staging ground for their Friday night festivities. Once inside, Connie found him, no more than mere seconds after he had walked in the door. *Was she waiting for him?* He wondered if there was some eagerness on her part that extended beyond a corporate orientation.

"Ray!" she called out and waved him toward a back corner. "Come over here!"

Bobbing and weaving his way through the swarm of power suits and assorted cocktails, he found himself no more than a foot or two in front of her.

"You found us okay?" she asked, in a tone that came close to shouting.

"Yes," he said, in a matching volume. "No worries…Did you want a drink?"

"Sure," she smiled. "Gimme a Jameson's on the rocks."

Nodding, he turned around and cut a narrow path to the bar, where he ordered Connie's drink, and picked up a Budweiser for himself, waving off a beer glass from the bartender. He turned around and steadily tried to retrace his path, which had disappeared like footprints in Sahara sand.

"Cheers," he said as he handed her the glass.

She looked at him as he took a big swig on the beer, and then leaned in to talk.

"What are you doing?" she asked.

"Uhh…drinking a beer? Why?" he answered.

"You shouldn't be drinking that," she said matter-of-factly.

"What the hell are you talking about?" he said. "I'm not under 21, and I paid for it…"

"No, no, no. You don't get it," she said, moving in even closer to keep the conversation intimate. "Beer's too low rent for this crowd. You don't drink that around these guys. Go get another Jameson's for yourself, and I'll ditch this." With that, she took the bottle from his hand and headed with it toward the washrooms in the far corner. By the time he had returned with another whiskey, she was back to her old position.

"Sorry about that," she said. "I should have told you sooner. These guys are not from the old neighborhood. If you wanna run with the pack, you gotta drink with the pack."

"Well, I'm out a beer, and I don't get paid like the pack…yet" he sighed, trying to find a way to register his displeasure without coming off too badly.

"You'll be fine," she assured him. "Just consider this as part of your orientation."

"Yeah," he grinned impishly. "And I suppose a couple of little cartoon guys are goin' to jump out of that TV and tell me the history of highballs."

Connie shook her head and laughed. "Yeah, I know. It was lame, wasn't it? It was Hal's idea, and he makes me tell every recruit to watch it like their life depended on it. Just some cheerleading bullshit…I think some friend of his from Yale does these productions. I wouldn't be surprised if he got a kickback for it."

Ray gave her a curious look. "I get the impression that you don't like a lot of the people you work with," he said, taking a tentative sip of the whiskey – something that he had never tried before.

"Well," she explained, "I don't hate them if that's what you mean. They're just not my kind of people. That's all."

"So why work there?"

Connie raised her eyebrow, as if to confess some non-lethal secret that was obvious to everyone anyway. "At the time," she said, "I thought that's what I wanted. I mean, when you're on the outside looking in, it's pretty attractive. That was five years ago, and it's turned out to be nothing like it."

"Nothing at all?" asked Ray, not sure whether this was a bad omen for his own preconceptions.

"Well, the money and the perks are pretty good," she confessed, "but they can be real assholes, so they should pay you well to put up with their bullshit, shouldn't they." It was not a question, but a statement of belief.

"Well, they can't be all that bad," countered Ray. "I mean, that's all your own perception, isn't it?" He had learned from Robin St. John Roberts about the power of perception, and how it can help - or undermine - your life dreams. Maybe she was sabotaging herself by thinking the worst in others around her?

"Okay," she said, putting her drink down on the table. "You want proof? Come with me, and I'll show you some proof."

Ray followed her over to a discreet corner and pointed to a tall blonde woman who was holding court with a half dozen or so of the salesmen and traders. He watched her as Connie whispered what amounted to a play-by-play of the inaudible action.

Her name was Mel. Not Melanie. Mel. Of that tidbit of information, he, as the new guy, was surely required to know.

She was physically impressive – and intimidating – with a BMI that was close to textbook, and long, flowing, golden hair that probably made the chemists at Clairol swell with professional pride.

He knew her kind, but then again, so did everyone else with eyes and a pulse. Arrogant and conceited, they could only hold a conversation so long as they were the center of it. It was always in some elevated voice, so that those beyond the periphery of the audience could easily hear. And it always followed the same pathology – what they did, where they went, and who they met along the way.

Ray knew, however, what marked the transition from simple garden variety egotism to the full-blown neuroses affectionately known as narcissism. The egotist would at some point, shut their mouths when they ran out of fodder. They were natural braggarts, but they were honest ones, and even their embellishments had some grounding in truth. The narcissist, on the other hand, being the far more malignant of the two, would just keep on going. Running out of personal virtues to extoll upon, they would brag about their spouse's accomplishments as if they were their own or wax on about their darling children's' performance in preschool, inferring that this was a forgone consequence of having been the product of their own divinely blessed seed.

Of course, once having exhausted this reservoir of self-involvement, they would now ruminate on the problems of their lives, which were but a canvas to paint more vainglorious colors. Oh, my life is far from perfect, they would argue, and then cite the endless social functions, the continual travel to exotic locations, or the litany of awards and citations to them and theirs as some great burden to bear. Although they were never so crass as to openly articulate it, it was easily understood by all that this was but the price one had to pay for being marked for greatness.

Connie felt compelled to warn Ray to stay clear of her. She explained that Mel was pushing into her mid-forties, and with the kids already trucked off to some prep school, all that welcomed her home was her formerly Adonis-like husband, and a small, twitchy, rat-like creature she tried to pass off as a dog.

"I heard Raphaelson is banging her on the side," she whispered to him after Mel had passed well beyond hearing distance.

"How do you know?" he asked, just before he took a sip from his glass.

"You'll learn soon enough that we know everything," she replied slyly.

"Everything?"

"Honey," she said, with an exaggerated gesture, "the CIA ain't got anything on the secretarial pool."

He wondered whether this candor meant that she was, indeed,

willing to give him a chance – for friendship at the very least. "Should you be blowing your cover to the enemy?" he asked playfully.

Connie squinted her eyes at him and smiled. "I'm not so sure you're the enemy…at least not yet."

"Don't be so sure of yourself," he chuckled. "They might send Mel to interrogate me."

"There wouldn't be anything left of you if she did!" she joked.

She paused for a moment to take another sip of her drink, which was more of a swig. "Seriously," she began, "Rob is a pretty good judge of character. He must have seen something in you to bring you in."

"My smile and winning personality?" he joked.

"Naw…I doubt that very much," she laughed as she rose from the barstool. "Look, I'm tired, and you need to take me home."

"Excuse me?"

"I mean…I'm tired and drunk, and I'm a single woman alone late in Manhattan. You need to escort me home…or didn't your mother teach you all the rules of being a gentleman?"

"Of course, ma'am," he replied in an exaggerated gesture, as he got up to join her. "Besides, I start a new job next week, and I do have to suck up to the right people."

The two left the bar and headed to a corner nearby where their chances of hailing a taxi appeared to be better. Unfortunately, the chances were better for others, as a crowd of merrymakers had already lined the sidewalk in competition for a couple of taxis that were already pulling away with full complements of passengers.

"I knew we should have left earlier…Shit!" she muttered.

Ray was slightly amused by her state of agitation, albeit mild by the standards of home - and his father. Maybe it was the idea that his curmudgeonly spirit was being channeled through the body of a young woman that he found funny. Discretion being the better part of valor, he knew enough to obfuscate when she noticed the smirk on his face.

"You laughing at me?" asked Connie.

Ray reflected on how a witty and debonaire man about town would have answered that question. *What would Antonio Banderas do?*

"Naw," he slurred with added conviction. "Just drunk and

tired, I guess."

"Well, you could hail a cab," she suggested.

"I could," he replied. "But being a gentleman in the bar by buying you drinks has tapped me out. Unless you're picking up the tab, we'll have to take the subway."

Connie was lightly annoyed at the prospect. Nevertheless, she reached into her enormous bag and pulled out a pair of running shoes. She threw them onto the ground, then grabbed Ray's arm to steady her balance as she effected the change from pumps to Nikes.

"You know," she said as she knelt to tie the laces, "I'm not as bitchy as you think I am."

"I wasn't thinking any such thing," protested Ray. "The chip on your shoulder took years to build. I only met you today."

When she got up, Ray was expecting an unpleasant reaction, not the sly smile Connie sent his way instead.

"I'm sorry. I did it again...Look, it's nothing personal," she explained.

"Really? I don't see anyone else here," he said, craning his neck to the left and the right to emphasize the point.

She did not reply. Nothing in the way of an explanation would be appropriate, and anything else would only serve to inflate his ego by deflating hers. There was nothing to gain, so she kept silent as they walked. That, of course, lasted about a block and a half before Ray obliged her with an opening.

"Can I tell you something?" he asked.

"About what?" she replied, in a quiet tone.

"About me."

"Oh...something personal," she observed. "Well, we just met and like I already told you..."

"I'm scared," he said, purposefully interrupting her attempt at a monologue.

"What?"

"I'm scared," he repeated. "I'm scared of Monday, I'm scared of this job, and I'm really scared of all of you."

"Well, you should be," said Connie playfully, not comfortable herself with the direction that the conversation was taking.

"Seriously. I have no clue what I'm doing. People are going to see through me right away."

Self doubt - so what do I do with this? After five years at Tuckner

Wass, listening to this confession was as awkward as watching a big, virile man break down in a puddle of tears. You feel for them – honestly – but the sight makes you squeamish and uncomfortable. Wall Street does bourbon and trash talk, not tea and sympathy.

"Look," she began in a conciliatory tone, "Like I said, Rob is a pretty good judge of character. He wouldn't have hired you unless he saw something. And so long as you make him happy, you won't go wrong."

"Yeah, but you all seem like a pretty tough crowd."

"Best defence is a good offence – you know that" she said.

"But they seem so polished and so professional. I'm nothing like that," countered Ray.

"And neither are they…Look, they all graduated from the Eliza Doolittle school."

"Where's that?" asked Ray. "Is that some training place?"

"Geez, you really don't get out much…Hello? Eliza Doolittle? My Fair Lady?"

"What about it?" he asked, not sure what a musical had to do with selling corporate bonds.

"Okay, you know, the professor grabs a street woman, dresses her up, teaches her to speak a certain way, then passes her off for royalty – fools everybody."

"And?"

"And what do you think half of the people in our office do? Did they go to the best schools? No. Did they score high on their SAT's? Not a chance."

"So, what do they do?"

"Well, three things. First, they dress the part. That includes what they drive, what kind of watch, and where they get their hair cut. Second, they learn what to say. You know, small talk. They learn a couple of things about as many topics and throw them out as though they have something upstairs. Some of those assholes spend more time googling stuff than watching their screens for upticks. Then, lastly, they learn how to say things."

"Whaddya mean 'how' to say things?"

"Okay, the first lesson's free. Don't say 'whaddya.' You have to say all the words. Never shorten anything, and remember to say it slow, and clench your jaw."

"Okay," said Ray, and proceeded to follow Connie's

instructions. "What…do…you."

"Good start, now get used to doing that all of the time."

"I still don't get why I have to do this."

"Well…how should I put this? Okay, well there are people out there who are as dumb as a plank, see? Now, in the good old days, they knew they were dumb, and had the good sense to stay in the mailroom, or bag groceries, or something.

"Now, I don't know what changed. Maybe their parents would tell them how smart and beautiful they were all the time, even if they weren't. They would come home with a drawing of shit and their Mommy would pin it up on the fridge and call it a Picasso. The way I see it, there are a lot of morons who have been told how smart they are for so many years they've begun to believe it. What's worse is that they're too arrogant and stupid to recognize the truth."

Ray frowned. "That's pretty harsh, isn't it?" he observed.

"Not if it's true," countered Connie, ignoring the discomfort that she saw in Ray's expression. "I know it sounds rough, but you've got to call them as you see them. I mean, it's not like they're going to change, or something. It's just that you have to be on your guard. You play the game, just like everybody else. Talk like you have your jaw wired shut, and just blather on about bullshit. That's what they do."

While he knew that she was trying to help, trying to ease his jittery nerves, all this advice served to only make him feel more self-conscious about what he was walking into. "Well, sooner or later, everybody gets found out right?" he asked.

"Oh, yeah, like Mister "how big are your balls" Raphaelson is going to call somebody out on that. He's the biggest phony of them all…No, Bortelli is the brains of the operation, which brings me back to what I said before – keep Rob happy, and you're good to go."

Ray stopped walking and looked straight into her face. "And that's all there is to it, huh?"

"Pretty much," she replied. "That and keep on the good side of the secretaries, and you'll survive till at least your first annual bonus."

The two resumed their walk in silence for another couple of blocks, before Ray gave in to his urges, and turned to his travelling companion. "Do you believe in love at first sight?" he asked.

"What? You're kidding, right?" laughed Connie, taken wholly by surprise by the question.

Ray said nothing. He looked at her like a puppy that had been scolded for chewing a favorite slipper.

"Ohh," she said, changing her tone. "I'm sorry...I wasn't trying to make fun of you. Honest."

"Don't worry about it," he shrugged. "Nothing personal, right?"

"No, no... I mean, you can't really spring that kind of thing on somebody like that. I just met you this morning."

"And?"

"And…. Look, I...," she stuttered. "How am I supposed to answer something like that?"

"How about truthfully," suggested Ray.

Connie was starting to feel flushed from embarrassment. It was not that she did not find him attractive. She thought he was somewhat handsome in an average way - not stunning, but not homely. He was proportioned in a relative non-threatening way.

"I think," she hesitated. "I think that you are confusing some feelings here. I mean, I'm trying to be nice. You're the new guy and all that, but I wasn't coming on to you. Honestly. And besides, we are going to be working in the same office. That's my job. If we were ever to get involved, and things went south, well, I don't have a fallback. One of us would have to quit, and I'd be damned if it was going to be me."

"So," smiled Ray," you do believe it?"

Connie returned his grin with a playful one of her own. "I don't know. It's too early to tell...Besides, you have more important things to worry about."

Chapter 5

Over the coming months, Ray often wished that his career in the sales department was half as successful as his friendship with Connie. While she was adamant; she did not, and would not, date either salesmen or traders, she eventually relented and made an exception for Ray. Of course, this bending of her cardinal rule had lasted only seven or eight months, because while her cardinal rule covered dating, there was no clause that dealt with getting married.

As keen as Ray was on the proposition, he would have preferred a longer courtship. He still lived at home with his parents, while her apartment was not much more than a room in a boarding house. Whatever money he had saved for a larger place in the city was just going to end up in the pockets of the caterers, the florists, and the parish priest.

The solution to this problem was to be the first instance of substance where Connie and Ray were not simpatico. Unlike virtually every mother of every friend he had, Ray's mother liked her daughter-in-law to be. Of course, Connie, not being particularly close to her own mother, felt equally enamored with Missus Lulio.

The women had decided that the newlyweds would, for an indeterminate amount of time, reside in the Lulio house. The tenancy would, of course, depend upon several factors, not excluding the demands that children may pose on a young couple. The men, having never seen common ground on anything for the past twenty years, excepting the Mets, were equally opposed to the arrangement. It was far too open-ended for either of them. Of course, it had not been a fair fight, and the ladies had already set to work redecorating before Max and Ray had finally admitted defeat – an admission that was as muted as the objections that neither of the men dared to verbalize to their significant others.

Money was not the root of all evil, Ray had reasoned. The problem was the lack of it. More money meant an end to the living arrangement, and the kind of freedom he could only taste. Barring a winning Powerball ticket, the path that led to that extra money went straight through the office of Harold Raphaelson, and on to the Tuckner Wass trading floor.

Despite having been at the firm for over a year, the most time he had ever spent with the man had been on the day of his interview. That alone made him somewhat grateful for the lack of proximity, but that distance was a double-edged sword. It also meant a distance from the kind of advancement that would finance his master plan.

Bortelli could help, and in all honesty, would likely put in a good word on his behalf. He had done his best to earn Rob's trust and respect, just as Connie had told him, and reminded him several times over. That was all well and good, but Ray knew that the most that Rob could do was offer some moral suasion on whatever decision that Raphaelson would make. In the end, the CEO could take it, or leave it. Great if it worked, but an enormous waste of time and energy if it did not.

As it was, the sales department was the furthest place from the executive suites as you could get. Raphaelson never set foot on the sales floor, unless there was some big announcement. Even then, it was usually Bortelli who handled that detail. He was a more frequent visitor to the trading desks. Connie had explained that they were 'cut from the same cloth.' Of course, this is what she said at the reception desk, in front of the others. Ray knew that she implied something far less complimentary.

It was the reason why Ray, on occasion, would go out of his way and take a walk along the corridor outside Raphaelson's office. Out of sight was out of mind, and he needed to place himself first and foremost in the great man's sights if he were to have any hope of advancement. Eventually, one day, he got exactly what he was looking for.

"Hey, Lulio. Got a minute?" came the voice from the open door to Raphaelson's office. Ray stopped in his tracks and stepped back a couple of paces to see the Chairman waving him to enter while he was on the telephone to someone.

"Sure…," said Ray cautiously, before Raphaelson held up a hand to silence him. The CEO then held the receiver back to his ear and continued the phone call while Ray took a seat opposite.

Ray had never actually been in Raphaelson's office before, although he had occasionally peered in on his many trips past. Usually, Marguerite, his secretary, kept a tight vigil at the door, so one never spent more than two or three seconds rubbernecking past before she would give a rather efficient, monotone 'Can I help you?'

The office was large, and well appointed, as one would have expected. The walls were oak paneled, and brass wall sconces gave punctuation to the effect, which seemed quite incongruous with a building that could not have been scarcely twenty years old. The furnishings were of a classic style. Ray knew that there was probably some fancy term to describe the period, but he simply referred to it by a name he recognized – 'Bombay Company.'

There were wall hangings and other assorted ornaments that looked Japanese to Ray, although his own travels never took him further east than Atlantic City, and of that trip he had little recollection. He had heard that Raphaelson had spent a couple of years in Tokyo, heading Tuckner Wass's operations there, before he returned to Manhattan, so it was a safe assumption.

Off to one corner, beside Raphaelson's desk, was a dressing dummy adorned with a silk embroidered robe, black with a pattern of a dragon in gold and red – a kimono? The sideboard behind where he sat held a couple of ornate swords. Ray guessed them to be Samurai swords, as it was the only sword he knew that the Japanese made.

Ray sat nervously, trying not to make eye contact with the Chairman while he was talking to what sounded like the mysterious Missus Raphaelson, who, like the Loch Ness monster, was the source of endless speculation at Tuckner Wass, despite having been no evidence of her existence.

"…You'll have to take care of it…I can't be there…Well, until you get that faggy gardener you hired to plant me a fucking money tree, I gotta work…Sorry, I forgot that you would have to know what work was…Yeah? That's what you think it is? Well, if that's the case, then you're seriously overpaid…I could buy a whore a night for two weeks for what it cost to pay for one of your spa weekends…Yeah? Well, don't wait up!"

Raphaelson slammed the received down into the cradle, and without missing a beat, he looked at Ray and asked, "You married?"

"Uhh, yeah," replied Ray, in a rather confused tone. "Connie Gondela? Six months ago? You were at the reception?"

"Oh, shit. That's right…Anyway, don't ever show weakness. From the day they put on that dress, they want control."

"I'm sorry. I don't follow…" said Ray, hoping that by pleading ignorance, Raphaelson would quickly tire of the line of discussion. This, of course, was futile, given how the great man's mind worked.

"Okay, okay…so when my kids were younger, we had them in soccer, right? Well, I went to the first couple of games, but then I stopped going. You know why?"

"You don't like soccer?" volunteered Ray.

"Can't stand it! Faggy game – not like football…But no, that's not it…Wanna know why?"

Ray felt like a kid who was about to sneak a naughty peek at something he should not see, but could not help but look, like a car collision. "Uhh…why?" he asked tentatively.

"Yentas and eunuchs!" exclaimed Raphaelson.

"What?"

"Yentas and eunuchs!" he repeated, as though he were having some great epiphany that needed to be imparted. "All the parents were there. All I saw were a bunch of battle-axe bitches nattering at their husbands to do this and to do that. And while the husbands were busy with their kids, do you know what the women were doing?"

"I hate to ask," sighed Ray.

"Standing around gossiping! Look, I know I come across as hating women. I hear what they say about me, but they're wrong…I love women. My mother – she was a saint. She cooked, cleaned, sacrificed. My wife? Doesn't cook a meal, or clean off a table, leaves the nanny to raise the kids, doesn't hold down a job. I pay people to take care of everything. Hell, the only thing she ever did was fuck, and she never was any good at that! Now she won't even do that one simple thing!"

Well, who do you pay for that? Oh, wait – you have Mel for that, don't you!

"Anyway," continued Raphaelson, "that's not what I wanted to talk to you about."

Ray smiled meekly. Continuing this line of conversation was as palatable to him as watching an autopsy being performed live. Finally, there was a point to all this talk other than getting a front row seat to the epitome of dysfunction and animus.

"You've been with us for a while now, and don't think I haven't noticed your work."

"Thanks," replied Ray, not sure whether he was more appreciative of the compliment, or the merciful change of subject.

"Well, I understand that selling is a shit job, but, hey, we all start out that way."

Ray had seen enough in his time at Tuckner Wass to seriously doubt that statement, but his mouth displayed a gracious acknowledgment. It seemed Raphaelson was giving him the opening he craved, so he took his shot. "I was hoping that I might get a shot on the trading floor. I know that Tomlinson is moving to London, and I've been…"

"You'll get your chance," came the interruption," but I'm moving Burney into that slot. No offence, but he spent ten years moving mortgage bonds at Lehman before he came here. Besides, I gave him my word. Code of honor, you know."

Burney was a dinosaur, and not the good kind, either – the ravenous velociraptors that ate new recruits and crapped them out before the closing bell. He was from a time long past. Most of the traders, and a few of the salesmen, would openly joke that his first bond sale was probably a Victory Bond outside the USO the day after Pearl Harbor, and he hadn't done shit since other than terrorize the floor.

"Mister Raphaelson…" began Ray.

"Call me Hal."

"Okay…Hal…Look I really thought I should be up for a slot by now. Connie and me, well we wanted to move into a new place, and you know…"

"Yeah, yeah…Mom and Dad listening to the rusty bedsprings, huh?" he joked, with enough relish to heighten the crassness factor.

"I just wanna get ahead…and besides, my balls are as big as the day we met – even bigger!"

Raphaelson seemed particularly pleased by Ray's comments. "Well, that's what I wanted to talk to you about," he laughed. "If you're serious about getting ahead, then I have a proposition for you."

With that, he pulled out a business card from the top middle drawer of his desk, and, after scribbling something on the back, he handed it across to Ray.

"Eddie Moreton is an old friend of mine – we go back to the old days with Rainieri at Salomon. Anyway, he has a small shop and is always looking for talent. If you want to pull some extra shifts on the side for him until we open something up, then give him a call – and make sure you give him that card."

Ray looked at the card and gave a sigh. "Hal, I really appreciate this. Really…I do…but I'm already pulling twelve hours a day here. I mean, Thank God Connie works here, because I'd never lay eyes on her if she didn't. What I'm trying to say is that I don't know if there are even enough hours in the day to do this?"

Raphaelson grinned in a way that made Ray somewhat uncomfortable. "Okay, I know what you're saying…Shit, if it were me, I'd live here, but you've actually got someone decent to come home to. Look, I'll cut you back to eight a day, but keep you at the same salary, okay?"

With that, he got up from behind the desk, and sat down on one of the front corners, his knee no more than a couple of feet from Ray's head. "I'll level with you…You're doing me a favor…Eddie's a good guy, but lately, he's a bit of a fuckup…I don't wanna see him piss away his shingle, and if you can move some paper for him, I 'll owe you for it…Ray, I don't need to tell you how much my IOUs are good for around here, do I?"

Ray grimaced. As good as having Raphaelson in his debt was, the whole idea of moonlighting still did not set right with him.

"I gotta talk to Connie first," he said.

"No," replied Raphaelson. "Not if your huevos are as big as you claim they are."

A childish challenge, and not out of character as far as Ray had understood. Connie would tell him to walk away from it, and just say something pithy – anything to get the topic on to something else. But Connie was not the man. He was the man, and the challenge was declared. Boys would just taunt you and call you 'chicken' or 'pussy.' They were men, with the benefit of wisdom, education, and sophistication, and would never lower themselves to such a level. They would insinuate that if you were not a 'chicken' or a 'pussy,' you would take up the challenge in a heartbeat. A real man would never cower in this, their moment of destiny – of, dare he say it, of opportunity?

"Fine," he sighed. "I'll take it, but the next slot that opens is mine. Right?"

"Code of honor. You have my word," said the Chairman, as he grasped Ray's hand into his own fleshy palm.

Chapter 6

Max Lulio walked into the living room to find Ray sitting on the couch, watching one of his DVDs of Robin St. John Roberts, for what seemed to him to have been the eight thousandth time. "Santa Maria! You watchin' that crap again?" he growled.

"It's not crap, Dad," defended Ray, giving a sigh of frustration that he must revisit this issue yet again. "This is important stuff."

His father shook his head incredulously. "Important? All I see is some loud Limey with a headset prancin' around sayin' do this an' do that. Didn't George Washington kick them outta here?"

"Robin St. John Roberts is a motivational life coach," explained Ray, ignoring his father's sarcasm, which seemed to have been the only strategy that half worked on Max's tirades.

"Oh yeah? Well maybe he can motivate you an' Connie to get an apartment, heh?" A-ha! Max savored the dig and puffed out his chest as though he had won some award from the Knights of Columbus and was being feted by the parish priest.

"Max, you leave him alone!" yelled the voice from the kitchen. "Ray, you know you can stay as long as you need."

"Thanks, Ma," Ray shouted back, giving a knowing look at his father.

"Yeah, well turn that damned thing off – I wanna watch SportsCenter," snapped Mr. Lulio, having found that his verbal victory lap had been rudely cut short. "Besides, don't you have to go to work?"

"Not for another hour, an' I'm waiting for Connie."

"She's too good for you, boy – you know that" said Mr. Lulio in a much softer voice.

"Yeah…but so was Ma."

That brought a somewhat contemplative, if grimaced, smile to Mr. Lulio's face.

"Yes, son," he said, "an' she still is."

Within a few minutes of the exchange, Connie arrived home with a couple of bags of groceries. Ray got up from the couch and met her at the door.

"Here, hon," she said, almost out of breath from the journey home. "Your mom wanted me to pick up a few things. Can you take them in to her?"

Ray kissed her gently on the cheek as he grabbed the bags from her hands. "I'm glad you're home," he said. "I was afraid I'd miss you before I left."

He promptly headed for the kitchen and deposited the bags on the table, while his mother was busy peeling potatoes for the evening dinner. Eager to get back to Connie, he quietly sneaked out without her attention.

Coming back into the living room, he caught sight of Connie hanging up her coat in the closet by the front door. "I'm going to have to leave soon," he said tenderly.

"What time will you be home?" she asked, in a way that seemed to predict an unpleasant answer.

"As early as I can. Maybe ten-thirty or eleven at the latest."

She shook her head in resignation. "You can't keep this up, Ray – we can't keep this up," she insisted.

Ray gave a shrug and said "I don't like having to work all night either, but we need the money. We can't keep living here."

"I know, but you're never around. And I love your parents – don't get me wrong – but we're getting on each other's nerves."

"All the more reason for me to pull all these shifts. I'm able to make enough that we can get a down payment on a small place, here or maybe in Jersey. Just a little longer, and we'll have enough to get our own place."

"But if you were here more, you could run interference."

"With my dad…you're serious? He likes you more than me."

"That's not true. He's old school. He'll never tell you to your face how he really feels."

"But he's told you," said Ray, with disbelief clear in his voice.

"Well," hesitated Connie, "not in so many words…"

"Yeah, like no words, maybe?"

"He loves you, Ray," she argued, sensing that this was not a conversation that her husband wanted to have, especially just before he was heading out the door.

"I don't doubt he loves me. I just don't think he likes me very much."

"In any event, maybe I like having you near. What's the point of doing all this for us, when 'us' is always just you?"

"Not fair. Besides, Hal's gotta open up more for me on the day shift, if I prove myself on this."

"Oh, it's Hal now – not 'Mister Raphaelson' anymore."

"I dunno. He told me to call him Hal. He's the boss."

"He's a snake. Look, I've been around that company longer than you. Any trade who ever got that cozy with him ended up with their ass in the street - or worse."

"He's your boss, too. I can't afford to piss him off, or we're both gone. What are we going to do then?

"I'm not saying you should tell him to go to hell – I would have done that myself years ago," Connie frowned. "All I am saying is that you have to watch your back. The only thing he never keeps for himself is the blame, and he'll only give you a taste of the good stuff, so you'll jump when he says to jump."

"Look, I gotta go," said Ray. "Believe me, I know what you're saying. At this point, this is all I got. When you're stuck out in the water, you don't question who throws you the rope – you just grab it, that's all."

He leaned in and gave Connie a kiss on the cheek.

"You worry too much," he said. "I'll be home no later than eleven, so don't wait up."

With that, Ray put on his overcoat, grabbed his attaché case, and headed out the door. He was surprised to see his father sitting on the front step, as he had not noticed him anywhere the front door to begin with. The fact that he would be there to begin with, though, was not a surprise. Max liked to smoke, and as Bertie had developed respiratory difficulties over the past few years, he had willingly taken his habit out of doors. He had also found this spot far more relaxing, as it felt to him as his home was only his in a legal sense, and in no other way - all the more so with the addition of another person, and the real prospect of even more to come. He had half-jokingly considered the possibility of buying a dog, for no other reason than to have a doghouse to be banished to.

This was his father's time, and even Ray knew better than to intrude on this makeshift sanctum sanctorum. Nevertheless, he had a train to catch, and that meant having to cross this virtual line. He knew enough to make it quick and to not say a word. Unfortunately for him, Max decided to break down the wall of silence.

"I see what you're doing," he said as Ray tried to maneuver himself past on the narrow staircase.

"What? I'm going to work," defended Ray. "You wanna break my balls for working now?"

"You screw people out of money. I don't call that work."

"Well, not every legitimate job involves a monkey wrench," countered Ray. "Just because you can't get your head around it, doesn't mean it's wrong."

Max took a long drag from his cigarillo, and then gave a sardonic smile. "Just because I can't get my head around it doesn't mean it's right, either."

"I haven't got time for this," Ray said, as he waived his hand as if to further accentuate his dismissal.

"Walk away...Your uncle did that. Only a matter of time before you do, too."

Ray stopped walking toward the street, turned around, and glared at his father. "Where the hell do you get off? I have been taking your shit for years, and truth be known, I would have punched your lights out if it hadn't been for Ma."

Max countered by saying "If it hadn't been for her, I would have dropkicked you to the curb."

"You hate me that much?"

"No, I don't hate you at all," he sighed. "I love you, son, and that's why you piss me off so much...You don't understand, but I've seen all this before. I saw what he did to this family, and I swore that I would never – ever – let it happen again. I thought I could stop you. I tried my best, but I couldn't. It's bad enough that you're going to do this to your mother again, but Connie? Bertie and I brought you into this world, but her? She married into this."

"You said 'again'. I haven't done shit to anyone. You just keep blaming me for what Uncle Ray did. I was born a bad seed, so that's it. Well, maybe that's easier than looking in the mirror and owning up yourself for what kind of father you were."

Max lowered his head and sighed ruefully before looking his son straight in the eye. "Every day," he began, "I look in the mirror, and if it makes you feel any better, no, I don't always like what I see. But that's the difference. I can admit it. Your uncle couldn't do it, and I don't think you can either."

"I don't have time for this," snarled Ray, as he attempted to leave the conversation, such as it was.

"Answer me something first," said Max, still maintaining a peculiarly controlled tone. "Where did this idea that the rest of the world owes you something come from? The rest of us had to work to get anything we have, but you and your uncle? No, that's not for you.

"You spend all your time listening to that guy on TV tell you 'you deserve'…What do you think you 'deserve' anyway? Why you and nobody else? I don't remember any wise men dropping off gifts at the hospital where you were born."

"I'm going," muttered Ray. He slipped open the gate and headed out onto the sidewalk, but not before he heard Max shout out his final word, or question, on the subject.

"When did people start believing they were better than they really are?"

Max watched his son walk off into the distance, with not so much as a pause or stumble in his pace. What he did not see was the pained grimace on Ray's face. His last shot had hit his target.

Anger fueled Ray's walk to the train station. He felt so flushed that the sting of a cold wind barely registered with him. Typical of him, he groused, with every pace, every stomp of his feet punctuating his feelings.

For a moment, as he stood on the station platform, he considered what would happen if he just walked away – just disappeared into the night. It was one thing for people to nag him for the things he had done, but what other choices were there? *Sure, Hal's an asshole, but I still need the money. Besides, I don't see Connie quitting her job any time soon. You should do this. You should do that. With what?*

The truth was that none of that bothered him half as much as what his father had said – or how he had said it. No yelling – at least not from him. In fact, Ray was taken aback by the whole thing. He had been the one that was doing all of the yelling, and his father all of the deliberate questioning. The worst of it was that he could remember everything that came from Max's calm and purposeful voice, and really nothing that came from his own.

Despite the commotion in the stations, the trains heading into Manhattan were eerily quiet. The great exodus from the city and into the surrounding boroughs and towns. The other sides of the platforms were packed from the back wall to just mere inches from where the subway cars would stop.

Ray's side of the track was, by contrast, sparsely populated. Shift workers and young couples heading in for a date or a show. Although he hated having to work these hours, he enjoyed the commute. It was a guilty pleasure to be able to sit down and stretch a bit on a bench, while the people across the way were crammed together like linebackers in a huddle. At least there was something going his way.

He stared at the massed crowd, still thinking about his father's parting words. Was he right? Did he think he was better than he really was? Working where he did, he had seen enough cases of people who seemed that stupid suddenly became smart if you were just aggressive enough about it. He knew that stupid plus pushy just equaled more stupidity, and that those fools confused other people's reluctance to call them out on it as some form of vindication.

He saw it in other people, but did other people see it in him? Was he a hypocrite or was Max just delivering another one of his patented cheap shots?

The sudden gust of warm wind shook him from his senses. The train slowed down to a creep as the doors opened in front of him.

It was at this precise moment across town that Rob Bortelli gulped the last mouthful of bourbon from his glass, leaned forward to his desk, and stared at the screen of his laptop.

They were going to come, sooner or later. A week, a month – it did not matter. Just because you do not know the date of your demise, or the circumstances of it, does not mean you believe you will live forever.

He had fought Hal every step of the way, hadn`t he? The

executive committee minutes would bear that out. But that did not matter. He was there and he knew it all. The excuse of ``just following orders`` did not work in the Army, and it was not going to work this time either.

He could stand his ground and plead his innocence. Sure, and the federal attorney`s office would never go on national television and hype their prosecution, and they would hardly spend millions of dollars to vilify him. And, of course, after months of legal inquisition, he would never be forced to give up on an exoneration, and simply decide between a plea bargain or having the book thrown at him.

Back and forth, back and forth, his brain bounced from scenario to scenario. Finally, his eye caught a small plaque hanging in the hallway, just outside his office door. It was one of those inspirational signs with a trite message, the kind of sign that are altogether too popular with unimaginative bosses who rely on slogans more than talent. The sign simply read ``He who hesitates is lost. ``

Not exactly a shoulder tap from the divine finger of God, but it would have to do. Rob picked up his Blackberry and he made his call.

Chapter 7

The offices were located on the main floor of a converted warehouse in an old industrial neighborhood. In its day, it had the roughhewn feel of a backdrop for a 'Bowery Boys' film. Today, though, the area was gradually being gentrified, with the odd coffee bar and boutique shop beginning to appear. Regardless, it still had the feel of a dark and foreboding place, like the dockyards after sunset.

Ray wondered why someone like Hal would associate themselves with people like this. *Loyalty - or pity?* As unconventional as he could be, he was still the head of one of the most prestigious firms on Wall Street. *Either these clowns travelled in higher circles, or Hal had travelled a bit lower on occasion.*

Nothing on the outside of the building indicated the nature or the purpose of the business, save for the small brass placard above the intercom that read 'Moreton Securities.' Unlike Tuckner Wass, this firm did not invite the public, or openly extol its virtues to the world.

He stopped and punched in the code that released the door lock. From there, it was a dozen feet or so down a nondescript hallway, which led to a large open area that looked vaguely like the trading floor at Tuckner Wass. There were no side or corner offices – just cubicles – no big board flashing numbers from the various exchanges, and no series of clocks that told you it was seven in the evening in Tokyo, or two in the morning in Dubai.

Everything at Moreton appeared to be a stripped-down facsimile of Tuckner Wass, Spartan and utilitarian. If the latter were akin to Tiffany's, then this was a strip mall dollar store.

Although Ray was loath to admit it openly, even the people there were a stripped-down version of their Wall Street kith and kin. Despite the obvious aspiration to something much greater, most of the traders there reminded him of a neighborhood wise guy, or local tough, trying to score big on that afternoon's trifecta at Pimlico. The place felt somewhat dirty, and it made him feel that way too. There were the odd faces he recognized from Tuckner Wass, but, like him, they were all low in the pecking order.

The floor boss was an old veteran of the days when trading meant standing on the floor of the exchange and screaming orders at the top of your lungs. Pete Kelly was a slightly rotund man, with salt and pepper hair greased back like a plastic helmet. Ray figured him to be slightly older than his father. He could picture Pete as a beat cop, or a truck driver, but not as a floor boss, or any sort of manager. The most successful of that generation of traders were loud and aggressive, and Ray had guessed early on that, by that measure, Pete should have already earned enough to retire several times over.

The fact that he had not faded away gracefully meant one, or more, of three things - either his proclivities were too expensive, his alimony was too restrictive, or he simply needed to keep playing, just as a shark needs to swim or die. From what he had seen of Pete in action, and what he knew of the operation, Ray was pretty sure that he could rule out the third possibility. Cream rises to the top. It does not congeal at the bottom of the barrel, feeding on the Social Security cheques of middle America. It seemed fair to assume that most of what Pete earned went straight into the hairy, outstretched paw of whatever monkey was on his back.

Ray did not like him – pure and simple. It did not extend into hate, or even loathing, though. It was more of an indifference aided and abetted by plain old-fashioned apathy. He just simply did not like the man. If he were to have ever met him on the street, he would likely look the other way, and pretend not to notice him. If he were cornered, he would acknowledge him, exchange a couple of pleasantries, and then quickly apologize for having to rush off so fast.

He made his way to a plain looking desk, where he set up shop. There was no cloak room, or even any cubicle walls for him to hang his coat, so he slung it over the back of his chair. An annoyance to be sure, as it always seemed to get tangled under the coasters, rolling from one spot to another.

The idea of making dozens more cold calls to prospects had depressed him more than a little bit. Even Moreton's clients were a complete juxtaposition to those of Tuckner Wass. While the venerable Wall Street firm dealt with blue chip stocks and experienced, well-heeled investors, this office's activities – as far as Ray could surmise – involved calling rather unsophisticated people and trying to peddle shares in somewhat dubious ventures. The typical Moreton client – if he could call them that - was probably an elderly woman, likely widowed, and with a decent enough nest egg. Possibly it would have been some sort of a pension, the proceeds of selling the family home, or the remnants of an insurance payout after the bills and the burial were attended to.

The share offerings were always portrayed as a unique, golden opportunity, available to only a select and discerning few. So golden and unique that nobody had ever heard of the damn things, he mused to himself.

Nothing traded above a dollar a share, and all were either on the Over The Counter market, the Pink Sheets, or on some foreign bourse. Some had foreign sounding names, particularly in Chinese or Portuguese, but that did not necessarily mean that they traded outside of the United States. A marketing ploy, to be sure. Most people being solicited would hear no less than a dozen news stories over the course of a week about how China, or India, or Brazil was going to be the next great economic engine of the global economy. Naturally, they saw these flotations as their ticket to play. Whether or not those numbers were entered in this lottery was an entirely different matter altogether.

They were so obscure that you could not find a Moody's or S & P report on one of them, lest some Moreton client happened to wonder how their five thousand shares in Company X compared to the rest of the sector.

The sales pitch had been devised to handle every objection in the same way. Depending on the sector, the Moreton salesman would mention whatever global behemoth dominated that specific market, and then would ask rhetorically if anyone had heard of them way back when. Who had heard of Microsoft back in such-and-such a year? What about Google? What about Apple or Amazon?

It was, to be sure, a fine line fib. You never actually portrayed these companies as the next you-know-what. You only asked whether anyone had ever heard of these major corporations back in the day. A lesson in sophistry, perhaps, but it was enough to provide some level of cover and keep the folks at FINRA or the SEC from nosing around too closely. Ray did not really appreciate all of that. He only knew of its importance in the context that Pete had communicated to him on his first day at Moreton – do it and you're ass-canned!

"Hey, Lulio! Since you're just standin' around, go pick up some coffees," yelled Pete.

Damnit thought Ray. Every time he was getting ready, or got on a roll, Pete was pulling him off the phones for some bull crap reason – and always related to food. It was the same situation for the first few weeks at Tuckner Wass, but he was not a rookie anymore – at least not in the overall sense. It was hard enough to make a decent commission from the nickel-and-dime nature of Moreton's business. It was damn near impossible if he was out fetching pizzas, coffee, and Chinese takeout every five minutes.

"Yeah, yeah," he said, getting up from his desk. "What's everybody want?"

The ten guys in the office all started to bark out their orders in unison, when Ray waved his hand and yelled "Hey, write it down. How the hell am I supposed to keep it straight?"

One by one, they handed him their preferences on pieces of sticky memo paper. "Great," he said, sarcastically. "And I suppose you clowns want me to pay for it too?"

"Take it outta petty cash," yelled back Pete.

Ray went over to the reception desk. "Anita, I'm gonna need thirty bucks," he said.

"All we got is twenty," the receptionist yelled, so that Pete could hear.

"I'll add the rest to your pay," came the echo.

"Yeah, right," yelled Ray, as he headed out the door. "Add it to the fifty you stiffed me last week for pizza."

"Uh, okay," came Pete's reply, which Ray could barely hear as he stepped out into the street.

It was roughly about this time that Connie had settled down to watch some television. Even though she was glad to be home, and away from the office, she felt some strange compulsion to switch the set to the business news channel. It was all the stranger for the fact that Raphaelson was appearing live. Sure, she had to suffer his presence from nine to five, but now? She was on her own dime. Still, she felt she needed to watch. Maybe to curse at the set, or to feel the power of pushing the mute button every time he would speak? It was juvenile, but it felt good anyway.

"*...From the NASDAQ trading site in Times Square ...*" boomed the television set, just as Ray's father came in the front door.

"I picked up the stuff, Bertie," he bellowed. "Verrazano's a goddamn crook. You wouldn't believe what he charged me for these tomatoes!"

"Just bring it in here and quit complaining. Connie's trying to watch her program," came the answer.

"So," he said, turning to his daughter-in-law, before he made his way to the kitchen, "I take it Diamond Jim has left to make another million."

"He's trying, pop. Why won't you give him that?" she asked, in a tone more appropriate to a statement than a question.

"Humph," he muttered as he left the room.

No point. Maybe Ray is right after all, Connie said to herself as she went back to her show.

"*...tonight, we have the CEO of Tuckner Wass, Hal Raphaelson, in the studio. Thanks for joining us at the desk.*"

"*Good to be here, Sarah...*"

What a greaseball. Here he is on TV blathering on, while Ray won't be home until God knows when.

"*...Now, you really have to let us in on your secret. Amid all the carnage on Wall Street, your firm is posting some solid numbers for this quarter. You guys are made of Teflon or something...*"

"Or something," muttered Connie.

"*...no, no. Tuckner Wass doesn't have any magic formula. We have good analysts, good traders, and we just stick to the basics. Above all, we're value investors, and...*"

It was just at that very moment that a half-dozen police officers burst onto the studio set, showing viewers just how live that live television could be.

"Harold Raphaelson. We have a warrant for your arrest!" yelled the lead plain clothed detective.

Connie's eyes became as big as saucers. Her jaw was frozen open. What the hell…

At that moment, Raphaelson, true to form, began to spout a line of obscenities at such a rapid-fire rate, the beeping seemed to be a continual tone. With a degree of athleticism that was surprising for a man of his age and habits. He hurled himself on top of the anchor desk and started throwing objects at the officers. Laptops, desk monitors and papers went flying in a frenetic flurry. Police and panelists alike were attempting to grab him by a foot or ankle as he hopped back and forth like an exotic dancer attempting to evade the reach of her more rapacious admirers. What seemed to endure for ages, ended abruptly when a couple of them had pulled him off and wrestled him to the ground.

As the mayhem subsided, the host gained control of the set, and slightly off-kilter, he said *"Sorry, folks. I'm not even going to try to explain that one…Best to move on with our Chart of the Day…"*

After the high-tech graphic and musical fanfare, up came on the television screen a pre-loaded stock chart for Tuckner Wass.

"Shit," said the voice on the television.

Connie was stunned silent by what she – and the world – had just seen, looked up for a moment to notice Mr. Lulio, who had been standing there for quite some time.

"Well, it looks like Junior's gonna be looking for a job," he said matter-of-factly. "Maybe he should go to work for another crook like Verrazano…Did I tell you what that sonofabitch charged me for those tomatoes?"

She said nothing. It was though the hand of fate had clasped firmly around her mouth. *Oh, my God!* Her brain started to flood with a torrent of fears and premonitions. *Our jobs…Ray…Where the hell was he? Does he even know?*

Meanwhile, Ray fumbled ever so slightly as he attempted to balance the cardboard carry trays of coffee while walking across the street. He muttered to himself about how he was getting royally screwed out of earning some commissions, let alone out of whatever this snack run was going to cost him out of pocket.

So far, this 'favor' of Hal's was costing him more than he was earning. He had been embarrassed by this fact and had neglected to tell Connie that he had already withdrawn about a thousand dollars from their savings to cover the shortfall. But what could he do? Quit? Not only would he scuttle the possibility of making money at Moreton at some point, but he could probably kiss goodbye any chance he had of getting to the Tuckner Wass trading desk. Hal had promised him the first available opening, did he not? Code of honor – that is what he said.

A sudden gust of cold wind brought him back to the here and now, and nearly toppled his precious cargo in the process. Damn it, he muttered to himself, as he repositioned his balancing act. I should be home with Connie. His dislike of the current living arrangements was more a dislike of living under Max's roof, and at a time like this, it was pretty hard to justify killing himself and upsetting his wife just to avoid that particular annoyance.

It was when he had come within a few doors of the office that he noticed the commotion. The exhaust of the two large NYPD vans blazed red with the reflection of the flashing lights, looking more like the dance floor of a 70's discotheque than a city street. He slowed his pace to a near stop when he caught sight of Pete and the others being led out of the building and into the waiting vehicles.

"Shit!" he muttered in a panic. He had always had a bad feeling about what went on in that office, but the need for money outweighed his fear of the possible consequences. Not wanting to catch the gaze of Pete or any of the others, he quickly turned around and headed back in the direction from where he came.

He felt a shiver of panic run down his spine, making him shudder as he walked briskly away. It was high school, and Kevin Cortese waiting down the street with a knuckle duster all over again. Flight over fight. He threw the coffee down a staircase to a basement entrance and picked up the pace, wondering whether they would notice him running away. *Just a few more feet to the corner… Just a few more feet, then…*

As Ray rounded the corner, he ran into a group of men standing beside a black Lincoln. It gave him what he could only describe as a 'bad vibe.' This situation did not appear to be much better than the one he was avoiding, so he quietly turned to retrace his steps.

"Hey, you!" yelled one of the men. "Stop right where you are!"

Ray felt the blood drain from his face. His chest felt like it had been weighed down with a large piece of iron slag. In a rare moment, he was at a loss for words, or an idea.

Mercifully, it seemed, another man spoke up before Ray collapsed in a sobbing heap on the sidewalk.

"My apologies," he said to the man who ordered Ray to stop, "but my associate's English is not so good. He glanced at Ray, giving a fleeting, but knowing, gaze. The look that said to him to just play along - *for God's sake - play along!*

Ray took the line instinctively, and, giving a meek smile, shrugged his shoulders.

The first man, who had yelled for Ray to stop, looked at him carefully for a moment, and then turned to the gentleman who had intervened on his behalf.

"Consider this due notice," he said as he handed him an official looking document. "You have 48 hours to comply with the order, but I'm sure you know that already."

"Yes," came the reply, calm as could be. "Thank you. I shall forward this to my superiors, and they will give you their answer."

Ray was not sure what to make of this. *Shit, most people would be trying to hide from a process server – that, or beg their way out of a repo…Hell, he's not even taking their car? Maybe it's just to appear in court – but for what?*

The official looking men got back in their cars, and drove away, leaving Ray standing with the strangers.

"Well, uh, thanks, guys," he said, still not sure what just happened. "Anyhow, I gotta get going. My wife is probably worrying about me, and…"

"We'll give you a ride home," said the lead man, sounding more like a command than an offer.

"No…really…it's okay," assured Ray. The awkwardness began to disappear, only to be replaced by something that felt even worse. "I can get home on my own. Besides, I need some time to figure out what to tell my wife."

The lead man repeated his words – we'll give you a ride home

– as one of his associates opened the back door of the limousine. Clearly, he was getting a ride home whether he wanted it or not.

The hairs on the back of Ray's neck stood up as he climbed into the back seat of the car. "So," he asked, with a slight nervous tone, "what kind of business are you guys in."

The man who had spoken on their behalf gave a few brief words to the driver in Spanish, then turned back and smiled at Ray. No answer appeared to be forthcoming.

"Look," Ray continued, fighting his growing anxiety with a determined resolve not to lose control of himself. "I don't know what that was about back there, and I appreciate whatever you did for me, but I really should be heading home. Just drop me off at the next corner and I'll get back on my own."

Still nothing, No response. Not a word, or even a grunt was directed his way. The only noise came from the conversations among the men in Spanish, which were clearly not meant for him. Ray quietly admonished himself for not paying attention to his parents when they tried to teach him the language before, when he was not contemplating the situation at hand.

"You didn't ask me where I live," he said nervously. They have to answer that now, don't they?

"Excuse me?" said the lead man, as if he had forgotten some important detail or information.

"You didn't ask me where I live. How are you going to drop me off if you don't know the directions?"

Ray's question caused the man to relax his facial muscles from the frozen expression they had had since he had walked in on their business, or whatever it was. "We need to stop at our office first," he explained. "I need to file a report before we take you home. I hope that it is not a great inconvenience."

"Naw…it's probably quicker than the train. Besides, maybe I could call my wife when we get to your office – just to let her know I'm okay."

The man said nothing. He smiled and looked out the window.

Within twenty minutes, they had made their way to an upscale neighborhood close to Central Park. The car pulled up to a wrought iron gate, which opened to reveal a large brownstone complex with a circular driveway. Above the front entrance hung a large flag – red and white stripes, with a single white star on a blue background.

"You guys from Texas, huh?" said Ray, now feeling a little more at ease. "Yeah, I love Texas – the Alamo, the Cowboys…Hey – don't mess with Texas!"

Still no reaction from the other passengers, beyond the odd quick phrase in Spanish, which was fast becoming a source of renewed anxiety. Ray remembered that his parents only spoke it when they had something to hide away – like getting behind in the household bills, or some marital tiff. From as far back as he could remember in his childhood, Spanish equaled bad news, and nothing thus far showed itself to be good.

Chapter 8

Once inside the front entrance of the mansion, the man led Ray through an expansive foyer, which also seemed to function as a reception area. Despite the utilitarian style of the furnishings, the entrance still retained the character of an older era. One could picture horse-drawn lacquer carriages ferrying the scions of Knickerbocker society for some gala. To Ray, they appeared to be foreign relics of an ancient era, assigned to the ranks of old Indian arrowheads and Peter Stuyvesant's tomb – here first, perhaps, but here no more.

The man led Ray into a large banquet room that had been filled, instead, with work cubicles – about a dozen or so – with a narrow corridor leading out into another room. Making their way past, they entered the last chamber.

This room, a formal private office, seemed to be the only place in the building that had preserved any semblance of its intended function. Oak bookshelves lined much of the wall space. The rest was comprised of lathe and plaster cloaked in a sumptuous, silk-like, red wallpaper, all held off the floor by three feet of rich oak paneled wainscotting.

"Beautiful room, isn't it? Apparently, it was the private study of some descendant of an old New York family – Vanderbilt, Astor, I can never remember. Anyway, he lost it all in 1931, and our predecessors in the government bought it quite cheap. Some want to sell it, but I think it is worth keeping…Ivan, please close the door."

Startled, Ray snapped his neck around to catch sight of one of the men from the car, a stocky, muscular fellow. While he had been taken up by all the sights and sounds in the old mansion, Ray had not noticed the man who had been no more than five feet behind the whole time.

"Jeezus, you snuck up on me!" he said to the man called Ivan.

"Please," the man in charge said as he gestured for Ray's attention. "Have a seat."

Ray dutifully lowered himself into the large leather padded chair opposite the desk where the man took position.

"Maybe we should get to know one another?" he said.

Ray looked confused, not knowing why these formalities were necessary. After all, he would be up and out the door in a matter of minutes. On the other hand, he felt as if he did owe the stranger some courtesy for having spared him a ride downtown with Pete and the rest of what used to be Moreton Securities.

"Uh, yeah…my name is Ray Lulio, and I work for Tuckner Wass."

"Tuckner Wass?" The mention of the firm seemed to create some glint in the man's eye, like he had stumbled upon some eureka moment. "I didn't know they had an office in that part of town. I would have thought they were closer to Manhattan?"

"Well…," hesitated Ray.

"Never mind. I am being a poor host. My name is Raul Rodriguez, and this is the Cuban Permanent Mission to the United Nations. I serve as the chef de mission."

"Chef? So, you cook things up around here?"

Rodriguez began to laugh. "I've never quite heard it described that way. Actually, I assist the ambassador in his duties in the General Assembly."

Ray seemed satisfied, for a moment, but then his expression changed. "What mission did you say this was?" he asked very cautiously.

"Cuba," replied Rodriguez.

"Ohhh, shhhiiit!" stammered Ray, as he got out of the chair, like he had been singed by hot coals. "Sorry, buddy, but I gotta get home. No offense."

Without missing a beat, Rodriguez smiled and calmly said "Sit down, Mister Lulio."

At that moment, Ray saw him nod to the back of the office, where a man pulled shut the door and locked it.

"You can't keep me here," Ray said defiantly. "This is the United States of America."

Rodriguez rose from his chair, walked slowly around the desk to Ray, and patted him on the shoulder. "This is a diplomatic mission, so, technically, you are on Cuban soil…Just sit down and relax, Mister Lulio. We've got much to discuss."

"You can't kidnap me! I'm an American!" yelled Ray, becoming more agitated by the second.

"Who said anything about kidnapping?" replied Rodriguez. "All I want to do is talk to you about a very lucrative opportunity."

Opportunity. That word, so imprinted on Ray's brain for so long, was like a hypnotic suggestion. It froze him dead in his tracks.

"Opportunity?" he asked. "What do you mean by 'opportunity'?

"Yes, of course. We understand that this situation is confusing for you. If you will give me a moment to explain things, then I am sure you will be interested in my offer. Then we can figure out what to do next."

"Like for me to go home?"

"All in good time, but I must explain how things stand."

"Like what?" asked Ray. "What was going on back there?"

"A simple misunderstanding," explained Rodriguez. "You see, our two countries do not have a very good relationship, and misunderstandings do tend to crop up from time to time."

"What kinds of misunderstandings?"

"Oh, some agents of your government are under the impression that we are involved in espionage…"

"You're spies?!" exclaimed Ray, only marginally calmer at this point.

"No, no, no…not at all. We represent our country in the United Nations – nothing more," assured Rodriguez.

"So why do they think you're spies?"

"A misperception, fed by those in your government who are pushing an agenda."

"You say they're lying?"

"No, I would say that they are laboring under assumptions that are not wholly accurate."

"So, they are making a mistake, then?" asked Ray.

"Tell me, did they ever find those weapons of mass destruction?"

Ray paused for a moment.

"Point taken," he sighed.

"Anyway," continued Rodriguez, "your government's authorities have accused our trade advisor, Antonio Vasquez, of being a spy, along with three other staff."

"Umm...sorry?" said Ray. "I still don't know why this is any of my business?"

"Mr. Lulio. The men who detained us back there think that you are Antonio Vasquez."

"But I'm not."

"But they *think* that you are," said Rodriguez, as he sat down on the edge of his desk.

"Well, they're wrong, and I'll be happy to set them straight," said Ray, as he rose from the chair. "All you need to do is let me go home, and this will all get fixed."

"Maybe, maybe not," sighed Rodriguez.

"What do you mean 'maybe not'?"

"Well, Mr. Lulio, let's say I agree and let you go. Let's assume that they buy whatever story you have for associating with Cuban government officials – I'm sure you have already worked that out – but assuming you have convinced them, then what?

"I heard the news tonight, and I know what happened at your firm, Tuckner Wass. The head of your company was arrested on live television not more than an hour ago..."

"That's bullshit!" argued Ray. "You're just saying that because I told you where I worked. If I had said any other name, you'd have used it instead. I'm not stupid."

"I never said I believed you to be stupid," said Rodriguez, maintaining a cool and placid demeanor, despite Ray's increasing agitation. "You appear to be a shrewd man who tries to limit the potential downside of any situation. I can only guess that your reaction when you saw us was because you were trying to avoid trouble elsewhere.

"Clearly, however, trouble is surely on its way. A fish may rot from the head, but the stench does travel beyond. This Mister Raphaelson may be given some inducement to share his misfortune with colleagues to receive some leniency. Maybe he will share it with you?

"I believe that the end result of your plan will be that you will be charged with fraud, and attempting to leave the country, while my colleague will be sent home on a trumped-up charge, and unable to do the work so vital for my country. This is not what you want, is it?"

Ray frowned, slumping back down in the chair. It was almost impossible for him to believe that Tuckner Wass was guilty of a fraud, but Hal was not the company – just a man, and one for whom scruples seemed to be some meaningless decoration trotted out to appease the board and shareholders every so often. And then there was Moreton. The police raid was not some trumped up story. It was real and he saw it. Faster service at the coffee shop and he would surely have been a part of it. He also could not forget that it was Hal who had recommended him to Moreton in the first place, and neither was he the only Tuckner Wass trader moonlighting there. These notions rushed back and forth through his mind like the shimmering flecks in a snow globe after it has been violently shaken.

"I don't believe you."

Rodriguez shrugged, then reached for a remote sitting on the credenza behind his desk and pointed it toward the large television mounted on the wall to Ray's right.

"...futures in the financial sector are dramatically down with the arrest of Tuckner Wass CEO Harold Raphaelson in dramatic fashion on live television earlier this evening. This is in connection with an eighteen-month investigation by the SEC and the Office of the District Attorney for New York's Southern District..."

Rodriguez shut off the television, then turned back to Ray. "And you work for Tuckner Wass."

Ray remained fixated on the television. After a moment, he raised his left hand, combing back from his forehead and up so tightly it looked as though he would yank out some of his hair. He let out a deep breath. "So," he sighed, "let's have it. What's your plan?"

"Simple. As I said before - be Vasquez."

"Be Vasquez," repeated Ray, in a monotone of disbelief.

"Yes," Rodriguez replied. "The FBI took your picture. They think you are Vasquez. So be Vasquez."

"What do you mean by 'be Vasquez'?"

"Vasquez has been ordered to leave the United States in the next 48 hours. The FBI thinks you are Vasquez, so you leave in his place," said Rodriguez.

"To where?" asked Ray.

"To Cuba, of course," came the answer.

Ray was not sure what seemed worse to him – the idea of going to Cuba, or the suggestion of the scheme in the first place.

"Now hold on a minute. Assuming I agree to go – and I'm not saying I do – but assuming I agree, you seem to think that it's going to be easy. They spend billions of dollars to track who is coming and going. They'd see through this in five minutes flat!"

Rodriguez rose from his chair and turned to look out the window behind his desk, his back turned to Ray.

"Your Pentagon buys toilet seats for ten thousand dollars each," he said," while your major corporations have staff who steal office supplies and long-distance phone calls. You assume that big organizations have big abilities. We all do – even us Cubans. But I have learned that the bigger the machine, the more moving parts you need to pay attention to. The problem is that no one actually does it.

"We show up at Teterboro, and some poor, overworked security guard has to figure out who you are. They have a picture from the FBI that says that you are Antonio Vasquez, a Cuban passport that says you are Vasquez, and three colleagues who swear that you are Vasquez.

"Now, consider that this person is nearing the end of their shift. They have others to screen, but they are going to ignore everything you say, we say, all of the documents, because they know deep down that it is all false?"

Ray sighed as he raised his eyebrows. "I suppose not," he said, "but you haven't answered me why I should even do this to begin with."

"The same reason anyone does anything," explained Rodriguez. "We will make it worth your while."

"Which means what?" asked Ray, sensing that the momentum

of the conversation had changed, and that he was not the only one in the room bargaining from a position of weakness. "You expect me to put my neck on the line, you're going to have to give me some details."

"Well, we would put you up in a resort for two weeks – a nice place with impeccable service – and then we fly you to Canada, where your wife can meet you with your passport and ID. This situation with your employer - chances are that the authorities won't bother with you directly after enough time passes. Maybe you get called as a witness – maybe not, but you likely won't get charged yourself."

Ray frowned. "What makes you think that my wife will want to meet me after I disappear for a couple of weeks, then show up with a tan?" he asked.

"Because you will have fifty thousand dollars in an account in the Cayman Islands," replied Rodriguez.

Ray stared at him for a moment, trying to get his brain around all of this.

"Uhh…I'm still not sure about this whole thing," he said, hesitating nervously.

"What's to be sure about?" asked Rodriguez "You stay in a luxury villa in the Caribbean for a couple of weeks and come back fifty thousand dollars richer. You stay out of jail, and you allow my colleague to continue his work promoting trade. Who gets hurt?"

"Assuming this thing works," interjected Ray.

"It will work," said Rodriguez. He then turned to the man at the door and gave some instructions in Spanish.

"Ivan will show you to your room, where you can get cleaned up. We will take your passport photo tonight, so we can have things ready for tomorrow afternoon when we leave."

He walked over, and gently placed his hand on Ray's shoulder.

"In two weeks, you will be back with your family, and you'll have the money to begin a new life. Just try and think about that," he said.

Ray got up from the chair and gave a nod of resignation to Rodriguez. He was, of course, right. Options were not that plentiful. He was boxed into a corner, and if there was an opportunity to see, his sight was far too clouded to pick up on it. And after following the man named Ivan into a room to get his picture taken for his new Cuban passport, he was escorted to a guest room on one of the upper floors, where he would stay the night.

Never in his life had he experienced such a fitful sleep – not before his interview with Bortelli, not even the night before his wedding. It was not that Ray was oblivious to the happenings around him, or that he was immune to worry. He worried and fixated as much as the next fellow. The thing was that Ray always had the innate sense that everything would eventually turn out in the end. In the end, he believed, everything works out as it should. After all, did he not get the job and the girl?

This time, however, was different. He tried to rationalize, to strategize, to get his head wrapped around the situation he found himself in. A man who is quick on his feet will be fine – provided on his feet is where he remained.

It was not fear. That would have been an exaggeration. Concern, yes, but not fear. A very strong concern to be sure.

He looked out the window, beyond the bars, out into the night. The front of the mansion was so overly endowed with foliage and tree cover, it would have been pitch black had it not been for the glow of a late and full harvest moon. He began thinking about Connie, and how it was a good couple of hours past when he said he would be home.

She would know about the arrests at Moreton. Ray predicted that she would have gone to whatever precinct the rest of them were being held at. There was also a good possibility that she had found out that he was not among those picked up in the raid. His avoidance of the NYPD would be no consolation.

The first reaction of someone trying to track down a missing person is to call the police. Connie would know that if they found him, he would be arrested on the spot. She would avoid filing a missing persons' report if it would lead to a one-way ticket to Ossining.

Ray sat up on the edge of the bed, placing his head in his hands. He hurt her, and he knew it. She, Bortelli, and at least a dozen others told him that no one ever survived the experience of being one of Raphaelson's lackeys. In a rare moment of introspection, he considered the possibility that it had never been about the money, and that just maybe it was about feeding something deep inside his head. That ruminated in his brain as he finally drifted to sleep.

Chapter 9

The darkened room was quiet and comfortable, so much so that it took more than a gentle tapping on his shoulder to wake Ray up. For a few moments, he felt as though he were laying snugly in his own bed, with Connie giving him a slight tap to wake up.

"Senor Lulio, it will be time to go soon," said Ivan. "I have left you some clothes, and when you finish, there is breakfast in the dining room."

Still groggy, Ray rubbed his eyes and grunted his assent. He remembered where he was, as well as the circumstances that had led up to this point. His mind now flooded with a jumble of worries and concerns. *Connie! I need to call Connie…My job – our jobs – shit!*

It took almost a half hour for ray to settle his mind enough to get on with things. A quick shower and shave followed by getting dressed. A set of clothes, namely a linen suit, had been placed at the foot of the bed for him. They were not an exact fit, but close enough. They were as comfortable as the clothes that he used to wear before he got married, when he had to buy his own.

He headed down the hallway and descended the staircase. The gentleman at the base of the steps politely pointed him in the direction of the dining room, where he informed Ray that Senor Rodriguez was eager to discuss the finer details of today's agenda. Once in the room, he was greeted by Rodriguez, who invited him to sit down and enjoy a hearty breakfast as, in his words, he would be needing it.

The next couple of hours had rushed by in a hurry. In between mouthfuls of poached eggs and toast, Ray was questioned and rehearsed, over and over, until it had become as natural as walking or breathing. Over and over, he repeated the mantra. I am Antonio Vasquez. I am a trade analyst with the Cuban Permanent Mission to the United Nations. I was born at Santiago de Cuba on May 21, 1974. My wife's name is Marta and I have two children – a boy and a girl. Whenever he happened to make a mistake, Rodriguez instructed him, kindly - but firmly - to do it again three more times.

He did it so many times that it began to become meaningless to him. They were just words without context. Unfortunately, it made Ray start to treat the whole thing as a big joke. The constant rehearsing and instruction of 'again', reminded him of an old Saturday morning cartoon where Bugs Bunny was forced to repeat over and over *"I am Elmer J. Fudd, millionaire. I own a mansion und a yacht."* It made him chuckle like a schoolboy, which served to do nothing but confuse and annoy his host.

Once breakfast had finished, and Rodriguez was reasonably satisfied that Ray would not crack under pressure, it was time to organize their departure.

Ivan presented his boss with the newly minted passport for Ray, replete with all the stampings that he presumed had shown up in the original – London, Barcelona, Tunis, Caracas, and, of course, New York. Rodriguez examined it carefully before handing it to Ray. "Do not lose this – whatever you do," he cautioned.

"Don't worry," said Ray, slipping the booklet into the inside breast pocket of his suit jacket. "I know the routine. My neck's on the line, too, you know."

Rodriguez rolled his eyes. *There is no comparison.* He knew the difference between an American prison and a Cuban one, and he harbored no illusions about what the downside of this plan really was.

In the meantime, Ivan had supervised the loading of the luggage and other sundries into the back of the Lincoln, as well as another car – a simple, nondescript sedan that would follow them on their way out to Teterboro. Within the hour, both cars were fully loaded, passengers and all, as they pulled out past the gates and onto the street.

Compared to his journey to the Mission, this was a relatively talkative affair, with most of the discussion now taking place in English. Unfortunately for Ray, it almost exclusively consisted of Rodriguez continuing to quiz him on every aspect of Antonio Vasquez's existence. While he argued that he knew as much about Vasquez as he did his own life, it was Rodriguez's contention that the only real proof of that assertion would be whether they were able to board the plane without incident.

It was only about a fifteen-mile drive from their location to the New Jersey Meadowlands. Through the Lincoln Tunnel, then jog onto Route 3W until they would hit I-95. After hugging the Hudson for a stretch, they would get off at Winant, and then it was straight in to Teterboro. Unfortunately, fifteen miles really meant nothing. New Yorkers learn to measure in time – not distance – and for that, it was somewhere between forty-five minutes and three hours. It was frustrating if – like the Cubans – you were from out of town and expected a correlation between speed and length.

Ray, on the other hand, was raised to take these things in his own stride, and as a result was the least stressed of the group. Besides, as he rightfully reasoned, the only things that he would have otherwise been rushed to do were all exceedingly unpleasant and complicated. Barring a cavity search at the airport, or a subsequent nosedive into the ocean, the flight was the more agreeable of his options. The trip ended up being closer to an hour, so everyone felt as though they had not been particularly ill-used.

The nature of the trip and the passengers involved required a quick detour to the northeast corner of the airport. Homeland Security operated out of a non-descript building on Fred Wehran Drive. Ray stayed in the car while Rodriguez and one of the other men paid a courtesy call. Another twenty minutes and they were back on their way, heading back up, then southwest on Industrial, past a row of aircraft hangars and other assorted outbuildings.

Rodriguez pointed to one of the buildings and instructed the driver to pull up to the entrance. As they slid in under the canopy of this mini terminal, he turned to Ray and said with more than a degree of sangfroid "You need to get this right. Understand? Make a mistake and we're all done for!"

"I know, I know," insisted Ray, tired of the constant lecturing. "The only thing that'll screw me up is getting nervous from all your nagging! Just let me do it, okay?"

Rodriguez nodded and got out of the car, with Ray and three others in tow. A deep breath, and in he went.

Despite the assurances, as the men approached the INS officers, Ray felt as though he was about to lose the breakfast he had eaten earlier. The bile was backing up into his throat. He tried to look calm and relaxed as he choked it back.

Rodriguez introduced himself and the others, explaining that they were complying with an official request from the State Department. With that, he handed a plain brown envelope to one of the men behind the counter. After a few agonizing moments where a man directed his attentions back and forth between the Cubans and the documents, the nod was finally given to proceed.

Ray had never flown anywhere before in his life. That did not mean he was unfamiliar with airports. From time to time, relatives from Puerto Rico would come to visit his parents. He also had a friend in high school, Mark Krazinski, whose father was a luggage handler at La Guardia's main terminal. Before 9/11, they had been, on occasion, allowed to come in and see how the whole set-up ran – the maze of conveyor belts, the strange looking trucks and their loads of knapsacks, duffle bags and suitcases that resembled some exotic desert caravan plying its way across a concrete Sahara.

But now, he was on the business end of things – but exactly what kind of business? A drowning man may not necessarily care what motivates the person throwing them a lifeline, but, at some point, one does consider that nothing, including charity, comes without a price. Ray might not have ever given a second thought to what he owed his mother and father for perpetual room and board, but he did start to calculate what he was into Rodriguez for. All he knew was that it was not going to be cheap.

One by one, the men passed through the metal detector after having emptied their pockets into the grey plastic bins that were slid through an X-ray machine.

Ray glanced momentarily at the security guards operating the machine. He avoided direct eye contact, for fear that they would see right through him. Despite Rodriguez's haughty dismissive of them, he knew that they were not as overworked or underwhelming as they might appear. Even lazy thinkers have a coping mechanism. If you cannot discern the guilty from the innocent, then just assume guilt in everyone you meet. Even if you are occasionally wrong, the criminals will never go free. The only downside would be those who took their moral outrage to the powers that be, but even their rage could never stand up to the Byzantine workings of the bureaucracy. He wondered if the people they were dealing with at this moment subscribed to this philosophy.

"Walk through, please," came the emotionless command from one of the guards, a middle-aged woman, whose government issue uniform did not flatter, but profanely insulted, her physique. Ray mused to himself that the women who should wear dresses rarely did.

One by one, the Cubans took their turns slowly walking through the metal frame – in a couple of cases, more than once – until the attended staff were well satisfied that all threats to the Republic had been duly thwarted.

The runway side of the terminal was windier and colder. The open fields provided no break or cover from the elements. The Learjet 45XR sat like an oasis in the desert – or was it more like the getaway car after a bank heist? Ray still mulled over the reasons why Rodriguez's offer was so attractive. Regardless, he was as much excited to get on a luxury jet as he was to be out of harm's way.

He climbed aboard after Rodriguez, who had him sit at the front, in a seat facing directly toward his own. *Did he need to be watched?* Dutifully, he took his place and fastened the seatbelt.

The interior of the craft was simple, but elegant. Tan leather seats, highly polished wood that looked marbled, like walnut, and gold-plated fixtures all around. Ray reflected on the irony of it all. For years, he travelled less than modestly while Raphaelson made it a point of fact to travel in planes like this. Now, in the space of less than a day, he was the one on the jet while his boss was likely shackled in the back of a paddy wagon. Maybe this plan was not such a bad idea after all.

The opulence of the cabin distracted his mind from the fact that he had never actually flown before. While the gentle rolling of the jet to the runway did not feel much different than a bus plying down a street in Brooklyn, the stop and the shaking that came from the ready for takeoff began to rattle his confidence as much as it did the fuselage and everything in it. The sudden and rapid bolt forward, accompanied by heavy rattling and deafening noise made it feel as though he were on a roller coaster from hell.

Within seconds, and after he steadied his stomach from the momentary push upward and swallowed to clear his ears, things were remarkably calm. Not serene, but better.

Luckily for Ray, the jet had been a charter, so the reading materials aboard were not only in English but were geared to a particular clientele – *Architectural Digest, Forbes, The Economist, the duPont Registry*. For a moment, he began to dream of what he would do with his windfall. *Of course, it was more like seed money, but still, it was a substantial enough stake to put him and Connie on the fast track, to do something nice for Ma, and Dad...and Dad...* The thought of his father snapped him out of his reflections and diverted his attentions to the goings on in the plane, which were less interesting than just staring out the window into the clouds. He decided it was as good a time as any to lean back and take a nap. After all, it was bound to be a busy day.

His mind replayed the night at Shaughnessy's, their wedding day. Hope for the future. Then Max...Good old Max come to rain on his parade...

His slumber was eventually interrupted by Rodriguez giving his shoulder a gentle shake, saying "We're going to land soon. You'll want to get yourself ready."

"Uh...okay," muttered Ray, as he reached down to adjust his seat. *So far so good. If this was how he got there, what would his suite look like?*

The takeoff had prepared Ray for the commotion of the landing, and he considered for a moment whether some of his forthcoming payout should go to paying for flying lessons.

Once the jet had taxied over to a large hangar, Rodriguez invited Ray to step out onto the tarmac. The heat from the outside hit him like a blast of forced from a boiler room. Unlike his fellow passengers, he had no sunglasses, so the glare of the sun was blinding for a moment or two. His eyes adjusted to the sight of a distinguished, well-dressed man, waiting beside a late model black Mercedes. An E63 AMG, he judged only because he knew a trader who had bought one with last year's bonus money. Used, mind you, as that was all the fellow could afford after the IRS took its cut.

"Julio," said Rodriguez, reaching out to shake his hand. "It is good to see you."

"Good to see you, Raul," the man replied, in a tone that

seemed neither familiar nor official. "The Minister wants to see you immediately."

Rodriguez's face showed a mixture of confusion and concern – something that Ray had yet to see since he made the man's acquaintance. "I already filed my report in full," he explained. "Did he not get it?"

"Yes, he received it," sighed Julio. "Look, I can't get into it right now. We can't keep him waiting."

"I am not going to like this, am I?" observed Rodriguez.

"Probably not…Is this the fellow?"

"Yes, this is Senor Lulio," he replied, making a quick introduction.

"This is Julio," Rodriguez explained to Ray. "He works for the Foreign Minister. He's come to take us to his office to set things up for you."

Ray was too busy paying attention to Rodriguez to notice Julio's facial expression, a cross between a cringe and a frown.

"We've got to get going now, Raul," insisted Julio. "I'll have someone take your bags to your house. Just bring your briefcase."

The men climbed into the back of the car and left the grounds of Jose Marti for the city proper. Ray tried to engage Rodriguez in conversation, but to no avail. It was as quiet as the drive to the Mission the night before, but somehow different – and far more disconcerting. He could see a tensed strain on the Cuban's face, a clenched jaw. Whatever the cause, neither did he attempt to relax it, or explain to Ray what was wrong.

Ray could not take his eyes off Rodriguez the whole time that it took to reach the front entrance of the building where the Foreign Ministry was housed.

Finally, Rodriguez spoke. "We need to go up and speak with the Minister. He's expecting us."

The Minister was a distinguished looking man, whose comportment and demeanor were not typical of his generation of revolutionaries. Indeed, he happened to be the only member of his family who did not leave for Florida when the change came. His father may have been wealthy, and invested heavily in the regime of Fulgencio Batista, but he was an ideologue. Blood may be thicker than water, but nothing is thicker than a true believer to a cause.

Like the proverbial bull in a China shop, he fought tooth and nail to help Fidel become the new President. It was only then, prattling around alone in his family's now vacated home, that he began to appreciate what his actions may have represented on a personal level.

That had been the first revelation. The second began with his first posting and continued to this day. It was that, despite the detail of Marx and Engels, and the steady sloganeering of Fidel and Che, people still needed to eat, factories still needed to run, and people still had to ensure that water would flow through opened faucets, and that lights would illuminate when their switches were flipped.

After some time working in agriculture and health, he was more than ready for the move to the Foreign Ministry. There were too many years working on annual plans for the production of this and that, and too many frustrating meetings where he was forced to argue how hurricanes, the embargo, and a lack of one thing or another ruined each consecutive forecast. He welcomed the chance to work in the one department where, in his estimation, he was not set up for failure.

It had presented its own unique set of challenges, to be certain. For the first while, the focus was almost exclusively on the Russians. He had been enrolled in some courses of study at Moscow State University, where the standard of instruction was, arguably, superior to what was available back home. Beyond that, there had been the advantage of meeting one's counterparts in the Soviet bureaucracy.

Then came the early 1990's – *glasnost, perestroika*, and all that. These were particularly trying years as the nation's largest foreign benefactor was turning westward. Harried diplomats who had spent years learning the unique attributes of the Cyrillic alphabet now entered crash course studies of Mandarin in its written form. That was bad enough, but for him, it really was not the worst of it. In twenty years, he essentially lived a live not discernably different from whence it began. His Soviet colleagues, however, who had been in similarly modest conditions, were now known as 'oligarchs' – these hyper capitalists who owned private jets, mines, factories, oil companies, newspapers, and teams of the English Premier League.

While he remained philosophical about this divergence of destinies, he displayed the gravitas necessary to hide his bitterness away. Most of the time, it never entered his mind, excepting for those occasions when things went wrong, and one naturally wished to be somewhere else. Unfortunately, Raul Rodriguez had laid before him one such situation.

Reckless and sloppy – that is what it was. Sloppiness in exposing Vasquez, and recklessness in seeking to fix the situation in this harebrained way. But why should this have been a surprise to begin with? Rodriguez may very well have been the most talented official the Ministry had trained in a generation, but Rodriguez, himself, seemed all too aware of this assessment. The Minister had hoped that experience would mute those tendencies, but after almost a decade, they showed no signs of abating. Humility would make him a legend in the Ministry, but the lack thereof made him no more useful to the Republic than a mid-grade clerk.

He considered his options and set his resolve to the point where his secretary had paged him to announce the arrival of Rodriguez and the American. He gave word to admit Rodriguez alone, then stood firm, behind his desk, as his protege entered the office.

Rodriguez determined that he should be cautious. He offered his hand to the Minister but received only the look of a father so sorely disappointed in his child.

"Sit down, Raul. We need to talk."

"Yes, Minister. Thank you," said Rodriguez as he took a seat opposite his boss.

"To be honest," began the Minister, as he opened his briefing booklet "I'm not sure what bothers me most – your sloppiness, or your recklessness."

"Excuse me, sir? I don't understand."

"It is bad enough that Vasquez and the others were exposed, but to enlist an American citizen?! Have you taken leave of your senses?!"

"Not at all. Senor Lulio was very cooperative throughout, and he has his own reasons for doing this. Besides, it allowed us to keep Vasquez in place."

"Vasquez," muttered the Minister. "What good is he to us? He's been exposed. What's worse is that we have to hide him in the mission!"

"Hide him?" asked Rodriguez.

"Raul, did you ever ask yourself what would happen if the FBI ever were to stop Vasquez on the street? They would take one look at his identification and say, 'Didn't we already send you home?' Then they would compare photos and the like and figure out that we sent a decoy home and left the real Vasquez there. Did you consider that?"

"The Americans have no coordination," defended Rodriguez. "Too many people doing too many different things. They have a saying that 'the left hand does not know what the right hand is doing'."

The Minister removed his glasses and rubbed his eyes.

"Raul," he said, "I've been in politics for a long time, and I've seen a great deal. The one thing I've learned is that if you leave incompetent people to their business long enough, they will stumble onto doing the right thing. Even an imbecile can have a stroke of genius, and once is all it would take for your plan to fail."

"Minister, with all due respect, I do not believe that this plan will fail. I am willing to stake my career on it."

"Then you are a fool. Even I would not make such a claim over something I was dead sure on. Besides, if you are wrong, it won't be just your career. This country risks an escalation with the Americans that we can ill afford. Spying plus detaining one of their citizens will set us back to the Missile Crisis. You may be too young to remember those days, but I'm not."

With that, he pressed a button on the intercom and said, "We're ready."

Within moments, a uniformed officer came into the office and saluted.

"Sanchez," said the Minister, "please escort Senor Rodriguez to his home."

Turning to Rodriguez, he said "You are suspended indefinitely, and confined to your residence pending a hearing...I'm sorry, Raul. You don't give me much choice."

"What about Senor Lulio?" asked Rodriguez.

"I will deal with him. It's no longer any of your concern."

Over this time, Ray had been sitting, rather nervously, in the anteroom with the Minister's secretary. He was not sure why he did not go in with Rodriguez. Did the Minister not want to meet him? When was he supposed to go to the resort? When was he supposed to get his money?

It seemed like it was taking forever. In the meantime, he sat quietly and tried to take in every possible detail. He did not know why, but it seemed important. It did not take long, as a man in a military uniform came into the room, nodded to the secretary, then stood near the door into the Minister's private room. He made no eye contact with Ray. He did not even acknowledge his presence. Conversely, though, Ray could not take his eyes off the soldier. He took particular note of the holstered revolver and handcuffs. *Was that necessary? Was that for him?* Ray began to shudder.

The intercom on the secretary's desk began to crackle, with some Spanish phrase that Ray was not sure that he recognized. Whatever it was, the secretary nodded to the soldier, who opened the door, and went straight into the room. *What the hell is going on? What do they need with this guy anyway? Just send me to my hotel and give me my goddamn money. What is up with this?*

At that moment, the soldier reappeared, this time with Rodriguez by the arm.

"What's going on,' demanded Ray, caught between disbelief and a growing panic.

Rodriguez did not respond. With his head held high, and his gaze fixed forward, he accompanied his escort out of the anteroom and out into the hall.

"What the hell is going on?!" yelled Ray. "Rodriguez!"

The Minister stood in the doorway, and once Ray's attention turned to him, he said calmly, "Please come in, Mister Lulio."

Ray cautiously rose from his chair and walked tentatively toward the Minister, who had already taken a pace back to hold the door.

"Please. Come. Sit down."

Ray entered the office and took a seat in front of the desk and waited for the Minister to assume his place. Is this where Rodriguez sat, he wondered. *Am I next? It's a Communist country, after all. People like me go to prison, or they get shot, don't they?*

"Mister Lulio, it appears as though we have a small problem."

"You gonna shoot me?" he blurted out in a panic.

The statement caught the Minister by surprise for a moment but became the source of laughter on his part.

"My dear boy," he chortled, "you have been watching too

many spy movies. Why in heaven would we do such a thing?"

"Well…Rodriguez…"

"Rodriguez broke the law, and he is under arrest. Surely law breakers get arrested in your country too."

Yeah, but they're not always guilty, and only when they don't flee to Cuba! Ray wondered whether a prison in upstate New York might not be preferable to the situation that was now unfolding.

"Anyway," continued the Minister, "we are left with a rather difficult situation."

"What do you mean – difficult? I made a deal, and I kept my end of the bargain," said Ray who, now assured that he would not end up being offered a blindfold and a cigarette for his troubles, now found the courage to argue his case.

"Senor Rodriguez was not authorized to make such an agreement with you," said the Minister matter-of-factly. "He went beyond his authority, and now he will be censured for that."

"That's not my problem," countered Ray. "I don't know what you gave permission for or didn't. All I know is that your guy made me a promise, and you're not keeping it."

"The terms are not acceptable. They never were, and Rodriguez knew it. I regret that he misled you, but that is not my problem."

"You kidnapped an American citizen!" yelled Ray. "I'll make it your goddamn business!"

The Minister gazed at Ray from over the top of his glasses, like an old school headmaster ready to launch into a lecturing of a disobedient pupil. "Mister Lulio, we both know you were not kidnapped. You are a fugitive from your own country's justice, and you have sought asylum here in Cuba under an assumed identity. Regardless of what you say – or believe – those are the facts."

"Bullshit," spat Ray. "I'll contact my embassy, and you'll be sorry!"

"Mister Lulio," the Minister said calmly, "I understand your upset. Senor Rodriguez betrayed us both. The question we must ask ourselves is what is to be done about this?"

Ray paused long enough to gain his composure, then said "Forget the money. Just send me the hell home, and I'll say nothing."

The Minister grimaced. "I'm afraid that is not an acceptable option," he replied.

"What do you mean? I want to go home – so send me back!"

"No."

For the fourth or fifth time in the last forty-eight hours, Ray felt as though someone had punched him hard enough in the stomach to knock the wind out of him. He could not speak.

"Let me explain," continued the Minister. "Your presence in Cuba is awkward enough to explain, but your return would pose several complications for our government, as well as yours. Now, you could go back and face many years behind bars, while our two countries argue as to whether you defected or were deported. It might even make the politicians in both our countries more hawkish for a war – nobody wins.

"On the other hand, you could stay here for a period of time and, when the situation allows, you could return to America."

"A period of time," replied Ray. "Exactly how long are we talking?"

"I would say to give it a year or so…"

"Nothin' doin'!" shouted Ray.

"I assure you, Mister Lulio, the time will pass by very quickly."

Ray got up from the chair. "I gotta call my wife! I gotta…"

"I'm afraid not. That would defeat the whole purpose of what we are trying to do."

"But she – everybody – they'll think I'm dead, or something!" he pleaded.

The Minister softened his voice further to bring down the level of anxiety being exhibited by the American. "This will only work if you blend into your new surroundings. Not forever, but just long enough to allow this situation to right itself."

"But I need to call my wife," protested Ray. "You're not going to deny me that, are you?"

"Your country has spies everywhere – even here," insisted the Minister. "Besides, what do you think they would do if someone in New York was receiving a long-distance call from Havana? No, it is best for you to be, how you say, inconspicuous."

"Okay…okay," he sighed, "so, where are you putting me up?"

The look on the Cuban's face told Ray exactly what arrangements would be made on his behalf.

"Well, where the hell am I supposed to live?" he demanded.

The Minister reached into his desk and extracted a large plain brown envelope and slid it across the desk toward Ray.

"Inside, you will find identification in the name of Antonio Vasquez, ration cards, and one thousand pesos. What you do with it is entirely your business."

Ray looked for a moment at the envelope, then straight at the Minister. "That wasn't the deal. You can take your Monopoly money and shove it up your ass!"

"Mister Lulio," intoned the Minister, "I have been very patient with you, given the circumstances, but my patience is wearing thin. Take the money, be Vasquez, and bide your time. It is either that, or you can share Senor Rodriguez's fate. You have ten seconds to decide before I call in security."

Eight seconds in, Ray made a huffing noise and reached to take the envelope. "Fine," he growled, "but you bastards better send me home the first chance you get!"

The Minister smiled, and, under the circumstances, felt the need to offer a carrot to this stick. "In your country, there is a statute of limitations regarding how long they have to lay charges. Stay long enough to run it out, and you can return a free man. You just need a bit of patience, yes?"

Ray was now resigned to the situation and nodded his approval. He shook the Minister's hand and waited for the secretary to come and escort him from the building.

Chapter 10

Ray stepped out into the street, not sure where he was, and even less sure on where he was going. He opened the plain brown vellum envelope that the Minister had given him. *One thousand pesos – how much was that?* In Mexico, that would get you a Big Mac and a Coke. What the hell would it buy here?

He looked at the ration cards. Antonio Vasquez. *This is bullshit! I'm an American – I need to get to the Embassy!*

A group of people were walking toward him. He stood in front to block their passing.

"Excuse me. Does anyone here speak English?" he asked.

A couple of them nodded their heads and answered yes.

"Great!" exclaimed Ray. "I need to find the American Embassy…"

One of them started to translate to the others, which caused a round of laughter, while the other asked "What do you need that for?"

"I'm an American, and I'm trying to get home."

Still more translation, and still more laughter.

"Are you drunk?" asked the man.

"No!" Ray shouted. "I need the US Embassy. Are you going to tell me where it is or not?"

"Head that way, to the Malecon," chuckled the man, as he pointed to the right.

"Will I find it there?" he asked.

"Well, you won't miss it," came the reply, as the laughing group made their way past.

"Wait - - what the hell is a melon..."

The group ignored his call and kept walking away.

Great - some melon thing that way...Maybe I'll see a big flag somewhere...

Ray took the advice and headed in that general direction for what seemed like a couple of hours. More than once he was tempted to hail a taxi – one of the coconut-shaped motorized tricycles that seemed to be everywhere – but he did not know the address, or whether the money he had would be enough to cover the fare.

Eventually, he made his way to a small square shaded by an overgrown forest of palm fronds. Escaping the heat, he found a bench to sit and rest. The bottoms of his feet were throbbing with pain.

In the middle of this square was a statue, surrounded by an open area paved with cobblestones and bordered by large stone blocks in a grid pattern. A group of men were gathered in one corner, engaged in what appeared to be a rather heated argument.

Ray debated whether to approach the men for help, or to keep his distance. After some tussling back and forth, he decided that whatever the problem was, it had nothing to do with him. He walked over to the men.

"Hello…excuse me…does anyone here speak English?" he asked.

Much to his surprise – and relief – about half of the group answered him.

"Great," he continued. "Look, I know this is going to sound really crazy, but I'm an American, and I'm trying to find my country's embassy."

"Americans aren't allowed here," observed one of the men. "How did you get here?"

"I know, I know. You don't let Americans into the country, but…"

"We don't stop Americans from coming here," interrupted the man. "It's your government that says you can't come."

"Yeah, well, you guys are Communists and you hate the States, so…"

"No," the man said. "We are socialist – not Communist – and we don't hate Americanos…Hey, does anybody here hate the Americanos?"

The men muttered among themselves and shook their heads. One man spoke up and said "I have a brother in Jacksonville. He sends back money every month. I've got no problem with Americans."

"I don't get it," said Ray.

"Senor," said the first man, "we like American people, but we don't like your CIA and your Mafia – they made life very bad for us before the revolution."

"You don't hate us?"

"Hate you?" the man laughed. "Senor, we just met you. How do we know if we hate you or not?"

Strangely enough, Ray felt a sense of calm he had not known since he had arrived. It was one thing to be a stranger in a strange land, but quite another to feel as though you were despised by every person you met.

"Great," he said. "You know where the US embassy is?"

"No embassy. Just the Information Office, out along the Malecon…along the shore of the harbor." And the man pointed north. "You are not that far."

"Thanks…uh, *mucho gracias*," replied Ray, as he turned to head in that direction, but not before one of the men spoke up.

"Hey, man," he asked. "Where in America are you from?"

"New York City…Queens, to be exact."

"So, you like '*beisbol*?"

" '*Beisbol*?…Oh, baseball…sure, I like baseball. My dad used to take me to games," answered Ray.

"You watch Yankees?" asked the man, in a determined way that sounded more like a statement than a question.

"Naw, don't like the Yankees," smiled Ray. "We're Mets fans…"

There came complete silence, save for the rumble of car engines in the street. Ray looked at the faces of his newfound friends, who stared back at him like a vigilante posse ready to string up a cattle rustler.

A self-identified Yankees fan stepped forward and spit at Ray's feet.

"What the hell?" shouted Ray, shocked by this sudden turn.

"Mets are garbage!" yelled one of the other men. "How dare you insult Yankees!"

"You're crazy! I didn't insult anybody!" defended Ray. "My dad raised me a Mets fan! What's your problem?!"

"Your father is an idiot – that is my problem!" shouted the spitter, his eyes wide with anger.

As scared as he was getting, Ray was enough of a New Yorker not to let the comment go unanswered.

"You've all been out in the sun too fucking long!" he snapped. "Your brains are…"

"Come on, honey. You promised to take me out," interrupted a female voice out of nowhere.

Ray turned to suddenly find a woman take him by the arm and lead him away from the group, amid the jeers and catcalls of the men.

"Who the hell are you?" he whispered to her, surprised by the intervention.

"Somebody who's saving you from a beating, that's who," said the woman, tightening her grip and picking up her already brisk pace.

"Where are we going?" he asked.

"I heard you say you were American, and you were looking for the Information Office, so I am taking you there."

"You believe I'm American?"

"I believe anyone stupid enough to argue 'beisbol' with them can't be from here," she replied. "Now, let's get on."

Chapter 11

It was strange that Ray had only noticed the physical attributes of his escort when they had already gone halfway to their destination. She was in her late twenties, by his guess, and in pretty good shape as well. Wearing a tight tee-shirt and what looked like a mini skirt and pumps, she could not have carried it off had she not paid some care and attention to her person. She reminded him of some of the 'working girls' back home.

Most of the women he saw along the way, however, were similarly attired. Ray reasoned that the heat and humidity made a more conservative dress somewhat impractical - even as he was feeling its effects, and he was wearing only the light linen suit that Rodriguez had supplied to him. Besides, it was wrong to infer anything of that nature about someone who had been kind enough to intercede on his behalf.

It took about half an hour before they reached their destination. Given the current situation between the two countries, it was explained to him that the US did not possess an Embassy *per se*. Instead, they operated what was referred to as an 'Information Office.' This 'office' was in a rather plain looking tan brick high rise building, surrounded by a tall mesh fence topped by curls of razor wire. A solitary Stars and Stripes fluttered in the breeze. Had the building been in the middle of the city, it may not have caught the attention of onlookers. This building, however, was not within a couple of thousand yards of any other structure, save for a strange looking park that consisted of at least fifty flag poles, each festooned with a black banner. According to the woman, the government built this display as a monument to the victims of 'Yanqui imperialism.' At this point Ray was sure that he did not want to stay on this island a moment longer than necessary.

"So," he asked. "Where's the entrance?"

The woman pointed to one side of the complex. "I don't know," she said, "but I think it is where those guys with the machine guns are."

"Good," said Ray, turning to the woman and shaking her hand. "Well, thank you so much." He grabbed fifty pesos and handed them to her. "I won't be needing these, so here you go…Goodbye."

The woman said nothing. She smiled, took the money, then sat down on the stone wall on the harbor edge. Ray did not take long in wondering what she was doing - after all, he was going home. The Marines and their machine guns did not bother him. They were American machine guns, held by proud, young American men. *They were probably corn-fed Iowa boys - the kind that address everyone as "sir" and "ma'am."*

Running frantically to dodge the eight lanes of traffic that lay in his path, he finally made it to the gate where the two servicemen the woman had spotted were keeping vigil. "Thank God! I am so glad to see you guys!" he exclaimed.

The guards, on the other hand, did not reciprocate this display of fraternal bonhomie. "State your business, sir," said the one Marine, in a brisk and efficient tone.

"Okay, my name is Ray Lulio – from Queens, New York – and I'm stuck in this godforsaken country. I need to see the Ambassador."

The guards looked at one another for a moment. The silent one smiled and rolled his eyes in an expression that seemed to infer that Ray's case was not, in fact, unique, and that dozens of displaced Americans would request meetings with the Information Office on a regular basis.

"Sir," said the first Marine, "you will need to show me your passport and identification."

Ray hesitated, then opened the brown envelope and extracted its contents. "You see," he explained, "all I have are these things. My ID is back home, and I don't have a passport anyway."

"Sir, we need to see proof of your citizenship…"

"But I'm telling you that I don't have it with me! It's back in New York!"

The Marine said nothing, but held out his hand, palm up, and moved his fingers in a gesture to hand the documents over.

Ray let out a sigh of frustration and relented. He handed the various items to the Marine and explained "They're all made up by the government here. It's all fake."

The Marine took the items through a small hole in the mesh gate and investigated them thoroughly. He flipped them back to front, over and over, then passed them back through to Ray.

"Mister Vasquez…"

"My name is Ray Lulio," protested Ray.

"Your papers say your name is Vasquez and that you are a Cuban citizen," replied the Marine in a voice that was neither emotional nor otherwise confrontational.

"Do I sound Cuban to you?!" he yelled.

"People learn languages and accents every day, sir," declared the Marine. "It doesn't prove who they say they are. Besides, if you were an American, you'd have a hell of a lot of explaining why you're here…I'm sorry, but I'm going to have to ask to move along."

"You can't do this!" he yelled. "I'm an American! I can prove it! Ask me what train takes you from Queens to Penn Station!"

The Marine snickered. "Buddy, I'm from Montana. I wouldn't know if you were lyin' or not…Tell me which Interstate takes you from Billings to Butte, and I might consider letting you through."

Ray went quiet for a moment, then asked "If I did, would you really let me in?"

Now both Marines were openly laughing at him. "The answer is 90, and no, not a chance, Senor Vasquez. Now, move along."

Ray looked over his shoulder to see a policeman moving in his general direction from about thirty yards away. "Shit!" he muttered, as he turned around and walked briskly back toward the highway, making a late running dash to avoid the speeding traffic.

The woman who had escorted him thus far had not moved an inch from her perch on the harbor wall. The only discernable change seemed to be the look of bemusement on her face. She reached out to hand him back the fifty pesos he had given her. "I think you need this more than me."

Ray took the money and shoved it in his pocket, then sat down beside her, staring longingly at the tall building and the Stars and Stripes fluttering in front. He felt like he was seven years old again, with his nose pressed against the display window at FAO Schwarz. See it, hear it, but never touch it, and certainly never possess it.

His mood was a mixture of seething rage and suicidal despondency. If there had been something handy that he had wanted to kill, he could have easily done it, and the absence of a satisfying target gave him a melancholy the depths of which he had never felt before.

"You can't stay here," said the woman, trying to distract him back to the here and now.

"Why not," he muttered. "Somebody going to arrest me?"

"No, probably not, but it's hurricane season and it always rains hard this time of day," she said.

Ray let out a heavy sigh, but not the kind that lowered the tension in his body. *Great - why not add a freaking hurricane to it all. That would just be the icing on this shit cake1.* In any event, he was here, in this place, and for the foreseeable future. There would be other opportunities, but for now, he better make himself at home.

"What's your name?" he finally asked the woman.

"Sofia Avecedo," she replied. "What is yours?"

"Raimundo Lulio, but people call me Ray."

"With a name like that, you cannot speak Spanish?" she laughed.

"You sound like my parents," he observed dryly, not appreciating the observation in the least.

"Sorry, it really is funny," she said as she attempted to contain her giggling.

"Tell me, Sofia Avecedo," he asked. "How far will a thousand pesos take me?"

Sofia assumed a reflective expression, then after a moment or two, declared "A month or so. It depends on where you stay, or what you eat while you are here."

"What if my stay is indefinite?" he continued.

"Indef...sorry, my English is...," she explained.

"What if I can't leave?"

"Oh," she laughed, "you will need a job and a place to stay

for sure!"

Ray frowned. "I know I'll need a job. I just don't know where I'll find one."

After a moment of silence, Sofia turned to him and said, "What if I could find you a job?"

"Doing what?" he asked.

"What did you do at home?"

"I bought and sold shares in companies on Wall Street."

"You won't do that here!" she laughed.

"Well, that's all I know," he sighed. "I don't know anything else."

"How do you buy and sell these shares?"

"It's pretty simple," he explained. "Clients call up and ask me to get them so many shares of this or that, and I get them. I also tell them about good deals on other stocks, like…"

"Okay, okay," she interrupted, "so you are like a waiter. You take orders and you tell them about the specials."

"Well, it's a little more complicated than that," he protested, somewhat insulted by the comparison.

Sofia said nothing. She looked at him, skeptically, with one eyebrow raised.

"Okay, so it is like a waiter," he answered, "but I can't speak Spanish. How can I do any job here?"

"Everybody here speaks Spanish," laughed Sofia, "and those who speak English – not so good. Very few can speak it good…I mean, well."

"Great," replied Ray. "I have this wonderful skill that is completely useless."

"I told you I can get you a job – a good one," she insisted. "It might take a couple of days, but I will do it."

Ray shook his head, not entirely sold on this idea. "You know, I ended up here because I trusted one of you. Why should I believe you aren't going to screw me over?"

Sofia shrugged and got up to walk away. "Believe me, don't believe me," she said. "It makes no difference. I am sure you will do just fine."

She had only gone about fifteen feet or so before Ray said, "Hang on…wait up!"

She turned around, hands placed on her hips, in a gesture of defiant judgment.

"Look," he explained. "I have no idea what to do. I don't know this place, the language, or the people – except for you, of course…What I mean to say is that I have to trust you, even if you screw me over too. I don't have any other options."

She smiled ever so slightly, touched by his candid admission, as well as his obvious state. "I will not – how you say – screw you over," she assured him. "This is not charity. I will do you a favor, and you will do for me too."

"Agreed," he sighed, as he got up from the stone wall. "So, what do we do now?"

"First," she explained, taking him by the arm, "you will treat me to a drink, and then we will discuss business."

After a short taxi ride, they arrived at a restaurant tucked on a corner from a secluded boulevard. The establishment looked, at least from the exterior, as though its decor had not been altered since the early 1950's. It was a small, single story building, its stucco and brick exterior painted in a dark pinkish hue. Slabs of jade colored marble adorned the frame of the entranceway.

Above it, hanging out on the end of a grey metal rod, above the street, was an antiquated looking neon sign, in shades of navy blue and gold that read "*Restaurante Bar Floridita – La Casa Del Daiquiri*". Beside the words was a stylized crown perched above a shield, emblazoned with the letters 'RF' – a pattern replicated on the exterior wall of the building.

Along the top of the exterior wall were a series of white plexiglass panels, designed to be backlit. On them, in bold green lettering read "*MI DAIQUIRÍ…EN EL FLORIDITA*" followed by what looked like a reproduction of a signature, in the name of Ernest Hemingway.

Once inside, Ray looked around the bar. The patrons appeared to be mostly tourists. Given that the bar charged around five pesos for one of their legendary cocktails, they were likely the only ones who could even afford to drink there. There were the recognizable accents from Britain, as well as the more guttural European ones, like German and French. There were also those who spoke English in a voice that sounded like an over pronounced version of upstate New York speak. Ray guessed them to be Canadians, as nothing else seemed to make any sense.

The two sat down at a table tucked in near the back, and Sofia instructed the attending waiter to bring them two daiquiris. "They were invented here, in this bar, you know," she informed Ray.

"No, I didn't," he declared, in a slightly grumpy tone. "I've never had one before in my life. Besides, my father says it's a ladies drink."

Sofia smiled politely and shrugged her indifference to this observation. This, in turn, made Ray, once again, somewhat conscious of his current state of vulnerability. He knew that it would be far better for him to at least try to be sociable to this woman.

"So, where do you work?" he asked her.

"At a cantina my family owns here in the city," she replied. "I also have a business I do on the side."

"Sounds interesting," said Ray, in a tone that clearly indicated the opposite. "I suppose that you didn't have many options – you know – education, money, and all that."

Sofia knew exactly where this conversation was going. "I have a degree in marine biology from the university in Matanzas," she said matter-of-factly, and with no shortage of pride.

Ray would freely admit that he was not the best at reading people, but even at his most oblivious, he would have known not to continue down this path, lest he dig himself an enormous hole. Sofia, on the other hand, could recognize the smell of blood in the water.

"You think that because I serve drinks, I am not that smart?" she asked.

"Uh, no," he defended. "It just seems odd that you would be doing that if…"

"You Yanquis have a thing about that," she interrupted. "You are what you get paid to do."

"That's not quite fair," argued Ray. "The job you do sometimes reflects who you are."

"Who you are always reflects who you are," observed Sofia. "Too many smart people who have to take orders, and too many stupid ones who get to give them."

"Is that what happened to you?"

Sofia gave a slight grimace. "A woman I worked with, Gina Ramirez, she made things very hard for me. Figured she was better than the rest of us. She was not even our boss, but her husband was *la policia*, and she assumed she could bully us around."

"So how did you handle it?" he asked.

"I put up with it for a very long time – years – but she must have believed me weak because I said nothing. One day she confronted me. No matter what I said or did, she kept yelling and carrying on. The only thing I could do was to get up from my desk and knock the bitch out cold. I lost my job, but she lost her front teeth. My loss was easier to replace."

"Remind me not to get on your bad side," laughed Ray. "I've lost every fight I've ever been in!"

Sofia laughed, then paused for a moment, giving him a kind, considered look. "You look relaxed, Raimundo."

"I look drunk," he corrected her with a chuckle. "Inside, I am a suppressed ball of nerves."

"I do not understand," she said.

"I mean that deep down I'm scared shitless," came the explanation, the ease of which shocked even him.

"You don't have to worry, Raimundo. I know many people, and some owe me favors. I am sure that I can get you something to get you through."

"Well, I need enough to get me the hell outta here," he replied. "I don't need to set down roots or something."

"You need to talk to your government," she advised. "That is the fastest way to go back."

"I can't do that," he frowned. "I realize that now – especially after what happened with those guards."

"I still do not understand," she said. "You want to go home, but you don't want to talk to your government. You are not making any sense."

"It's kind of complicated – really, really complicated," came the slurred reply. "There are some…some…issues."

"Issues? What are these issues?"

"Well," he explained, "there are these people back home who are under the impression that I broke the law, and I don't think that they are in the mood to listen to what I have to say."

"You broke the law?"

"Naw…my boss did…but the sonofabitch is gonna blame me and a whole buncha others…I just know it…He's probably doin' it right now…as we speak."

"I think it is time to leave," said Sofia, sensing that Ray's increasingly loud and slurred speech was drawing far too much attention from the bar's patrons.

"Uhh…okay…where we goin'…Hey, you know you're kinda beautiful? If I wasn't married, I'd…"

"Come on," she ordered. "You need sleep."

Ray began to bob and weave as he lifted himself up from the table and, in a slightly serpentine pattern, followed Sofia out the door.

They had only walked a block or so before Ray felt the overwhelming urge to vomit. Sofia, ever conscious of onlookers or the police, maneuvered him to the entrance of a back alley, behind a collection of garbage pails. The putrid smell of old grease from the restaurant helped give Ray's stomach the incentive it needed to carry out the task. She held him upright and did her best, under the circumstances, to hurry him on toward home.

Chapter 12

Ray was not a morning person by constitution. Given the fitful rest he had – which barely qualified as such – he was even less enamored with this particular sunrise. After hours in a strange bed with strange people, he faced a day of still stranger sights and sounds, and smells.

No essence of bacon and eggs wafting its way gently toward his nostrils. Just some odd mix of fish and cooking oil that felt like it was singeing his sinus cavity. Even the coffee did not smell like coffee. The pounding in his head and the delicate nature of his stomach did nothing to enhance the experience for him.

The early rays of light were enough to illuminate the room. The walls were a dingy tan color that made him wonder if it was by dirt or by design. The floor was covered with reddish brown tiles, visibly clean and maintained, save for the missing chunks of grout and hairline cracks that became darker as they collected dust and grime.

The furniture was old and Spartan – maybe as old as his father. He now realized that he had shared the room with two others, and that his mates had already made their beds and left for the day. The idea that he had not noticed that he had been sharing the room with two complete strangers, in the dark, felt very disconcerting.

It was cool, but far from cold. The sun had yet to bring on the heat in any serious way, and a light breeze was fluttering the sheer curtains that dangled in front of the open window. He groaned as he sat up and shifted his feet over the edge of the bed. He was not a big drinker, and he began to appreciate the wisdom of that lifestyle choice.

The tile beneath his feet felt warm, like there was some electric element embedded in the terra cotta. Even in the summer, they never got this warm back home.

Stumbling out into the hall, he spotted the bathroom, where he spent a good half-hour attempting to clean himself up. He then returned to the room, and finally noticed his clothes neatly folded over the footboard of the bed.

For a moment, the idea of someone having stripped him down to his underwear was disconcerting. His dry mouth and pounding headache, however, vetoed any real examination of his exact condition the night before. Dutifully, he got himself dressed and made his way down a short hall to where all the sounds and smells were coming from.

"*Buenos dias*, Raimundo. How are you today?"

Ray took notice of an older man sitting at the kitchen table, while Sofia stood at the stove, furiously stirring a concoction of ingredients in a large cast iron pan.

"Uh…fine…gracias," he mumbled.

"Jour friend does not like mornings" observed the man, in a heavily accented, yet precise, English.

Sofia turned to the man and said something in Spanish that Ray interpreted, by tone and demeanor, to be a respectful admonishment.

"Raimundo, this is Orlando. He is – how you say – the brother of my *papi*."

"Uncle?" volunteered Ray.

"Si, yes, uncle," replied Sofia with a big grin. "He has said you are welcome to stay."

Orlando was a stocky man of medium height, much like his own father. He wondered if the two did not share some distant relative who had ventured across the ocean centuries before with the first conquistadors. The man's hair appeared to be naturally curly but had grown out to the extent that it fell in unkempt bunches past his ears. It resembled the kind of mass of hair that a poodle from the Westminster Kennel Club show might sport in a competition. He sported a healthy moustache that did not hide his full upper lip, as well as what could be taken as the premeditated beginning of a beard, or simply the benign neglect of a morning razor for a couple of days.

Unlike his father, however, there did not seem to be any guarded pretense – not a single clenched muscle in the man's face. Just a pleasant and contented grin to greet this unexpected houseguest.

"Uh…thank you…*mucho gracias*. I should be no more than a week," he said to Orlando.

"A week, ees eet?" observed Orlando. "Jou have another place to go?"

"Well, I expect to be back home in New York once this whole mess is sorted out, but don't worry. I will pay you for any inconvenience."

Orlando laughed, and then turned to say something in Spanish to Sofia, causing her to laugh as well.

"Look, my friend," he began to Ray, "Sofia has told me all about jou and jour situation. I do hope jou make eet back to jour home, but right now, until then, conseeder thees jour home. We have a leettle, but we are happy to share."

Ray gave a condescending smile. "Sure, and I really do appreciate this. Really, I do, but I'm an American citizen, and I have rights."

Orlando stared at him as though he had not heard a word. "Jou are welcome here for as long as jou need," he repeated to his guest.

Sofia scooped out some of the mix she had been stirring in the pan, and put it on a plate, which she deposited on the table by an empty chair.

"Sit down and eat," she instructed.

Dutifully, Ray sat down in front of the plate, which appeared to be filled with a mix of rice, vegetables, fish, and – as far as he could tell – anything left over that was about to go bad.

"Gee…thanks, but I'll just stick with coffee," he said, gently pushing the plate to one side.

Without missing a beat, Sofia reached over and pushed it back in front of him and handed him a fork. "Eat," she ordered. "No food until lunch."

As she turned back toward the stove, he muttered "No food until lunch whether I eat or not."

Orlando smiled as he leaned in toward Ray. "Jou know," he said, "my brother – her father – was a quiet and gentle man."

"Really?" asked Ray. "So deep down, she's actually very easy going?"

"No," he answered with a laugh. "She's like her mother – that one was – how jou say – a battle axe."

"Great," Ray grumbled. "Very funny."

Ray's face turned sullen, as Orlando chucked aloud. Had she turned around he would have seen that Sofia was also quite enjoying the breakfast table banter.

Doing his best to ignore to pungent odor of the food, Ray began to gingerly pick away at the bits of fish and vegetable dispersed in the mound of seasoned rice. It took three or four mouthfuls for him to realize that this dish was not altogether bad. It also took him that long to realize just how hungry he was, and before he knew it, an empty plate lay before him.

"Good," observed Sofia, as she picked up his plate. "Now, go – both of you. I need to clean up."

Orlando got up from the table. "Come with me," he said, motioning Ray to follow him out a back door that led from the kitchen out to what looked like a fire escape.

The two men climbed down the steep incline to the ground. Orlando stopped at a door, and after fidgeting for a moment with a key fob, was able to unlock it. He flipped on a light switch near the entrance to reveal what looked like a bar.

"Mi cantina," he said proudly. "Please come in."

The place was clean, although it could not be cleansed of the sickly-sweet smell that came from years of spilled alcohol. It looked grossly out of date. Ray could easily imagine his father, as a young man, coming to a place just like this. He half expected someone dressed like the Fonz to come in and order a bottle of Bud.

"Very nice place," Ray said wryly, attempting to be more encouraging than his natural demeanor allowed.

"I took it over from my *papi*," explained Orlando. "The government does not really care about a little cantina, so they do not bother. In fact, some of them have been known to come here on occasion."

Ray noticed a small stage in the far-right corner of the bar. "You have live entertainment too," he said, trying to sound positive without condescension.

"Oh, *si…jes*. Sometimes we have singing, some *danzon*, and karaoke…"

"Karaoke?" asked Ray. "You actually have karaoke in this place?"

"Si, we do," replied Orlando. "Some *turistas* from Japan used to come here – they sent eet for me. Eet does not get used much by customers. People here love to dance, but some do not like to sing. Eef they do, they prefer our songs. The only one who seems to use eet ees me."

"So…what songs do you play on it?" Ray asked, not entirely sure if he wanted to know the answer.

"It ees American music from 1980's. Jou know – Wham, Flock of Seagulls, Cyndi Lauper – those people."

Ray's face went expressionless at the idea, but he still had to ask. "You sing songs by Cyndi Lauper?"

"Oh, *si*," answered Orlando, seemingly quite proud of the accomplishment. "I know the 'Girls Just Want To Have Fun' and the 'She-Bop', and …"

"I'm sure you do," said Ray, with a contorted smile. The idea of a greying, bearded, middle-aged Cuban man belting out those songs in a thick Spanish accent seemed as much tragedy as comedy. Strangely enough, however, it hardly felt out of place for what he had seen of this country. "So, you make a good living from all this."

"*Si*," replied Orlando. "I make enough to pay for theengs, to help Sofia, and to have some fun. That ees important too, *si*?"

Ray shrugged in agreement. Fun did not seem like an even remote possibility for him, let alone for his host. He was a stranger, and at some point, would be able to head home, but this man lived the life he was destined to lead for the rest of it – however long that was. Then again, if every night was drinking and dancing, then one's mortality might be the furthest thing from mind.

"Well, I am keeping you from theengs," declared Orlando. "Sofia has jour day planned. We should go up back."

"Back up?" asked Ray.

"Oh, *si*, as jou say, back up."

By the time the two men had made their way back up the

steps, Sofia was putting the finishing touches on the lunch she had prepared for their outing. Noticing the sandwiches, and thinking back to the breakfast she had made, Ray had offered to treat her to lunch at a restaurant. This brought a polite, yet firm dismissal. There was no telling how long he would be there, or how long it would be before he saw any income of any kind, she argued. It was best to preserve what cash he had on him for as long as he could. Knowing that there was no point to arguing about it, he nodded and went about helping her in her task.

For some reason, the same streets that he had walked without noticing the day before seemed to take him by surprise. Everywhere were beautiful facades that had faded with age and neglect. It was a curious mix – some were beautiful and well maintained, while others looked like some of the worst burned out tenements in the Bronx. What made it even more disconcerting was that two such buildings were often next to one another. *The Lower East Side and Hell's Kitchen all on the same block!*

The traffic was no less schizophrenic. Fifty-year-old Buicks and Cadillacs shared the road with new Citroens and Peugeots, while shiny Chinese made tour buses made their rounds. They, in turn, shared the less busy side boulevards with horse-drawn carriages and the coconut shaped mini taxis he had noticed the day before.

Ray remembered an old Saturday morning show he used to watch – 'Land of the Lost' – where everything was a jumble of different times, like dinosaurs and spaceships together. One look at Havana and he believed that he had stumbled upon the capital of that world.

Sensing that Ray's primary challenge would be the disorientation of being in a foreign place, Sofia had decided that the day would be simply about exploring the city. Despite the American's eagerness to leave, she knew that he would be there for some time, even if he was eventually successful in his aims. Given that he knew virtually no Spanish, he should at least know the layout of the city. If he were to become lost, he could not necessarily count on finding someone fluent in English who could put him in the right direction. Such people were out there – mostly on account of the recently created, and very lucrative, tourist trade – but he should not use it as a crutch.

They walked all around the streets of Havana, from the old presidential palace, past the Granma memorial, down by the opera house, to the old legislative chambers, the Capitolio. Along the way, they would occasionally stop for a coffee, or a bottle of water.

Deciding to make their way back to the Malecon, they hired a taxi to the Hotel Nacional. The Nacional was, despite its obvious age, one of the better maintained establishments in the city. It sat on, arguably, the highest outcrop of land in Havana, overlooking both the Malecon, as well as the mouth of the harbor. The light tan walls of its art deco façade gleamed like an amber diadem in the warm Caribbean sun.

Sofia explained to him that before the revolution, it had been the preferred residence of Mafioso and Hollywood A-listers alike. Now, in an irony not lost on Ray, the government had expended the resources to painstakingly preserve a symbol of the very regime it had overthrown. Not just preserve it, mind you, but actively promote it to those foreign tourists who hailed from the very types of places that were anathema to the local ruling class. The hotel even housed the Tropicana, where young nubile women clad in sequined outfits that left little to the imagination, performed a nightly revue worthy of a show in Las Vegas or Atlantic City.

The Tropicana had become the source of some misunderstanding between Ray and Sofia. She had confessed that she had once applied to join the squad of chorus girls, but had, unfortunately, not made the rather exacting and competitive cut. Ray's initial reaction was to ask why she would have bothered to have applied in the first place. While his intention was to question why a trained marine biologist would give up her career in order to prance around, half-naked, in front of a crowd of licentious tourists, Sofia had interpreted it as some questioning of her physical attributes, and why she would think that they would be up to that standard. Ray apologized for the misinterpretation, but still had a great deal of trouble getting his brain around the notion that cabaret dancers outranked scientists in the local pecking order.

In the late afternoon, as the sun set to a rich, reddish glow, Sofia hailed a taxi and suggested that they go to her favorite place in the city.

Passing the old Presidential Palace, which was undergoing some refurbishment project, they descended into a tunnel that banked into a rather steep incline under the harbor. She had explained that a French engineering firm had built it in the fifties, and that it had been state-of-the-art for its day. If the imparting of this trivia was designed to relieve Ray's anxiety about plunging into a long, deep tunnel under millions of gallons of water with cars speeding past, it had the opposite effect. *Fifty years ago, a black and white television that took up half your living room was also considered 'state-of-the-art'!* Rather than take Sofia's advice and enjoy this engineering marvel of the Caribbean, Ray nervously scanned the smooth ceramic tile walls for signs of cracks or fissures and shuddered when he saw the occasional glistening trail left by condensation.

Much to his surprise, as well as her expectations, they emerged unscathed on the other side of the harbor, and began to climb a hill toward El Morra, the old Spanish fort that once guarded the port from gunboats and privateers.

As the taxi turned onto the road that extended in and behind the fortress, Ray saw three or four green army trucks with what looked like rockets mounted on the back. The trucks looked old, with patches of rust here and there. Two of them had their front tires removed and were sitting on large wooden blocks. All of them were parked on a patch of grass beside the road, backed up against a tall mesh fence. They looked like the kind of vehicles you would see, parked and rusting in front of your stereotypical redneck domicile.

"Is that your defense against us?" Ray laughed dismissively.

Sofia shrugged. "It used to be," she said matter-of-factly.

"Well," he continued, "I hate to tell you this, but they don't look like they could hit the broad side of a barn."

"I suppose," she sighed, staring out the window at the sight. "Then again, your President Kennedy was prepared to start a war over them."

The comment forced ray to turn for a double take. "No," he said with some derision. "Those aren't the same ones. Couldn't be."

"I've always been told that they are," defended Sofia.

"Well, how do you know that you were told the truth?"

"I don't," she replied. "How do you know that I was told a lie?"

Ray did not know how to answer that question, although his gut told him that he was in the right, so he muttered about how they should have been taken better care of if they were so important.

The taxi finally stopped at their destination, about a hundred yards from the trucks. It was a large scenic outlook that gave an unobstructed view of the entire city, from the edge of the harbor to the inner shore where cranes and warehouses were situated. At the apex of the ridge stood a massive statue of Jesus, his arms extended outward, much in the style of the larger, more famous version overlooking Rio de Janeiro. Ray looked at the plaque at its base, and with what understanding of the local language he possessed, he saw that it had been completed by a famous sculptor only a year before the revolution.

Sofia beckoned him to sit on a nearby concrete bench so that they could eat. Ray noticed that the bench itself was, like much of what he had seen that day, in an obvious state of neglect and disrepair. Chunks of the cement had broken off, exposing the metal reinforcement bars to the corrosion of the salt water laden air.

"You know what this place reminds me of?" said Ray, taking his place beside her. "It reminds me of Ginger Rogers."

"Ginger Rogers?" asked Sofia, who took a few moments to figure out who it was "That woman in the old movies? She used to come here too."

"Yeah, her," he answered, not paying attention to Sofia's embellishment.

"That doesn't make any sense."

"No, no...hear me out," explained Ray. "Ginger Rogers, when you see her in all those old movies – she's very pretty. I mean, I know it's all in black and white, but you can tell she was gorgeous."

"I still don't get it."

"Okay, so when I was a teenager, my mom had a magazine with a recent photo of her in it. Now, you could tell it was her, but she looked rough – white hair all over the place, wrinkles..."

"Well, everybody gets old," said Sofia.

"I know, but when you compare the pictures, it kinda makes you sad. Maybe nostalgic."

"So, you think Havana is like that?"

"Sort of. I mean, there are all these beautiful old buildings and stuff, but they look like they haven't seen a coat of paint since the fifties – "

"1959, to be exact," answered Sofia.

"Well, you would think that somebody would take it upon themselves to clean it up."

"With what? The Mafia and the CIA took everything that wasn't nailed down, and your government blocked anything else from coming in."

"Okay, okay…I don't want to fight…"

"Too late," replied Sofia.

"Look, everything you've shown me today that you're all so proud of –it was all built before the revolution. It doesn't look like you've done shit since then. All I'm saying is if your great leader can end hunger and teach everybody to read and write, can't he get someone out there with a can of paint and a fucking brush?"

By now, Sofia was doing her best to hold back, but was fighting a losing battle with herself. She crossed her arms and said sarcastically "O, *si*, so that would fix everything? Maybe we put up big signs too? Maybe we buy hamburger from clown, or chicken from old man in white suit? Maybe we put up *mucho grande* signs for little pills that help you *Yanquis* please your women? Is there anything else, O great captain of American commerce?"

Ray thought the better of this exchange. "As a matter of fact, yes…yes, there is, "he said meekly, as he pointed to the large statue that stood behind them. "That thing, that pole running up Jesus' back."

"It's a lightning rod. What of it?" she snapped, still stewing over his civic advice.

"Well, it's Jesus…Kind of ironic that he needs to be protected from a bolt of lightning, don't you think?" he said with a mischievous smile.

Sofia's look softened as she dropped her hands to her sides. "I don't understand you at all," she said.

"What's not to understand?" asked Ray. "I'm an open book."

"Everything. How you got here, how that brain of yours works…"

"No one in my family has figured that out yet. Odds are you won't either," he smiled. "Look, I'm sorry for upsetting you. I sounded a bit like my old man when I think of it…You've been my only true friend since I got here."

Sofia smiled and replied "I didn't do it out of friendship. You'll be paying me back."

"So why come here with me, then? Face it, you're a nice person," he argued.

"A nice person who wants to practice her English," came a still pouting reply.

"You're very stubborn, Senorita Avecedo," said Ray.

"And you are trying too hard to get on my good side," she said playfully.

"Is it working," he asked.

"I think," she said, as she rose from the bench, "that it is best if, as they say, we agree to disagree. Yes?"

Ray got up to join her.

"You are my only friend here, Sofia. I apologize if I don't sound grateful…I am, really…It's just that I don't have any clue where I am or what I am doing. What I know doesn't apply here. I don't like how that feels."

"Maybe you think you had more control than you really did? I know many people who think they are master over their own lives, but they are not. They feel better when they think they are in control, so that is what they believe. Even if it is a lie."

"You appear to be very much in control. Maybe it is possible after all," he observed.

Sofia began to laugh.

"Control is a lie you tell others, but never to yourself," she said. "There's what others believe, and then there is what I know to be true. It is dangerous to confuse the two. Never, ever, believe the lies you tell others, Raimundo."

"You think I am?"

"I don't know. I only know what I see, and that does not go past yesterday. You know better than I ever will."

"Well, maybe people have no choice in the matter. They have to play along."

"You live in a land of freedom, but you are not free to live for being happy? Maybe I do not have the kind of freedom you speak of, but Fidel does not tell me how to be happy, or who to love. That belongs to me."

Chapter 13

Ray was not sure how, or when, it happened. What was supposed to have been a simple detour away from his normal life was now fast becoming a new life unto itself. The moments of introspection were few and far between – after all, the business of living in the here and now had become mentally taxing. Regardless, they still came flooding in whenever his mind eased up on its need to be vigilant.

One day, though, seemed to be worse than the rest, when it came to home. Ray woke to realize that it had been two weeks since he had landed in Cuba. Two weeks. Rodriguez had promised his return within two weeks. All things considered he should have been arriving home that very same day. Arriving home to meet his wife and assure her that no harm had come to him. It would not be easy to explain it all, but once he had shown her proof – and the money – she would understand.

He sighed as he looked out onto another Caribbean sunset and wished so much for it to be a cold, drizzly dusk in New York.

Tomorrow was the day that Sofia had arranged for him to start work. After much cajoling, and some none too subtle arm twisting, she had set up an interview with a manager at a resort in Playa Gomez, about halfway between Havana and Matanzas. The three met at La Floridita, and after a couple of Bucaneros, he was duly convinced that Ray would be an asset to the resort.

Ray wondered if the man knew Sofia's ulterior motive for him. *Surely, he knows what she does for a living?* And yet, not a word, or even a hint, of his intended 'freelancing' was mentioned. It was a strange way of doing business. Back home, it was direct and to the point, with few social niceties involved. Here, it was all social, with scant detail. Most of what was agreed on was never articulated, and yet, by his perception of it, everyone understood what they had signed on to. Ray was curious as to whether this 'business by stealth' approach was a function of operating in a Communist regime or was it true that Yanquis were loud and pushy, and that this was the way the rest of the world operated.

The man, who Sofia had referred to as Jorge, was a thin man, of slender build, whose coarse salt and pepper colored hair was slightly receded above the forehead. He was dressed rather casually by his estimation, with a bright yellow polyester golf shirt and a deep tan pair of khaki pants. Ray surmised that this was likely the mode of attire for the staff at Playa Gomez.

The resort was, according to Jorge, one of the newer such facilities in Cuba, and it prided itself in selecting only the finest people to join its retinue. Like all such resorts, it operated as a joint venture between the government and some foreign based hotelier – often Spanish, Italian, French, or Canadian. Similarly, while the front-line staff and some area supervisors were Cuban, the senior management was almost exclusively drawn from those countries, or from somewhere like Jamaica, Barbados, Mexico, or Belize, where such resorts had been operating successfully for quite some time.

While Ray remained somewhat passive during this de facto interview, he was left with the impression that getting in was not quite the cinch that Sofia had led him to believe. Despite the overtly amicable meeting, he sensed that what was up for grabs was for more valuable than he had estimated. Tuckner Wass did not screen middle managers as thoroughly as Playa Gomez selected cabana boys. Baseball, old cars and killing yourself for a minimum wage job - the old man would think he had died and gone to heaven, Ray mused to himself.

It was only after Jorge had left that Sofia had explained the situation to him. In fact, while, according to American standards, the job did not seem all that great, it was, in fact, quite prestigious and profitable in the eyes of most Cubans.

Those who secured employment with a resort made far more than the average salary, and were often able to receive some additional perks, like free meals and on-site housing – both of which were far more opulent than the norm. This, of course, did not include the generous tipping by guests that, while officially frowned upon, would occur nevertheless. There were also the gifts that were left behind, such as shampoos, toothpastes and other toiletries that were either not available or too expensive for the average person to buy.

It was no surprise that one often found fully trained and qualified doctors, lawyers, and engineers among those who served drinks, made beds, and bussed tables in the restaurants. The competition for these jobs rivalled anything Ray had seen on Wall Street. Sofia had not told him of the situation prior to the meeting, and could not explain things during it, and so there was a lot of added diplomacy needed to explain away both his lack of enthusiasm and his apparent lack of gratitude for being given this opportunity.

Ray was not so oblivious to his environment not to realize that his attitude may have been perceived as too prideful by Jorge. Sofia's postmortem only confirmed in his mind the need to be humbler in his demeanor – especially when he started at Playa Gomez.

Although the resort was no more than an hour's drive from Havana, Sofia had counselled that leaving the day before was necessary. Ray, being used to the schedules of the Long Island Railroad and the New York Transit Authority, figured that she was being overly cautious. *It was like taking a week to get from Queens to Yonkers. Hell, I could walk faster than that!*

It was barely ten minutes into the drive before Ray realized why Sofia was so insistent. While the road to Matanzas and Veradero was as busy as a four-lane highway, it seemed to be missing something that the Interstates back home all had – four lanes.

Ray was, of course, used to this kind of congestion. No one who had spent any portion of their lives in New York, the five boroughs, or even the tri-state area, for that matter, would have been unfamiliar with the phenomenon of urban congestion – the bumper-to-bumper traffic, cars so close to one another that a bike courier had a hard time slipping through. He knew gridlock, that was true, but he had never seen it move in unison at sixty miles per hour on pitted pavement that weaved in and out of mountain passes and deep gorges.

An eclectic mix of motorcycles, classic cars, more recent European subcompacts, as well as tour buses intermingled in a rapid dance with huge trucks hauling their wares from place to place.

For a distance, the road opened slightly as it hugged the coastline. To the north, Ray saw open water beyond the short beaches that ended abruptly on jagged rock. Every so often, there was a rest stop whose amenities ran the gamut from a full-service cantina to a paved patch adorned with a single forty-gallon metal drum for garbage. Also dispersed among these 'scenic' areas were oil pump jacks that raised and lowered their hammer heads in a monotonously methodical rhythm. Ray figured that the folks at Greenpeace would have a field day with these wells, and that the authorities would have one with them.

On the inland side, it could scarcely have been called better. Along the highway, factories and industrial facilities of every shape and size were scattered, with smokestacks that were either burning off some fuel, or belching out some other effluent. It gave the surrounding area that strong pungent odor that you find in a garage where a mechanic had been tinkering with an old diesel engine.

Each had the usual signs that carried some apparently patriotic exhortation. There was the "*Socialisme o muerte*" which even Ray could figure out, and then there were the ones that had the word "*Volveran.*" Although he had no idea what it meant, it made him laugh, because it reminded him of the name Wolverine from the X-Men comic books. Despite the strange looks from Sofia, he did not bother to explain. She probably would have felt he was off his rocker anyway.

There were other signs, of course, but they were written in either English or in Chinese. Sofia had explained that, as in the case of Playa Gomez, the government had partnered up with companies from different parts of the world, and that many of their nationals were supervising the operations. Ray made the comment that they would not need foreigners to come in and run the places if communism were so effective, but Sofia pretended not to hear. They had already gone over that ground, and she did not feel the need to revisit it. Besides, did she not hold all the cards where he was concerned? Despite all the big talk and braggadocio, he was as dependent on her good nature as a small child.

The bus turned off the main road and ventured down a narrower one that was one step above a graveled surface. The asphalt was old, and cracked, and despite the obvious repeated attempts at repair, large pits and holes were everywhere. Large palm trees and dense underbrush crowded so close that one could not tell where the road ended and the jungle began. This did not appear to be an encouraging sign to Ray. How good a place could it possibly be if the only road in was not fit for anything with four wheels?

His heart sank further as they ventured down this road past a couple of camp sites. Despite their best efforts to make them more attractive, one could not disguise the fact that they looked as rough as a refugee camp in some movie. The cabins were merely a series of small cinder block buildings painted in gaudy tones of pink, purple and lime green. Ray began to wonder how some of the camp's patrons lived in their normal situations, assuming the old truism about one going on vacation to get away from it all.

The truck slowed down as it entered a small, rather rough looking village. Sofia indicated that this was Playa Gomez, causing Ray to wryly remark that he could not see why wealthy Europeans would pay good money to sleep in a shack and contract dysentery. Ignoring his sarcasm, she told him that the resort itself was located on the beach, just beyond one of the mountains that bordered the settlement.

They pulled over to a gas station with a huge sign that read "Oro Negro" – or "Black Gold", as Sofia had informed him. The driver wanted to fill up the gas tank, check the oil, as well as let the radiator cool down a bit. He had noticed a spike in the temperature gauge and did not want to chance a crossing through the pass until he had topped up the water as well.

In any event, they would be there for a while, and had at least a solid half hour to kill off. Sofia pointed to a roadside stand beside the station and said "We can go over there and wait. That is a good place."

The stand looked to Ray more like a vegetable cart on Delancey than an actual drive-through. It consisted of a roof of thatched palm fronds supported by a solid back wall and two wooden posts, one on each of the front corners. Between the posts was erected a makeshift counter. Ray could not tell what kind of wood it was made from but guessed that it did not start out as the best quality. Years of obvious use, and abuse, had well-seasoned it, giving it a nice warm patina. It reminded Ray of home, and how butchers in Little Italy would pour extra virgin olive oil onto their chopping blocks and rub it right into the grain.

He and Sofia each sat down on one of the stools provided for the clientele. When the man turned to acknowledge their presence, she said *"Dos piña coladas, por favour."* She then turned to Ray and declared "He makes the best Piña Coladas in all of Cuba. You have to watch how he does it."

The man behind the bar, with unflinching precision, took what looked like a miniature machete, and, with a single steady and confident blow, sliced off the top quarter of the coconut. Then, without missing a beat, he took the blade to a full, fresh pineapple and made a clean cut at its equator.

He took the pineapple half and impaled it on what looked like some ancient contraption. Within seconds, a full bodied, pulpy juice bled through to a clear plastic container, which he immediately poured into a blender. Once the contents of both halves of the fruit were sufficiently extricated, he moved to the decapitated coconut, and poured its contents in as well.

The old chrome blender whirred loudly like some ancient vacuum cleaner that had gotten a throw rug caught in its beater bars. Inside the translucent chamber, the liquid and bits of pulp and meat were gnashed into frothy foam. After a few moments, the man brought the pitcher around and poured its contents into the two tall glasses where Sofia and Ray sat. Then, after setting the pitcher down on the back counter, he slid a full bottle of Havana Club toward them.

Sofia took a mouthful from her glass, and then poured enough rum into it to bring the level back up. "You can mix it as strong as you want," she explained to Ray, who seemed to still be fixated on the rather involved ritual of making what she had decreed as 'the best Piña Colada in Cuba.'

Ray followed Sofia's example and quaffed a good mouthful of the milky liquid. Then, after she had topped up her glass, he did likewise. The result was, in fact, what Sofia had promised. Although he had never had the drink before in his life, he could easily imagine that he would never experience a better one elsewhere.

"Sofia," he began, "I really don't know what to say. You've been so decent to me since we met. My own family wouldn't have done this much. I know I'm a stranger here, but I really want to pay you back for all of this." With that, he pulled out his wallet and took almost the entire contents out, offering it to her. "This is only a down payment. When I get back to the States, I will send you more - and in US dollars too."

Sofia laughed. "I don't want your money, and besides, if you ever go back, you are better off sending shampoo and deodorant! No, you are going to pay me back all right."

"I don't see how if you won't take any money," said Ray.

"Okay, now that you are going to be at Playa Gomez, I'm going to fill you in on your end of the bargain." She had said in such a way that it made everything up to this point – including their meeting – as some prelude that led up to this moment. *Bargain? Was there a bargain? There had always been some sort of quid pro quo that had been implied, but a bargain? Weren't people supposed to be up front with bargains? Agree on the terms up front, and then everybody follows through?* She may have vaguely hinted at a payback, but it was not a bargain without details. Ray was confused but listened to her intently. He knew that whatever interpretation he had lent to the relationship, he was indebted to her and that meant the terms were moot where he was concerned.

"You are going to be meeting a lot of *turistas*, yes? And your English is perfect."

It was a statement of the obvious for affecting some purpose. That was clear even to him. "Uhh, yeah," he replied. "I think that goes without saying."

"Anyway, what I want you to do is to arrange it for me to meet some of them – you know, how you say, introduce me to them."

"But…you are going back to Havana," he said, in a confused voice. "Why do you want to meet someone in Playa Gomez?"

"You are going to arrange dates for me," declared Sofia.

"Dates? Like going out?"

"*Si*… like that," he replied with a slight faltering lilt that belied a self-consciousness behind the words.

"Why? I mean, you're an attractive woman, and I don't think…"

Ray stopped talking and stared into her eyes for a moment before having his epiphany.

"You're a pros…"

"Prospective employee? Why yes!" she declared loudly, while giving Ray that look that told him to shut up immediately.

She leaned in close to Ray and muttered in a low tone.

"Don't say that word!" she hissed. "I don't know about America, but I can get into a lot of trouble here!"

"Well, you can get into a lot of trouble there, too!" he replied in an equally hushed tone. "I'm not stupid! I know exactly what you're doing! You're asking me to be a pimp, aren't you?!"

"I don't know what this 'pimp' thing is," she said. "I am asking you to introduce me to dates."

"Like a pimp," argued Ray.

"No, it's not," countered Sofia, sensing that he truly did not understand the intricacies of what she had in mind. "You work for me, and not the other way around."

"That's not what I meant! I mean, you take money, and in return…"

"I know what I do," she interrupted sarcastically. It was clear that no explanation on her part was going to convince him to give way on his objections. "It's you that needs to learn what your end of the bargain is. You introduce me to *turistas*, and I take care of the rest."

"How the hell am I supposed to do that? They're going to nail my ass and throw it into some gulag, or whatever the hell you Commies use!"

"A fifty peso fine?" volunteered Sofia, with an eyebrow raised.

"Uh…Look, I'll be happy to do whatever you want. Really, I will, but not that. Not that."

Sofia leaned back and crossed her arms. "That's not the bargain," she declared. "You don't get to change the terms on me – not now."

"You never told me what those terms were!" argued Ray. "If you had, do you think…"

"Think what? Think that you would have agreed to them? Yes. Yes, I do…What choice did you have? I saved you from getting beaten up, I gave you a place to stay, and food to eat. I even got you a job. Did you have a better offer from somebody else? Why didn't you go with them?"

Ray lowered his head and stared at the ground. She was right, and they both knew it. Bargain or no bargain, terms, or no terms, with or without full disclosure – he was completely dependent on her, and he would only defy her demands at his own peril.

"Sofia," he muttered, "I've never done this before. I don't know how, and even if I did, I'm scared to death to do it. Honest."

As tenacious as she could be, Sofia also knew when to recognize when she had won the day, and to not be too arrogant with the upper hand. She wanted his help, not his dignity, regardless of how he would end up interpreting this deal of theirs. "Look," she said in a calmer voice, "the *turistas* will approach you. Trust me. You don't have to ask them."

She then reached into her handbag and extracted what looked like a dozen business cards. She handed them to Ray and explained "If one of them asks you if you know someone they can party with, you give them one of these."

"That's it?" asked Ray. "That's all I have to do?"

"Well, yes," she replied. "I mean, don't let the management find out, and if you're going to get caught, get rid of the cards."

"Okay," he said, feeling somewhat better about his role in this enterprise. "Shouldn't you give me more? You only gave me twelve."

Sofia's facial expression turned to disgust. "More than twelve?! What do you think I am? A slut?! How many men do you think I could date in a week?!"

"A week?"

"Si, a week," she said. "I will see you in seven days. Do you think I need more than twelve dates in seven days? Santa Maria!"

"No, no, no. I'm sorry…I didn't mean to offend," assured Ray, fully aware of how absurd it felt to apologize for the apparent insult to her virtue. It did make him curious as to what the dividing line between a prostitute and a slut actually was, but he rightly abandoned that philosophical quest as being as useful to him as the 'how many angels can fit on a head of a pin' was for others.

"Anyway," she declared, noticing that the driver of the truck was paying for the fuel, "we are getting ready to go. Raimundo, I need to know. Are you going to keep your end of the bargain?"

Ray contorted his face into what could have been interpreted as either a frown or a pout. Either one, in truth, would have been a window into his soul at that very moment.

"Yes," he huffed reluctantly. "I'll do what you ask...but I have one condition of my own."

"What is it," she asked.

"If I get arrested, you better get me out," he said.

Sofia patted him on the shoulder and laughed. "Come on," she said. "Let's get aboard."

Ray dutifully followed her to the truck and helped her climb back aboard. He climbed up and sat beside her. She smiled at him warmly, and yet the only thing that stayed in his mind was the fact that she had not given him an answer.

Within twenty minutes, they had arrived at the resort. For the first time in a long while, Ray felt a degree of optimism creep in. The resort was as beautiful as any he had seen in any brochure or on television. The main building was a massive structure, whose front wall was made up of large ornate glass panels, shaded by a large canopy that covered the area where guests would be picked up and dropped off. The floor, from the edge of the front sidewalk, and in and throughout the lobby was a sea of terra cotta squares, crisscrossed by a pale salmon colored grouting. The walls were similarly painted in this muted tone. The front reception desk, as well as the lobby bar along the far wall, were made from heavy slabs of pine, stained to the dark, caramel hue of mahogany and polished to a glaring sheen.

The staff was all similarly attired, with bright yellow cotton shirts adorned with a tropical motif - palm fronds and tropical birds of paradise – and black slacks or Bermuda shorts. They would have easily fit in with the guests, except for the fact that they all wore the same thing, and that their shoes were heavy, intended for work. *No one in such surroundings should have to wear black socks and orthopedic shoes.*

Sofia gestured to a door to the left of the reception desk and said "You have to report in there. I'll go in with you to make sure things are still okay."

Ray felt the need to ask whether the man they had met in Havana, Jorge, was in on Sofia's plans. It seemed to make sense if he was. After all, why else would he have hired him to work in a place where people were prepared to surrender their first-born just to get an interview? Then again, maybe it was a favor for a friend, or a relative? He would have asked – wanted to ask – but the time for that was back on the truck, and not in a crowded lobby, a few feet from the manager's office.

Chapter 14

The day began with an orientation session, which consisted of two parts – lectures done completely in Spanish, and a rehearsal of conversational English.

The prospect of sitting through a class he could not understand caused a momentary panic in his mind, but after an hour or so, it did not seem to matter all that much. The classes were not interactive at all. A man stood at the front and, without asking or answering any questions, proceeded to go on about some subject or another. Ray spent more time observing his fellow pupils to see when it was appropriate to laugh, smile, or applaud. A couple of times, a video had been played which gave some sort of instruction or etiquette on issues of health and safety. Given the heavily pantomimed nature of the acting and the situations portrayed, he was able to follow along. It was like watching a silent movie without the dialogue cards.

The conversational English session was a veritable walk in the park. To make it a truly authentic experience, staff had been prohibited from lapsing into Spanish. Nothing but English was allowed, with the questions and situations seemingly pulled from the pages of a fourth-grade reader. While the instructor found Ray's diction and comprehension to be flawless, he did find fault with his seeming lack of enthusiasm for the exercise.

The instructor had warned Ray that although his skills made

him a good prospect for the resort, he would need to improve his attitude to be entrusted with the more prestigious positions that allowed one to interact directly with the guests. Ray tried his best to display the right amount of contrition and concern for this determination, although he could have cared less about it. He felt like a high school kid sweeping floors at some fast-food place on weekends, while some poorly paid assistant manager was attempting to motivate him with the promise of some marginally less crappy job. *Maybe he could aspire to cleaning out the deep fat fryer?*

In a way, he resolved that it might be better not to interact with the paying customers. It was too much of a reminder of life back in New York, and the fact that he would be around people just like him, yet free to come and go as they please. What he did not realize was that his orientation review portended, in his case, the worst of both worlds. His English guaranteed him the kind of interactions that he so dreaded, but the lack of an outgoing and 'ready-to-please' attitude consigned him to the lower rungs of the staff ladder. This was made abundantly clear to him when, the next morning, he was met again by Jorge, who led him out into the grounds of the resort.

The two men walked past the tuck shop, the cigar store, and the large dining hall where the buffets were served. Beyond some immature palm trees sat the resort's pool and jacuzzi tubs, surrounded three rows deep with chaise lounge chairs and umbrella topped tables.

"All right, Vasquez. I will start you out with something simple, yes? Today, I want you to change the beach towels," said the manager, as he led Ray around the circumference of the pool. "Now, just don't take them. Each guest is responsible for one towel, and we will charge them if they do not return one before they leave."

Ray was half-listening to the instructions as he followed along. Everywhere, there were happy, well-tanned people frolicking in the water, and sunning themselves on the deck. A couple of the women even looked like Mel, the office hedonist who, at this point, would have been a sight for sore eyes.

"Vasquez! You need to listen!" growled the manager, snapping him back to the here and now. "I'm only doing all of this as a favor to Sofia. I can have someone else in here - *rapido!*"

"I'm sorry, sir," said Ray, attempting to portray genuine remorse for his perceived lack of professionalism.

Jorge gave a grunt and proceeded to lead Ray over to the far end of the pool, beside a Jacuzzi tub. "It is better if you stand here," he instructed. "From here, you can see all the guests, and when they will need your assistance...Now, remember. Playa Gomez has a great reputation to uphold, and our patrons have certain expectations for service. You are a representative of the company, and, of course, of the *Republica de Cuba*. Always remember this. Okay?"

Ray nodded in recognition, and assured Jorge that Playa Gomez would be hard pressed to find a better ambassador than him. Then, the two men parted company, with Jorge just as skeptical of this promise as was his new employee of keeping it.

As Ray scanned the poolside, he caught a glimpse of what seemed like a mirage. It might as well have been, as it represented the only thing recognizable from his life back home.

Although partially obscured by a pair of Vuarnets and a large straw hat, there was enough of the face that was visible to be readily recognizable. After all, he had seen that profile so many times that it was as familiar to Ray as his own reflection in the mirror. "Oh, my God," he said under his breath, as he came ever closer to the first familiar face he had seen since he landed in Havana.

"You're Robin St. John Roberts!" exclaimed Ray, startling the man on the lounge chair from his siesta. The scene was so loud and noticeable that virtually everyone along that side of the pool had craned their neck to take notice.

"What?!" snapped Roberts, as he sat up on the lounge chair, clearly annoyed by the interruption.

"Oh, Mister Roberts," Ray continued to gush. "I am such a big fan. I have all your books and DVD's, and..."

Roberts casually removed his glasses and gave Ray a thorough scan from head to toe, taking notice of what he was wearing. "You couldn't afford them, even if they were legal here...," he coolly observed, not making any attempt to hide his displeasure at the sudden intrusion on his planned solitude.

"Oh, no... I have them all. Really!" protested Ray.

"Sure you do," sighed Roberts. "Let me guess. Somebody's selling some bootleg copies down in the market, and...Never mind, just get me a Cuba Libre, and don't water it down, *comprende?*"

"Sorry?" asked Ray. In all his excitement, and the feeling of having been transported back to New York, he forgot that he was not in New York. He was in Cuba, and he was dressed in the uniform of hotel staff. Roberts saw what he saw and reacted accordingly. That did not mean, however, that Ray was not taken aback by the terse response.

"*El drinko, por favor!*" yelled Roberts. "Geez, don't you understand English? You talk like you do!"

"Of course, I understand English!" said Ray, shocked by Roberts' confrontational demeanor. *Even if I am the paid staff, why is he being such a prick? Wasn't he the one who said that your 'outer shell' does not define the real you? Granted, wearing the uniform of a cabana boy was not particularly helpful, but he made a living telling people to look past all of that. Was he having a bad day? Was he not used to the sun? Was he drunk? This was not the Robin St. John Roberts he knew so well.*

"Then go get me a frigging Cuba Libre! I'm drying out here already!" snapped his hero and mentor.

Ray dropped the wad of beach towels down on Roberts' sandals and book, eliciting a "Hey, what the fuck?!" that became ever so fainter as Ray scurried to the bar.

The manager, of course, had taken it all in. It was not his custom to leave a new employee totally unattended with guests in the beginning. If he did not subtly spy on the new person, he made sure that someone else would. He intercepted Ray as he made his way up to the bar to order Roberts' drink.

"Vasquez - you are new, and maybe you do not understand what your job is here. You are here for the guests, and not the other way around! Senor Roberts comes here because he knows he will be left alone. None of his fans from America can come here to ask for autographs or favors, and that is why he has been a loyal customer over the years."

Ray sighed in frustration. "I'm sorry," he said, "I really am, but he has been such an influence in my life. I have been following him for so long…"

"Yes…," said the manager in a low tone. "Sofia tells me you think you are from the United States, and so you seize on to all things American. Look, Vasquez, maybe this obsession of yours helped you to speak English very well without an accent. That is why I was interested in taking you on. But if you don't control yourself, and focus on your job, I will fire you. Am I understood?"

"I understand, sir," Ray said, feeling as though he had been kicked in the stomach and had all the wind knocked out of him. One quick comment and he learned three unpleasant truths – first, that he was nothing more than a servant; second, that his hero and mentor was an arrogant and rude jerk; and third, that Sofia portrayed him as being delusional. It would have been bad enough if she had said it to secure him this job, but who was to say that she did not believe this herself? Maybe she believed nothing that he had said since they met. The thought of that possibility seemed to hurt more than the rest.

For the rest of the day, Ray tried to keep his distance from Roberts. It was as much due to him not wanting to be reminded of his mentor, and his loyal tutelage under this man, as much as it was in trying to avoid a replay of their meeting. If he stayed away from him, Ray reasoned, he would not have to be reminded of the way things were.

As noble and logical a strategy this was, it was doomed from the start. How could he not be reminded of his present circumstances? He was surrounded by people who, up until his last day in New York, were indistinguishable from him. People, who a few short weeks ago, would have looked at him, now looked through him. He felt angry and sad all at once. *These people, they're judging me. How dare they? Just because I fold towels and fetch drinks, how dare they assume…*

He remembered the first conversation he had with Sofia, and how she argued that what you did should not define who you were. He had thought she was full of crap, or, at the very least, telling herself a fiction to feel better about things. Now, he was sold on her philosophy, and began to wonder about his own views. Maybe, just maybe, no theory on life is worth anything unless you can use it in the middle of a shit storm.

A couple of days into the job, and Ray began to do what he could to rationalize the current situation. His staunchly Catholic mother used to talk endlessly about the lives of saints, and the heavy burdens they often took upon themselves to obtain some sense of redemptive holiness. This married well with the natural streak of self-pity that currently ran through his psyche and became a game he played inside his own head.

This was his punishment for a life not lived well. It was the penance that he must pay for a sinner's bill of fare. He was Saint Raimundo of Playa Gomez, pledged to a life of simple servitude to cleanse his soul. That worked for another few days, until the self-wallowing fed upon itself and pushed him well up to the status of martyrdom. By the end of the second week, in his mind, he had become a latter-day Jesus, pushing garbage trolleys up his own Via Dolorosa, which ran from the eight person Jacuzzi up to the stage where nubile young dancers would demonstrate the samba every other evening.

At the end of his shift, after the staff had all pitched in at the dining hall for the supper sitting and had a meal themselves, Ray wandered down the concrete path toward the beach. It had already started to get dark, and he had nowhere else to go.

The others often went to a campground just off the resort grounds – a collection of cinder block huts painted in gaudy shades of pink and lime – where they would talk, laugh, drink, dance, and listen to their music. He tried it the first day, hoping that it would take his mind of the unpleasant meeting with his idol, but decided against doing it again. He had nothing in common with his coworkers, and they considered him both strange and arrogant for insisting that he was an American, and, by extension, no worse than the guests they catered to. Rather than helping him adjust to a new life, the social interactions merely served to remind him of the old one that he desperately missed.

He sat down on the end of a plastic lounge chair and, head cupped in his hands, slumped forward with his elbows pressing sharply into his knees. Off in the distance he could see some flashing lights – a freighter, or some other large ship – heading east and out into the mid-Atlantic. It occurred to him that in another time, a ship would just as easily have hugged the coastline, spotted him, kidnapped him, and pressed him into service. *If only something like that would happen to him right now. Then again, isn't that how he ended up here in the first place? No, he was as willing as they were insistent, wasn't he?*

"You're Vasquez, aren't you?" came the voice from behind.

Ray was too tired to be surprised. He stood up and turned around to the sight of Robin St. John Roberts. "Uh…yeah," he muttered purposefully, not looking forward to a replay of their last meeting.

"Relax," said Roberts, making a lowering gesture with his hands, like someone approaching a vicious dog that stole their paper. "I know you're off-duty."

Ray shrugged. *Off-duty, on-duty. Did it really matter?* He felt as drained as a dead man. He was neither in awe of his mentor, nor in fear of his rebuke.

"Anyway," continued Roberts, "I saw you here, and I thought we should have a talk."

"About what?"

"Well, you did cause quite a scene. I mean, I come here for privacy, and I spend a lot of money to keep it that way. Why do you think I come to a place where Yanks aren't allowed?"

"You don't need to worry," said Ray, with some bitterness. "My boss already chewed me out about it. It won't happen again."

"Yes, I'm sure of that," intoned Roberts, "but still, this is a pretty good job for you people, and it would be damn near impossible to get another like it."

Ray did not like the direction that this discussion was taking. "Well," he answered, "if I stay away from you, then you won't have any problems, will you?"

Roberts began to squint his eyes ever so slightly as he gave a churlish grin. "If you think that's what it'll take," he purred. "On the other hand, one word from me to the manager, and it wouldn't matter where you hide yourself."

Ray held the anger he felt welling up inside.   "What do you want?" he asked.

Roberts laughed. "Ah, straight to the point!" he said. "You might be a Yank after all."

"What do you want?" he repeated.

Roberts took a couple of paces forward, so that he was facing the ocean and not Ray directly. "It's a nice resort, but it's boring. I don't do samba, and I don't do volleyball."

"Then talk to the manager. He'll sort something out for you."

Roberts turned around and smiled. "No," he said thoughtfully, "he won't. At least not for what I have in mind. But I'm sure you could help me."

A moment of silence passed between the two before Ray

declared "I don't swing that way."

"No, you stupid bastard!" Roberts snarled. "I prefer the company of women. Not every celebrity that comes to a place like this is a pervert. I'm looking to go on a date, and I need you to introduce me to someone."

Ray felt empowered by what Roberts said. "So," he began, "because I am a stupid Cuban, I need to get this straight. You want me to line you up with a hooker, or you'll make up some story to get me fired. Is that about it?"

Roberts quickly turned his head from side to side, lest some couple on a romantic moonlight stroll heard a single syllable of what Ray had said. His facial expression was an odd mix of panic and anger. He was about to speak when Ray cut him short.

"Hold on," he said dismissively. "Don't get your panties in a bunch. I didn't say I wouldn't do it."

Roberts relaxed his face muscles and gained his composure. "So...you have someone?"

"Yeahhh...," Ray said in a thoughtful drawl. "I think I've got someone. Mind you, even in an all-inclusive, you gotta pay for the extras."

"Of course, of course," agreed Roberts. "But how much?"

"Well, I'll let her decide that, but there is the matter of a finder's fee."

"A what?"

"Finder's fee, unless you wanna bang on every door in Playa Gomez and ask if there's a whore for rent."

"How much?" said Roberts, clearly not amused by Ray's style of salesmanship.

"Two hundred pesos," said Ray.

"Two hundred pesos?!" exclaimed Roberts. "You're bloody daft!"

"I'm not the one who has an itch he needs scratched, am I now."

Roberts stared at Ray with even more contempt than he showed at the poolside a couple of days before. He gave a grunt, and opened his wallet, extracting ten twenty-peso notes. "Here," he spat, "now give me what I want!"

Ray nonchalantly reached into his pocket and extracted one of Sofia's business cards. "Call her. Tell her you met me and make your own arrangements."

Roberts took the card and squinted at it in the moonlight. "You drive a pretty hard bargain for a local."

This made Ray grin. "Well," he said, "I prefer to look at it this way. I saw an opportunity, and I chose to be the opportunity."

Despite the reduced light of the evening sky, Ray could clearly make out the expression on his face. *Oops, I hit a nerve.* Roberts paused, then let out a grunt like a wild boar before turning to walk back to his suite.

Although his parting words gave him immense satisfaction, Ray somehow knew that his time at Playa Gomez was limited. Indeed, the next morning, after the breakfast buffet had been served, he was called into Jorge's office. A complaint had been received, and although he, as manager, felt that Ray was an asset to the staff, it was beyond his ability to intervene successfully. Jorge gave him a week's pay, in cash, a free meal, and a seat on the next tour bus that was heading back to Havana.

It was obvious to Ray that Roberts was vindictive enough to have sandbagged him once he was assured of his end of the bargain. His services were no longer required, and what better way to put an insolent local in his place? Oddly enough, though, this did not bother him. He hated the place with a passion. It was not a prized job, but a torturous reminder of the life he once had and was desperate to get back.

He had an early supper and spent the rest of his time sitting in the lobby, reading the resort literature, as it was the only material printed in English. Shortly before seven o'clock, the bus pulled up and he loaded on with the rest of the passengers. Never had he been in less of a hurry to get to a destination.

Chapter 15

Given the crowd that had gathered in the cantina, Ray had assumed that his entrance would have been relatively inconspicuous. Indeed, that was what he had been hoping for. He was not expected back for another week, and while Orlando would have approached things in his typical laid-back fashion, he was under no illusions as to what Sofia's response would be like. What value did he have for her if he could not get her dates, not to mention coming up with the money for room and board.

Unfortunately, the ability to be fully aware of one's surroundings is an essential trait for commandos and bar owners. Call it situational awareness, but Orlando would not have stayed in business for long had he not developed the almost Ninja-like ability to eye the stage, the crowd, and the till simultaneously. It was certainly good for business, but, at this moment, not so good for Ray.

Orlando was on the stage, microphone in hand, when he saw Ray shifting along the back wall into a relatively darkened area of the establishment. "*Senors…Senoras*…I want to welcome my good friend, Raimundo. He ees very troubled, *sí*? But he ees like a son, so I seeng thees for heem."

The karaoke began to play a song that was a bit before Ray's time to have recognized, although the words on the projection screen told him that it was "Kid" by the Pretenders. Even if he had known the song in its original, studio enhanced, presentation, it was doubtful that he would have known it. Even the most tone-deaf person in the world could hardly have confused Orlando's song stylings for the smooth, yet edged tones of Chrissy Hynde.

"Keed, wha change jour moo…Jou've gone all saa, so I feel saa too…"

On and on it went, this campily macabre serenade. That was bad enough, but Ray knew that the old man was doing this free of pretentions or scruples, and out of a genuine affection. It warmed him to know that this man, while not cognizant of the fact, was still willing to create such a spectacle on his behalf.

After accepting his accolades from a few of the patrons, Orlando laid the microphone down and left the stage to make his way toward Ray. He placed a firm hand on Ray's shoulder.

"Raimundo, jou are back early, jes?"

"Yes," he sighed. "It looks as though I won't be going back either."

"No matter," shrugged Orlando. "Jou come and seet. I will bring jou something to dreenk."

He led Ray to a small oval table to the right of the stage and, after a couple of moments, he returned with a half empty bottle of Caney and a couple of tumblers. "Seet," he repeated his instruction.

For a moment, nothing was said as Orlando emptied the contents of the bottle equally between the glasses.

"Jou are very unhappy, my friend. I feel sorry for jou."

"Sorry for me?" asked Ray. "My problems are solved once I get the hell off this island. No offence, but yours won't."

"I'm not offended," smiled Orlando. "Besides, I don't have any problems."

"You're kidding me, right? I mean, you all live nine people to a house. You haven't got a pot to piss in or a window to throw it out of. And don't get me started on your government."

"By jour standards, I am very poor. I drive my grandfather's car, and I share my home. That ees true. But I never have gone a day without food to eat or worry about having a place to sleep. When I get sick, a doctor gives me medicine. I have many friends and family who love me very much. What I want and need, I already have.

"Jou, on the other hand, want money, but have none. Jou want fancy things but have none. And the ones jou love is a world away."

"I have opportunity," countered Ray. "That's what I have."
Orlando smiled and began to laugh aloud.

"Opportunity," he said. "Eet is just a word. Jou know, Raimundo, this opportunity, she is a blessing when you have it, but a curse when you don't. She is like the woman who does not love you anymore. You ache for her, but you cannot have her, so she consumes you and drives you mad."

"I was always told that you never miss what you never had."

"I think you are right, my friend. I have had food, drink, love, laughter, and a bed to sleep. I have not had this opportunity you speak of."

Ray smiled, as he took a large gulp of rum. "To be honest," he gasped, from the burn of the liquor, "neither have I."

"Then jou are a dreamer," said Orlando, as he refilled Ray's glass, "which makes jou an even more pathetic case."

"That's a bit harsh, isn't it?"

"Sorry, my English ees not so good," he said with a half-knowing look. "I think I meant to say 'tragic'."

Ray raised his eyebrow and lifted his glass. "Honest mistake," he muttered.

"Look," replied Orlando, "if jou are really ambitious, and jou want to make some money, I might have something for jou." With that, he got up from the table and gestured for Ray to follow him out into the back alley.

Parked behind the cantina was an enormous object covered with old canvas tarpaulins and fastened down with ropes.

"Here, help me with thees," instructed Orlando, as the two men unfastened the ropes and pulled back the shroud.

"What do jou think?" he asked.

Ray was not sure what to think, but at this point, being surprised was something that did not easily happen.

"Uhh…it's a giant hot dog…on wheels," he said, not sure what he was looking at.

"It's a Wienermobile," declared Orlando proudly. "My grandfather had eet shipped here from the States before the revolution. My father used to park eet down in the old market and sell food there. Now it is mine."

"Does it work?" asked Ray, not knowing what would qualify for 'working' on this odd-looking machine.

"*Si*," answered Orlando, "it runs fine. I have a cousin who works on cars, and I know a couple of guys who know how to make parts in their shop."

"Well, it's a fine-looking machine," said Ray, hoping that the dim light of the alley would prevent Orlando from seeing him roll his eyes in derision. "I can understand why you keep it here hidden away. Wouldn't want anyone to steal it."

"Steal it? No, my friend. Nobody steals it," said Orlando. "I keep it tied up, so it doesn't go out to sea."

"I don't get it," said Ray, giving him a confused look. "It's a car, not a boat."

"It's fiberglass," he explained, as he tapped the side of the vehicle with his fist, making a hollow thud like a ripe watermelon. "One time, there was bad hurricane, it got out into the harbor, floated out to the ocean. Some fishermen knew it was mine, towed it in. Ever since, I keep it here tie up - especially during hurricane season."

Ray nodded his understanding. "Well, it's a very fine machine," he repeated, not sure what else he could say to Orlando about it, or sure what this all had to do with him. If there was a point to be made, Ray hoped that he would make it, lest he had to spend a few more awkward moments making small talk about this strange looking contraption.

"Jou are smart businessman in jour country, jes?" asked Orlando.

"Well, uh, I don't want to brag. I mean, I've had some successes at business. Yes," explained Ray.

"Jes, so jou run thees for me, okay?"

"A hot dog stand?"

"Jes, jou run. I let jou keep some profit, but jou run," repeated Orlando.

So - it had come down to this. Six months ago, if he had been asked to define moving up the corporate ladder, he would have talked about going to a corner office at Tuckner Wass. Now, amid this dystopia, success was defined as moving from handing out clean towels to fat men in Speedos to serving fried food out of a giant plastic frankfurter on wheels. As much as Orlando's heart was in the right place, he could not understand how much worse it made him feel.

"Orlando, thank you, but I need to think this over. You understand?" he said, patting the man on the shoulder.

"Si, I understand," came the slightly dejected reply. "Jou are afraid jou are not going to be fair with me. I do not worry. Jou are a good man. I trust jou."

"Uhh…okay," said Ray in a faltering cadence, knowing that he had clearly not made his point. "Nevertheless, I would like to give you an answer in the morning, if that's all right?"

Orlando shrugged. "Si," he answered. "Eet doesn't matter to me. The truck seets here if you say yes or no."

With that, the men shook hands, and headed back into the cantina. Unfortunately, the good will and bonhomie he shared with Orlando was not something that he was going to share with his niece. While he knew that he would have to face her sooner or later, he did not plan on her angry visage being the first face he would see as he passed in through the door.

"You're back early," said Sofia. It was not a question.

"Uhh, they let me off early," replied Ray.

Sofia started at him for a moment, her left eyebrow arched in an expression of doubt. "You're lying," she said with a deathly seriousness he had never heard before.

"You don't believe me?!" he exclaimed. "Call the goddamn place, then."

Without missing a beat, she opened her purse, and extracted her cell phone. Three numbers into the dialing, and Ray asked her to stop.

"You bastard! You ungrateful bastard! This is how you pay me back for everything I've done for you!" she screamed.

"I couldn't do it, okay!" he yelled back. "This kind of shit might be easy for you…"

"Excuse me?! What is so easy for me?"

"You know…" he said, with some hint of sprouting what might resemble a vertebra.

"No, no I don't!" exclaimed Sofia, ready to throw down the gauntlet. "Why don't you come right out and tell me!"

"Screwing!" he yelled. "There, I said it! Screwing, screwing, screwing!"

Sofia felt flushed with rage. "How dare you!" she screamed, as she raised her hand and slapped him full on the face.

"Do it again! Go ahead! Do your worst!" he screamed back. "My life is ruined!"

She let her hand come within a couple of inches of his cheek for a return visit before she stopped herself. "I hate you!" she cried. "You have no idea how much I hate you!"

"I'd say the same," he growled, "but I don't care enough to do it."

Tears were starting to well up in Sofia's eyes. She gave him a look that he had never seen before in her face, and only in one other person. As oblivious as he could be in such matters, he knew what was happening, and he also knew his responsibility.

"Look, your uncle offered me a business proposition," he said, attempting to be reassuring. "I told him that I would give him an answer in the morning. I still have about three hundred pesos left, so I will be able to cover my room and board in the meantime."

She stared at him with the look of a scolded child and said nothing. Even she realized that she had also gone further than she had cared to.

"It's late," he announced. "I'm going to bed…Goodnight." With that, he leaned forward and presented a peace offering in the form of a kiss on the forehead. He pulled back only to be greeted with an expression slightly less surprised than his own. He muttered goodnight again and headed up the staircase.

Sofia remained in the cantina, alone, opening a new bottle of Caney and taking a generous glass full, one after another, until she exhausted both the bottle and herself.

Ray lay awake for the longest time staring at the window, its sheer curtains gently swaying from the breeze. Eventually, the hypnotic movements, the afterglow from the rum, and the utter exhaustion of the day overtook him and pushed him into a deep slumber. Ray's last waking thought was how the only person who ever really talked to him was Robin St. John Roberts, and he turned out to be a sonofabitch.

He never dreamed, and if he did, he rarely remembered it. It was even more so since he had arrived in Cuba. His mother, ever the spiritual soul, had always insisted that dreams were how our better angels spoke to us. That is how God spoke to Daniel and Joseph, she would say. Ray was not altogether sure he believed this to be true, but, in the back of his mind, he did think that the reason he did not dream was that God had nothing to say to him. There was nothing to say, no advice to import, no great insight into the workings of the universe, or his minor role in it. That father was just as communicative as the one who came home at six every night and demanded complete silence as he watched SportsCenter.

The dream came quickly and vividly. He stood on the stone wall of the Malecon, facing north. His heart was heavy. He wanted to jump, to flounder, to sink. In a split second, he found himself submerged in a maelstrom, pulling him down like dirty dishwater down a drain. Before he knew it, he was sitting with his father at Shea. His father, with an expression of kindness he had not seen in years, turned to the hot dog vendor a couple of feet away, and asked for two red hots, and keep the change.

He relaxed as he leaned back to enjoy both the hot dog and the game. He took a big rapacious bite, and then, out of nowhere, he was plunged back into the whirlpool, hurtling out toward a light. It was home, and there was Connie…

Ray woke to find it was already morning. He rose from the bed and rubbed his eyes and face. He remembered it all – the mish mash of images, all thrown together into some strange narrative, but why? It did not add up to anything remotely coherent. He brushed aside this psychedelic trip through his subconscious to attend to earthlier, and immediate, concerns.

Once it was clear, he went into the bathroom to clean himself up. He turned on the shower and adjusted the temperature until it was as close to perfect as he would get and prayed that Sofia was not about to run the kitchen faucet for the next couple of minutes.

The steam from the shower created a thick mist that he could taste. The needle like streams of water prickled the skin on his shoulders and back, like some acupuncturist tapping their slender metal shafts into raw muscle. It was the only time he would allow the forces of nature to beat him down, down to the point where he could scarcely think.

When he finally finished, he grabbed one of the large coarse towels that hung on a rack and proceeded to vigorously wipe the remaining moisture from his body. The roughness made it feel as though his blood was coursing up to the surface. He looked in the mirror, and after applying a generous dollop of shaving foam he had received from one of the guests at Playa Gomez, he began to carefully sculpt it away.

He remembered that he had promised to give Orlando an answer about his business proposal. He also began to think about why he was so reluctant to say yes. *Was it out of some embarrassment? No. After all, almost every day in this country had been a sustained shit kicking to his ego. Patriotism might be the last refuge of scoundrels, but pride was the first casualty for the refugee. But a business partnership seemed so permanent. It was tantamount to giving up. After all, a big fiberglass hot dog was never going to be his ticket back to the States...*

Ray paused and placing his razor on the edge of the sink, he leaned forward to stare intently at his reflection. He did not see his face, though, as his brain kicked into hyperactivity, darting back and forth through everything – his conversation with Orlando, his dream.

"See the opportunity...Be the opportunity," he grinned as he picked up the razor and resumed his shave. It had finally all come together in his mind.

He knew what he had to do.

Chapter 16

Ray had followed Orlando's directions which ended up taking him to a smallish cinder block house on the outskirts of the city. It sat alone at the end of a dirt road that skirted one of the more inhospitable parts of the coast. He had explained to his prospective partner that if he was expected to make a go of this new venture, there were some mechanical issues that needed to be resolved. After all, being the son of a licensed mechanic in New York City, you learn a great deal about how cars work – even those shaped like hotdogs.

The man who lived in the house had seen the taxi from a couple of hundred yards away and had already started walking out to meet his guest, hastily rubbing his greasy hands with an old rag.

Dausel was a cousin to Orlando. Although younger, his work added years. His torso had the same basic barrel-chested form, but his arms were massive. He could see the veins in the man's biceps and forearms bulged and pulsing with each swing forward. Ray knew that years of hoisting engine blocks and twisting torque wrenches could do that. He had seen the same squat, muscular forms among his father's mechanic friends.

"You the Americano?" he asked in well pronounced English, the precision of which shocked Ray. *Clearly Orlando's particular patois was not due to some family trait.*

"Yes. I'm Raimundo," he replied, as he walked around to the trunk of the car. The driver had already opened the lid and had deposited the wheel hubs on the ground. "Your cousin told me to come if I needed a mechanic."

Dausel stood for a moment, looking at the rims while Ray assured the driver it would only be a moment longer before they headed back into the city. "Orlando tells me the car needs fixing, and you bring me this," he said. "Where's the rest of it?"

"That's it," said Ray. "Just the wheels."

After studying the pile of hubs for a moment, he looked back at Ray. "Are they bent? You lose air from them?"

"No, not bent. But I need a welding job on them."

"Why," asked Dausel, not sure what this strange man that Orlando had sent was thinking – if at all. "I weld them, and they are ruined." He grabbed one and rolled it along the ground a couple of feet, bending down to look along the edges. "I do not see a crack. No welding. I will tap it out and it will work fine."

"No, no," said Ray, trying not to display any heightened emotion at Dausel's pronouncement. "I need them for something else."

"What?" asked Dausel.

What did it matter what it was? He was the customer, and Dausel was the mechanic. You do the job, you get paid. This whole business of asking why and what for, now that was the family trait that seemed strong among Sofia's lot.

"I…I…need them for a generator," said Ray, not knowing why he had just said that, or how he was going to explain it further. He took the piece of paper out of his pocket and gave it to him. "You see, I need to have fins on them…for water."

Dausel looked at the diagram and raised an eyebrow. "You know, we have electricity here in Cuba."

"Hahaha, yes, of course," Ray replied, "but I want to take the car to places where I can't tap in. If I have something that will charge the batteries, then I can go to more places."

"Yes," said Dausel, "but you need water. You gonna have water where you go?"

"Uhh…yes…I wanna go to the beaches…where the *turistas* are. If I park near the ocean, I can get power from the tides."

Dausel paused for a moment, staring at the hubs and the paper. "Okay, I know how to do it," he said. "You need those wheels, but you need a frame for it, and you need a small motor, like a starter. I can…"

"Oh, don't worry about all of that," interrupted Ray. "I've been working on the rest of it myself. This is the last part I need. Can you do it?"

"Uh, sure, I can do this…You need to give me a couple of weeks at least. I have to fix the grill on that De Soto over there," he said, gesturing over to a car parked in a large shed to the side of the house. "I will call Orlando when they are ready, and you can come and get them."

"Actually…" suggested Ray, "I would prefer if you just waited for me to come and get them. I don't want to involve Orlando."

"Why not?" asked Dausel. "It's his car, his wheels?"

"Yesss…but he took me on as a partner, and, well, you know how generous he is. He will expect to pay you for all this work. I think I should pay the whole thing, but if he knows, his pride will get in the way…You understand?"

Dausel shrugged. "Look, friend," he said, "You don't have to tell me what you're really doing with these things. Maybe it's for Orlando, or maybe it's for you – I don't care. All I know is that you're not making electricity."

"So, you won't do it?" asked Ray.

Dausel looked straight into Ray's eyes. He took the rag and wiped his forehead, replacing beads of sweat with a blackened streak. "I didn't say that - and I don't want to know your business either. I just want you to know that I know what bullshit smells like."

Ray nodded. "I get it," he said, as the two men shook hands on the deal.

With that, Ray got back into the taxi and headed back to Havana, more assured than ever that the fates had ceased their fickle ways with him. Once he arrived back at the cantina, he reported to Orlando that the weinermobile would be in ship-shape in a matter of a couple of days, and the two men celebrated their collaboration over a couple of Bucaneros.

There was much to set in motion, including the food – the hamburger patties, the frankfurters, the bread, the rolls, and the condiments. Orlando assured Ray that such details were trivial, as he could source it out of the cantina. This confused Ray as the cantina did not really run a food concession. Orlando, however, insisted that these were details better left for him to deal with. Ray soon learned that there were some shipments of food to various resorts that may have gone missing, or accidently fell off the back of a truck, or some other thing. Better not to ask.

Then there was the matter of permits and licensing. Getting a spot at the local market in Old Havana was almost impossible. Again, Orlando met all of Ray's concerns with a confident 'don't worry.' And again, Ray knew it was better not to ask.

Of course, he was right. The sweet, wily, old man knew best, and Ray's end of the bargain seemed confined to driving to the site, taking orders, cooking the food, taking the money, closing up, and coming back to the cantina well after dark with the day's take. Once back, he and Orlando would sit down and over a bottle of rum, they would do his version of 'the books'. Orlando would open a small, leather bound notebook, would cost out what he had paid for supplies and what he referred to only as 'other services'. Then, he would count out that much money and set it inside the cover of the book. What remained was counted out equally in two piles, one which was folded and placed in Orlando's shirt pocket, while the other was gently slid across to Ray. Then, at the end of every week, a still sullen, albeit chastened Sofia, would approach him with the bill for his room and board. While this took the lion's share of his earnings, it still left him with a few pesos to spend as he saw fit.

The opportunity to part with that money came a month later when Dausel paid a visit to the stand. He had planned to come to Havana to pick up some parts for a starter motor to a 1958 Studebaker. Having finished the project for Ray, he decided to simply bring the wheels in with him. Trying not to look nervous, Ray paid him the money, which he always kept on his person, as a precaution, and loaded them into the back of the vehicle. He placed some boxes of ketchup on top, and a couple of propane tanks in front, lest Orlando – or Sofia – catch a glimpse.

It would not matter much anyway. Tomorrow was going to be his last day on the job.

Chapter 17

A full moon was both a blessing and a curse. The ambient light that allowed him to work to attach the makeshift paddle wheels was also the light that would give the patrol boats a better view of the beach. He had moved the vehicle into the water just enough to gain buoyancy when the tides reached their maximum height.

Ray grabbed the wheel wrench and began to twist feverishly on the lug nuts. Although he had remembered to loosen them while he was on land, it still was not an easy proposition. Every twist would cause the entire wheel to turn on its axle. Also, the steady rocking to and fro from the cresting waves seemed to jostle him every time he found a secure foothold.

He had planned on no more than thirty minutes to make the change, but an hour into it and he had only attached three of the hubs. It was only dumb luck that he had not drawn any attention – or had he? Who could tell if some passers-by had noticed this odd sight on the beach, and had made their way to locate a policeman, or someone else, to look into it?

Regardless, he could not stop now. A fifty-fifty chance of getting offshore was better than a one hundred percent chance of being arrested. By now, he had gotten used to the rhythm of the waves and had found a stance and grip on the wheel that worked for him. The fourth, and final, wheel had been the fastest so far.

It was done, but would it work? Well, the hot dog would float

– Orlando's story, as well as Ray's own observations bore that out. The wheels should propel the vehicle forward. That was a matter of grade school physics and Dausel's abilities as a welder, which Ray considered better than average. That just left the motor and the steering. He reasoned that the steering would be okay, as the front hubs had paddles and the thrust from the back axle would help turn them as well. Once he had forward motion, he could steer – extremely hard, but not impossible. In the end, it did not matter how well it worked, only that it worked. Period.

He struggled to hang onto the open window near the vehicle's cockpit. The waves continued to batter the shell with the determination of a welterweight fresh from the spit bucket and a pep talk. The incoming waves would help propel him up towards the opening, but the subsequent undertow would grab his now waterlogged boots and attempt to pull him back into the surf. He needed to get the rhythm again, to make it work for him, but in learning the timing, he had made a couple of attempts that had left him physically drained.

One more time. One more time, or there was no point. The open sea or a locked cell – it was going to be one or the other!

Another heave upward, like a released spring when the crest of the wave hit, and his head plunged in through the window. He grasped frantically for the back of the bucket seat on the driver's side, and once in his firm grasp, Ray pulled his lower extremities in like a wounded soldier crawling across a battlefield. Once fully within the confines of the vessel, his foot tangled in the steering wheel, causing him to crumple to the floor. A sharp stab of pain shot up his leg from the ankle. A sprain? A break? It did not matter. Too far along, and too close to start. Grabbing the seat, he rested his foot from its precarious position and carefully raised himself into an upright position. It was time to go.

Sitting down behind the wheel, he turned the ignition. The moment of truth. While Dausel was constructing his paddles, Ray had busied himself with the task of waterproofing the engine, the fuel lines, and the wiring. He had also fashioned an up pipe for the exhaust which, given its location, he had hoped would not end up poisoning him before the trip was through. Through it all, he had racked his brain to remember everything his father and his buddies used to talk about. It made him feel good – and relieved – to know that a great deal of those discussions had sunk in. Still, actually doing it was the real test.

The first attempt was nothing more than a hesitating chug. Ray cut the switch immediately. *I can't kill the battery or flood the carburetor!* Staring at the switch, he counted slowly, methodically, to ten, and then…success! The old plodding diesel motor sputtered to life. He placed his foot gingerly on the gas pedal to give it a little revving. *So far, so good — but would it move?*

Ray gently slipped the gear shift into drive and let the engine idle. He glanced outside. Was he moving? Even a little bit? The waves made it so hard to tell. Back and forth. Back and forth. It was hard to discern any sustained forward motion in all of this. All or nothing, he decided as his foot pushed down closer and closer to the floor.

As the engine began to roar with increased fury, Ray could feel his makeshift vessel push forward in a deliberate manner. At the same time, his arms began to strain with the task of steering through water, although the paddles on the front hubs made the job easier as the speed increased. Once he had pointed himself out into open water, it was only a matter of keeping the wheel straight.

For the next half hour, Ray felt the tension in his body ratchet up. Until he could get out into the ocean without detection, there was no rest. When the time passed without incident, he said his thanks to his Creator and continued with a newly discovered sense of optimism.

What he could not have known was how close it had all come to going horribly wrong. Within moments of his heading offshore, a couple of local fishermen had spotted him and had reported him to the police who, in turn, had contacted the local military command. A small patrol vessel was dispatched to investigate and, if needed, radio in authorization for use of force. When the word came back about a 'giant, floating hot dog,' what transpired was not only a refusal to authorize any action whatsoever, but a rather lengthy and colorful lecture on the evils of drinking while on duty. The patrol was halfway back to its base by the time that Ray had finally crossed out of Cuban waters and into the open sea.

After the effects of the adrenaline rush wore off, Ray realized that he had not packed any food for the trip. Digging around in the back compartment, he found a couple of thawed out boxes of frankfurters, and a case of Havana Club rum. Not being a fan of either hot dogs or rum, he chose to wait it out for as long as he could. It was only ninety miles to the Florida Keys, and his paddle wheel invention seemed to be working fine. And, of course, he had a compass to point him home.

Never in his permutations did Ray consider that the gas mileage on the ocean might be a bit less than on the open road, and that even a full tank would not likely get him where he needed to go, let alone the half-full tank he had inherited. Thirty miles from shore, in choppy waters, was the last place where he wanted to learn the lesson of planning ahead.

As with any crisis, the first reaction is panic. Eager not to starve to death, Ray began to devour as many wieners and bottles of rum as he could before the Grim Reaper was to bang his sickle against the fiberglass hull. Luckily, in the process of eating his tenth wiener and quaffing bottle number two, did he reason that the mixture of rum and grease from the deep fat fryer was like mother's milk to a diesel motor.

After some re-engineering, he managed to pour the concoction into the fuel tank. Once the magic elixir was added, and an hour was spent begging, cajoling – and crying like a baby – the gods smiled and let him continue.

To keep up the production of fuel, Ray used what propane remained in the on-board tanks to cook up as many wieners as he could. The more he had cooked and eaten, the more grease there was.

For the next couple of hours, it seemed as though the fates had chosen to smile and bestow their graces upon Ray. But it did not last, for in his haste, he had carelessly invited a dark and brooding maiden aboard, and her name was Salmonella.

The brutality of the attack was in direct proportion to the number of partially thawed wieners he had polished off. At first, he blamed it on the rum, and his decision to reserve a swig for himself for every two that made their way down to the fuel line. But Ray was no stranger to the demon drink, and he understood quickly that this went far beyond the usual bender.

Standing precariously on a couple of crates, he punched out the screen for the roof vent, poked his head out of the opening, and began to vomit so violently, he lost his balance and fell back into the car.

He lay there for a moment, believing the worst was behind him, which, in a way served to be a cruel irony, as that was exactly where the worst was about to be coming from.

What came next was a testament to a degree of ingenuity and stamina that Ray did not believe he possessed. With a rope tied to his waist, and fastened securely to the steering wheel, he gave himself a heave-ho and crawled out of the vent.

The waters between Cuba and Florida are among the heaviest patrolled areas in the Atlantic. In any given year, surveillance would pick out a high number of curious sightings. Given that fact, one might wonder what the satellite imaging experts at Langley would have made of the sight of a man, naked from the waist down, and defecating, as he clutched on the side of a giant floating hot dog thirty-eight nautical miles from Key West. We will likely never know as no CIA analyst with ambitions of promotion would be filing that kind of report any time soon.

A haze in the morning air obscured the horizon where the shades of blue that defined both sea and sky intersected. No delineation existed, as though a blue blanket had been draped over the whole earth. So disorienting, Ray could not discern between feelings of claustrophobia and agoraphobia. He kept his eyes fixated on objects within his makeshift vessel to set a bearing for his brain.

Only the eventual coming of the reddish golden haze created some visual reference for him. By then, though, it mattered very little. It took all his remaining strength to clear a small place behind the driver's seat, where he curled up in a tight ball, hoping that the clenching of his muscles would somehow dull the pain and nausea.

Underneath him, he could hear the sloshing and gurgling of the water, rising to a height where it would thump against the fiberglass wall, creating a hollow thud like the noise of his mother tapping a melon for ripeness down at Verrazano's market.

He had forgotten a timepiece – a clock, a watch, anything to help him get his bearings. The rhythmic slosh and gurgle beneath his aching head were as close as anything he had to the ticking of a second hand. *Time? Hell – what day was it? Light, dark, light, dark.* He had lost track of the count. All he could focus on was the gnawing pit in his stomach, the sharp stabbing pain in his intestines. Why could he not just hurry up and die already? Yes. Die free. Alone, but certainly free.

It was time to sleep.

Chapter 18

"Oh, oh…hot dog!"

Manny Diaz sat laughing at his television set. It was a shade past eleven at night, and his typical Saturday ritual was to sit himself in his recliner and watch shows until the wee hours of the morning. His wife would be in bed by midnight, so his only companions would be a bottle of Bacardi, a plastic jug of generic cola he picked up at the local Publix, and – of course – whatever happened to be playing that evening.

Manny liked his comedy –a little too much by his wife's estimation – and a rerun of Mad TV on Comedy Central was the menu item on offer.

"Shit, that Bobby Lee's funny!" he hollered out to the kitchen.

"He's not that funny," yelled back a woman's voice from down the hall. "He's even more annoying than that guy selling those towels, whatever they're called – slam, sham…"

"That little translator guy he does? He's hilarious," replied Diaz, pretending not to have heard his wife's critique of his viewing habits.

"It's late and you're drunk," replied the voice. "You'd find a potted plant funny about now!"

"Yeah, yeah, sez you," Manny argued, as he turned to look out his window and out into the harbor. The quick glance, however, turned into a prolonged stare. He grabbed a pair of binoculars from the side table drawer to make out the blurred shape.

"Oh, oh, hot dog…" his voice trailed off quietly.

"It wasn't funny the first time!" his wife yelled, holding a towel as she entered the room. "So help me God, you're on the couch if…"

"Shh," Diaz said, as he motioned for her to come over and look out the window herself. She took the binoculars and obliged, looking out the window in the direction that he was pointing. While not on the harbor, the Diaz home was close enough that they had a decent view of the water – especially at night, courtesy of the flood lights that peppered the shoreline. It was by virtue of all this that she saw the object aimlessly floating in from the ocean darkness. She also noticed very clearly, much to her dismay, what it resembled.

"I really didn't need to see this," she muttered under her breath. "I really didn't."

Within an hour a large group had gathered on the pier, where the floating hot dog was moored. A couple of men, who had been doing some late-night work aboard their charter fishing boat, had noticed the peculiar sight and went out to investigate. They were not the first to spot the strange vessel – that honor went to Manny – but they were the first to make contact, and duly towed it to the pier.

Manny, having seen the boat first, and being somewhat of a *de facto* precinct boss – albeit a self-appointed one – decided to make a big show of thanking the men for their hard work, but that the situation was now under control.

This, of course, did not wash with the crew of the boat who, despite the use of profanities and some firm finger jabs into Manny's chest, made a forceful argument for Manny's fiefdom ending at the water's edge.

After some quick, hardnosed negotiating, Manny had agreed to part with an acceptable share of the valuables that may lie aboard before he took formal custody in the name of the neighborhood. After the handshake, all of them set out busily to claim their booty, lest the local civic authorities act in a provocative way as to disturb this détente.

Manny, armed with a flashlight, tied a rope around his waist.

"Hold it tight, guys. I'm gonna climb over to that hole there."

He slid onto the top of the fiberglass hull and straddling it like a horse, he leaned forward into it and shimmied his way down to the opening.

"Holy shit!" he exclaimed. "It smells like a sewer backed up in there!"

"Can you see anything in there?" asked one of the men holding Manny's makeshift safety line.

"Naw, not yet...Let me get a light in there."

By this time, the local network affiliates already had their mobile camera crews at the ready for whatever Manny and the men would find in this strangest of boats.

The bright light shining in Ray's face caught him by surprise. Still weak from the food poisoning, he began to moan.

"*Como esta?*" asked Manny, clasping Ray's face in his huge, calloused hands. "*Como esta?*"

"Uhhh...," he groaned, gesturing for the flashlight to be turned away.

"English? You speak English?" asked Manny.

"Eng...lish...Eng...lish," muttered Ray.

"Never mind," said Manny, "we better get you outta this thing." With that, he shouted for the men atop to lower down a harness to raise the stranger up.

Once it had been sent down to him, Manny propped Ray up against the back side of the driver's seat and attempted to reach around his back with the harness straps. Once secured, Manny tugged on the line and yelled for those atop to heave-ho.

With a jerking motion, Ray began to rise from his place of rest like some macabre marionette, his head hung down, with arms and legs dangling lifelessly, with the occasional spasmodic start that coincided with the rhythmic jostle of the pull from his rescuers.

"Jeezus, guys! Be careful with him!" barked Diaz as Ray's head emerged from the opening. Once his shoulders were above the hole, a couple of the men, feet carefully balanced on the slick fiberglass, grabbed him around the torso and hoisted him out.

An ambulance had pulled up minutes before and the two paramedics aboard had already placed their gurney on the dock at the closest point to the odd-looking craft. The lead paramedic instructed the men to deposit the castaway on the bed just as Diaz was climbing out the top.

"Where you takin' him?!" he yelled.

"The hospital. The man's dehydrated. Could be more."

"Not without my permission! I found him!"

"Found him?!" snapped the other paramedic. "He's not some fuckin' stray dog! Besides, if he's yours, then it's your ass if he dies!"

"Well…I'm goin' with ya," demanded Diaz. "I saw him first, so he's my responsibility."

The paramedics gave a quick look to each other, acknowledging that even though Diaz was a pain in their asses, that showing up with a John Doe would be a bigger pain, with hospital administrators, social workers, police, and the requisite paperwork.

"Come on, Dad," the first paramedic said derisively. "Gotta get your son to emerg…"

Chapter 19

Ray lay on the Diaz's couch for the next couple of days, drifting in and out of consciousness. *Home - he was home. The next two thousand miles would be far easier than the last ninety. Back to Connie, back to Momma. Even the sight of Pop would look good.*

Manny sat in his reclining chair, watching television. Ray noticed him there every time he drifted in and out. It made him wonder which one of them was confined to one spot.

"…for the latest on the trial of Harold Raphaelson, we go to Rebecca Symes in New York…"

Trial? Raphaelson? What the hell is going on…

"…the former CEO of famed Wall Street brokerage Tuckner Wass faces indictment on seventy-five charges, ranging from mail fraud to embezzlement. At the center of the prosecution's case is Raphaelson's use of off-site operations – often referred to as 'boiler rooms' – where traders for the firm sold fraudulent investments to shore up the company's balance sheet…"

"I'd love to get my hands on one of those bastards," said Manny, making a hand gesture to simulate a choking.

Ray coughed nervously as the gravity of the situation set in.

"Oh," said Manny, turning to his guest. "You're awake. How are you doing?"

Ray was in a panic, not sure what to say or do.

"Hey, friend," Manny continued. "Do you know English?"

It was then that Robin St. John Roberts' sage words creeped into his brain – see the opportunity, be the opportunity.

"Uhhh…*si*…a leetle Ingles," he stammered, trying to copy the speech pattern he had heard so many times from Orlando.

"You from Cuba?" Manny asked.

"…uh, si, yes, Cooba," replied Ray, probably laying the accent on a little heavier than necessary.

"Thought so," said his host. "We found stuff in your boat, or whatever the hell it is."

Ray nodded and smiled. He could only imagine what impression that his choice of watercraft had left on those assembled on the pier when he floated in.

"What is your name? *¿Cómo se llama usted?*"

Ray hesitated for a moment, then answered "Antonio Vasquez."

"Well, Senor Vasquez, don't mind me sayin' but you looked like shit when we got you outta your…uh…boat. Smelled like it too."

"Uhh…gracias," muttered Ray in a sickly moan, hoping that a good show on his part would cut the conversation short.

"Oh, sorry. Forgot my manners. I'm Manny Diaz. You're in my house…in Miami. I know you had a rough trip, but you made it. You're a free man now."

Free. Now there was a concept. Free to announce who he really was? Free to get up and go back to New York? Free to pick up where he had left off with Connie? Not likely.

He smiled meekly, lest he not show the requisite amount of gratitude for having been plucked out of the sea and placed firmly in the Land of the Free and the Home of the Brave.

"Tiiiime," he moaned, gesturing to the wrist below his left hand.

"Time?" replied Manny. "It's about eight in the morning. Are you hungry?"

Definitely no. His stomach was still a twist of knots, and while part of him would have loved to gorge upon whatever was placed in front of him, the other knew that even the most bland and benign morsel of food would set him off in another episode of dry heaves.

Diaz left about an hour later and returned with a stranger early in the afternoon. With Manny out of the house, Ray's only companion was Missus Diaz, whose toleration of him was not that different from what Max would have displayed, although hers was a more contained and deliberate brooding that, at its warmest, could be described as passive aggressive. He had learned that she was originally from Georgia and had no Hispanic roots – let alone Cuban. This meant that she would never dare attempt a conversation in Spanish, allowing him to sit quietly and not be directly assaulted by her complaining, although that left voicing her ire in good old-fashioned English, slamming kitchen cabinet doors, and emitting loud grunts of frustration. Having Manny back was a relief but having another ally would be even better.

"Antonio," said Manny, "this is Sammy Calderon. Your English is not so good, and my Spanish is terrible, so Sammy agreed to help out. He is going to translate for me, so you can understand."

Shit - what am I going to do now?

Diaz turned to Calderon and said, "Tell him that we are very glad to have him here."

Calderon nodded, then turned to Ray and fired off a patter of Spanish that he could never hope to follow.

Ray quickly realized that it did not matter what Calderon said. It was only going to be the Spanish version of what Diaz had already said out in plain English. All he had to do was to follow what Manny said, and then wait for Calderon to stop talking before he answered.

"Uh...gracias...*Mucho gracias*," he said, staring at Calderon. Diaz started up again.

"Sammy, tell him that he is a hero and a symbol for our community, and that we need him to help us in our efforts."

Again, Calderon dutifully translated Diaz's words, while Ray patiently waited for the right moment to answer.

"*Si...*," said Ray in a faltering tone, not sure what this help was going to entail.

"Good," said Diaz, "now there are politicians in Washington who want to lift the embargo on Cuba – maybe even go so far as to recognize the government. Unfortunately, there are younger people in our community who don't understand what's at stake. They were born here, and they don't see a problem with opening things.

"People like Sammy and I were born in Cuba. We saw what our parents lost, and we saw how close Fidel took the world to war.

Out of respect to our parents' generation, we can't give in or give up.

"That's where you come in. You came here to get away from all of that. Freedom means so much to you that you risked your life to get it. Our young people – and the politicians – need an example of sacrifice in the name of freedom."

Diaz leaned forward until he was no more than four or five inches from Ray's face. "You can say what the rest of us can't," he said.

Ray felt frozen with fear. *Say what exactly? Baseball, cars or getting Sofia her 'dates'? Was he supposed to say it in Spanish, or in the suddenly fluent English skills he developed from watching whatever Diaz had tuned in on at two in the morning?* He remained silent for what seemed like an eternity, weighing his options, trying to figure out the best way to extricate himself from a situation that was beginning to drain him both mentally and physically. Try as he might, nothing seemed to present itself.

Slumping back in the chair, he gave a look of confusion to the men, which they had interpreted as a complete lack of understanding.

"I mean," continued Diaz, "you were in this country for a while, in New York. That's what they said on TV. You were at the UN or something."

Finally, a lifeline! Of course, he could speak some English. Had he not already done so? It was hard to remember the last couple of days. They blurred into one another. He could have told them anything. Besides, was he not Antonio Vasquez? Would the Cubans send someone to the UN who could not speak any English? It did not have to be perfect, or great, but there could be something. *Thank you, thank you, Manny!* He sat back up and showed some life.

"*S-s-si*," he said, continuing his plodding version of Spanglish. "I lof thees country…I lof Amereeka…I weel help you."

"Terrific!" exclaimed Diaz, as he patted Ray on the shoulder. "Now, we aren't going to just throw you in. Sammy and I will be there every step of the way…You understand?"

Ray nodded with a wide grin that looked like that of a child who had just announced to the world that he had successfully gone to the potty. As afraid as he was of overacting, he was even more concerned about not playing it up enough and showing just a little too much familiarity with life in the States – more than could be explained away by a diplomatic assignment. Calderon responded with a toothy smile of his own.

He leaned in toward Ray and clasped his hands in a thoughtful pose. "*Senor Vasquez, como...*," he began.

"No, no," interrupted Ray. "Ingleesh, pleese...I must practice."

"Okay," shrugged Calderon. "I understand...What I was going to say was that I represent a group - *grupo*? It is called 'The Sons of Jose Marti.' We work to help our Cuban brothers and sisters who come here. We find them places to live and jobs."

Ray nodded his polite approval of this philanthropy.

"Anyway, we are only successful when people in our community understand what we do...Do you follow me?"

Ray nodded again. It was a general enough statement to grasp that required little or no preconceived understanding of the activity, whether it be selling widgets or rescuing children in the Third World.

"There are people who don't remember the sacrifices that have been made on their behalf. As the years have gone by, it gets harder to remind them. But you, you are different. You represent the essence of what we are all about. Manny and I are not asking for your help to put you on the spot. We understand that you are vulnerable right now, and we do not want to take advantage of you...Actually, we want to take advantage of the situation you have presented us. The opportunity, if you will..."

The magic word! Opportunity!

Ray smiled his understanding. Besides, what else could he do? After all, they did take him in, give him a place to stay, food to eat. Did he not have some moral obligation to honor his benefactors?

It was at this time, however, that Ray also began to feel some unease with it all. He had not exactly figured out how he would get out of Miami and make his way to New York. Actually, he had not figured out how to get to the Interstate, let alone travel out of Florida. It would be fair to assume that his sudden absence would be noticed and would be treated more urgently than a kid on a bicycle posting reward flyers for a missing Cocker Spaniel!

It also begged the bigger question - when could he stop being Antonio Vasquez? It had been so long that he thought he might forget his real name. Besides, why would Calderon and Diaz let him walk away when they had such plans for him to be the centerpiece of their campaign? What were those plans anyway?

After Calderon left, Ray spent the rest of the day - and a good portion of the night - preoccupied by that question. What had he signed on for exactly?

Chapter 20

The following morning, Manny had told Ray that Sammy and 'the Sons' had organized an outing for him. While it was to serve as a public relations exercise, in some capacity, the main reason, assured Manny, was for him to relax and to get a feel for the 'real America.'

Ray had interpreted this introduction to Americana as some neighborhood tour of the environs of Little Havana, possibly culminating in a drop-in at some local café or taberna. Sammy would lead this 'stranger in a strange land' around to the various community leaders, and after some rhetoric about the struggle for freedom and liberty, he would collect some cheques and that would be about it. One would have thought, by this point, that Ray would have left the business of forming expectations of what others planned, or believed, when it came to his participation in any activity. The only time in months that he truly was his own man – in charge of his destiny – had been aboard Orlando's Wienermobile, bobbing to and fro on the trade winds. The fact that it had been the closest he had been to death did not strike him as being the least bit ironic. Nevertheless, Ray began to ponder whether Spanish was the only language that Calderon spoke for which he had no comprehension.

In truth, Calderon was more obvious than Ray understood. He was, at heart, a political animal. While Diaz was a true believer, and a tireless workhorse, he lacked an appreciation for what Sammy had declared to be 'the bigger mission.' In the time he had spent as a community organizer, from the early years of watching his father, to assuming a leadership role in 'the Sons,' Calderon had learned that much of politics was done in the ethereal abstract. One could offer to pay every overdue utility bill and argue with city officials over every by-law fine levied in the neighborhood, but the real influence came from proselytizing the message. The less charitable called him a propagandist, but he saw himself more as an evangelist – a prophet for the cause of freedom, liberty, and repatriation.

The older generation needed no reminders, he reasoned, for they knew first-hand what they had lost. They had been the ones who rushed to collect their belongings and flee their homes for a new life in the United States, forfeiting anything that could not be carried by hand. They were refugees at heart, and no matter how many years would pass, or how much success they might enjoy in their new homeland, they would always feel like exiled peoples always feel, and would exhibit the two common attributes – a severe sense of grievance, and the uneasy feeling of life being arbitrarily temporary.

Their children, the generation of Sammy's peers, on the other hand, showed no such scruples. Their parents' grievances were not their own, and their feelings about the much-vaunted struggle were complicated and nuanced. While they understood the arguments, they had not lived them as viscerally, and their American born sensibilities found the old jingoism to be somewhat parochial and, on occasion, a little embarrassing. How could one dream of returning home when you were already there?

While Calderon understood this disconnect, he did not subscribe to it. Something had been stolen, and justice dictated that it be returned. Besides, one could never truly appreciate freedom without first understanding its very fragile nature.

No, it was when you believed all was well with the world – that is when it would go so horribly wrong. He would not neglect the hard-learned lessons of the past – he would keep the faith.

Walking around the neighborhood was all well and good, but it was self-limiting, and in his estimation, self-defeating. Most of the younger generation was more American than Cuban, and old-style appeals would be dismissed or ignored outright. No, Calderon knew that to get to the people he had to cast a far wider net.

Almost before the crack of dawn, he had arrived at the Diaz home, driving a black Chevy Suburban whose windows were tinted almost as dark as the rest of the vehicle. Two other carloads of men were parked immediately behind. *Geez - it looks like a frigging police convoy. Where the hell are they taking me?*

As Diaz and Ray made their way down the front path, Calderon exited the vehicle and opened the back door closest to them.

"*Buenos dias*, gentlemen," he said with a broad grin. "We have a pretty busy day today, so we should get moving. Now, Antonio – I can call you Antonio, right – well, I've taken the liberty of inviting some friends along for our trip. This is a big day for you – I thought you might want it recorded, for posterity's sake."

Ray shrugged. *Record what? I don't even know where you're taking me? How do I know if I want it recorded or not? Clearly, you think I do.*

Once everyone was loaded in, the caravan pulled away from the curb and headed north, toward the aptly named 'Florida's Turnpike'. For the next couple of hours, Ray sat back and let the never-ending parade of overpasses and gaudy billboards pass him by. The huge signs almost seemed to tell a story. First, there was the billboard advertising some pornographic enterprise, and then, a mile or two further, one that confidently proclaimed that 'life begins at conception.'

Then, still further along the way, he saw a grand plaque that exhorted drivers to exit to Mount Carmel Salvation Center to expunge their karmic records. Another one along the way that offered deals on bulk diapers and formula might come in handy, he thought to himself.

Ray spent much of the trip reading the billboards. The scenery was relatively flat and treeless, with smatterings of swampland, and after a while it seemed as though the same four or five miles were being run past his window like some film in a continuous loop. The only alternative would have been to engage the others in the vehicle in some conversation.

That was a non-starter for obvious reasons. He could not even ask where they were heading. That would imply a level of self-awareness that a Cuban refugee simply would not possess. Besides, based on the conversations that were going on around him, and the direction that they were heading, he was certain that Orlando was their intended destination.

It was slightly before nine in the morning when the caravan had reached its first destination, Gatorland Zoo, and proceeded to take up half of the parking lot. By then they had been joined by four trucks, each branded with the logo of a local station's network, along with a half-dozen sedans and other models of passenger car. It was going to be a circus, thought Ray. He wondered for a moment what act he would be performing in this show – as a clown, or up on a high wire without a net.

In the time it took for Ray to emerge from the black Suburban, a throng of reporters had already encircled him and began to yell over each other to make their questions heard. Most insistent of them all was the woman from Telemundo who, assuming that a language barrier made for a strategic advantage, fired off a staccato stream of Spanish that made him think, for a split second, that Sofia was back to exact her revenge.

Calderon and Diaz, ever the attentive minders, quickly whisked him forward, yelling back at the throng to hold their questions until they got into the park. So, like some strange globular organism with Ray as the nucleus, the pack moved toward the front gates.

Needless to say, the staff of the park, while entirely welcoming of Ray and his immediate cohort, were not keen on the prospect of having his whole entourage trampling through the park and upsetting the various creatures that called the place home.

Thus began an awkward negotiation. Yes, Vasquez and a couple of escorts were welcome, but certainly not the reporters. This evolved into a compromise to allow a camera crew, but that only served to inflame those who would be left to stand around the parking lot for a couple of hours while others would get the scoop.

Nevertheless, after enough wrangling back and forth about sharing feeds and offering side interviews later in the day as some sort of consolation prize, the group had been sufficiently pared down to an acceptable core. The remainder took the opportunity to get a bite to eat, read a newspaper, or hose down their vehicles at the coin operated car wash across the street.

Once inside the park, Calderon and Diaz led Ray and the others into the viewing area, which looked more like a network of sheltered wooden docks connected to a larger platform, all raised above one massive shallow cement pool where alligators would float and swim at their relative leisure.

Halfway to the platform, Calderon stopped everyone to officially declare the purpose for said visit. As the roof of the walkway reduced the Florida sun considerably, the one videographer allowed inside turned on the spotlight attached to his camera. The glare was so intense that Ray dropped his gaze to his feet. This, however, did not prove to be a good idea.

Ray's eyes focused on one particular resident of the pool that he could see through the gaps between the wooden planks. A rather large reptile, it had stopped swimming and parked itself directly under where he stood. Two eyes, like dark marbles, seemed to follow his every twitch and shuffle.

After weeks of evading Wall Street sharks and Cuban barracudas, now he had to contend with an everglades gator who wanted a chunk out of his ass. Calderon and company had started to move along before he had to seriously ponder that situation.

After a few minutes wandering around the various exhibits, Calderon led Ray to a small platform where a wooden bench sat below a park banner. "We should get your picture taken," he suggested, and instructed Ray to sit on the bench.
All part of the treatment, reasoned Ray, as he obliged and sat down firmly in front of one of the park's staff, who was operating a large Polaroid camera bolted to a wooden counter.

Behind her stood his retinue, who had dogged him every step of the way, even to the door of the bathroom stall where he spent as much time relieving his nerves as he did relieving his bladder.

"Okay, then," smiled the perky teenager. "Are we ready for some friends?" Friends? What the hell is she talking about, he asked himself. Just take my goddamn picture and be done with it. His mouth, however, emitted a meek and compliant "*si.*"

With that, the girl reached into an opening in the top of the bench, and extracted a small alligator - approximately three feet long, with its jaws taped shut. Holding it by the head and neck, she gently walked over with it to Ray.

"Now, hold your hands out, and don't be afraid," she assured him, as she deposited the reptile squarely on his lap. Gritting his teeth so as to not show his distress, Ray obediently held out his hands and took hold of the creature. The girl, having dealt with numerous tourists and children, sought to dissuade him of his evident fear.

It did not move as much as he thought it would, and after a moment, he was a bit more acclimatized to the whole thing. He, or she - it - felt like one of his mother's old leather purses - and just as heavy, he mused.

Then, on cue, the girl reached into another display case and extracted another one of Mother Nature's bastard offspring. As Ray was to learn, cuddling a gator was not a full and true experience without a four-foot boa constrictor dangling around one's neck. *Geez, what the hell are they trying to do to me? Couldn't they have propped me in front of some guy in a mouse or duck costume instead?*

The girl held the snake up with both hand to the height of her shoulders, letting the head and tail dangle toward the ground. She walked over carefully to him, like a waitress carrying a full tray of drinks. "Now," she cautioned, "just relax and I'm going to just place her around the back of your neck, like so."

Down it came, like some scaly, slithering scarf. He could feel every twitch of its sinews as it rubbed against his hair and the flesh on the back of his neck. He shuddered like a winter chill had suddenly blown in and brushed his bare skin. He watched the girl walk casually back to the camera, where she instructed him to give her a big smile.

Ray obliged, and through his gritted teeth, in a low and inaudible voice, he muttered "Just take the fucking picture already!"

At that moment, he learned that there was someone – or something – that happened to be more nervous about this situation than him. A warm, wet sensation began to spread on his lap, and then trickle down his bare leg. Within seconds, a small puddle was collecting beside his right foot. *Shit! The alligator! It's taking a piss! On my lap!*

The girl pulled back from the camera. "Ohhh, I am so sorry," she giggled. "Jessie gets a little frightened sometimes."

He clenched his jaw while the voice inside his head started to rant and scream. *Jessie?! It's got a name? It's a man-eating monster, and you coo over it and call it Jessie? Are you people insane!*

The girl came forward and picked up the gator. Turning to Calderon, she asked "Do you still want to do this? He doesn't look to happy about it either."

"He's been through worse," said Calderon as he draped a towel over Ray's lap and instructed the girl to put 'Jessie' back in position. "Besides, I really need for you to get this picture...It's a nice memento of his coming to this country."

Memento, my ass! You just want a photo op that you can pimp out to the press and your donors!

With Jessie and the boa firmly in place, and with no other complications or distractions, the girl once again instructed Ray to smile for the camera, and then...click.

Five minutes later, the masterpiece was on full display to the gathered reporters who giggled about the leaky reptile but were quick to point out that 'Senor Vasquez was such a good sport for putting up with all of this.' Ray saw it and thought the expression on his face was that of someone grimacing while they were holding in a bad case of flatulence.

Chapter 21

"Hey, Baker, that Connie Lulio is here looking for you."

Frank Baker was not having a very good morning. For that matter, good mornings were few and far between nowadays. He was on countdown to retirement, and the budding career that was his life's ambition was just another albatross around his neck.

While many from his graduating class had gone on to head their own offices, or return to Quantico as instructors, he continued to bide his time in the New York office. Despite what he considered his best efforts, Baker was never able to go beyond the level of functioning as a convenient foil for whoever happened to run the office at any given moment.

He was never entirely sure when the bitterness and cynicism set in. He felt like it had been a steady companion all along. He would be lying if he denied that the steady rises and promotions of some of his peers did not weigh in the back of his mind. On the other hand, he could rationalize a great deal of it. After all, there was some real talent there, and a lot of those guys worked hard to get to where they were. What he could not justify was the increasing trend of having to report to a boss who had started out as a snot-nosed kid fetching him his morning coffee.

Frank Baker was the only agent left in the New York office who had served under anyone who had personally known J. Edgar Hoover. That used to be a source of pride, or professionalism – a touchstone to the golden age of the Bureau, of fabled G-Men like

Eliot Ness, and those epic battles against the likes of Dillinger and Capone. Now, among this new generation, it served only as the punchline to tacky jokes that involved women's dresses or bugging the phones of Dr. King or the Kennedys. That kind of talk always got on his nerves. It was probably why it happened so often.

Now, he was resigned to what he considered as being a wetnurse to these agents, and counting down the days until he could pack up his modest belongings and move out to the cabin he had purchased upstate, near Saranac Lake.

Of course, he knew that he was getting close to that time. Why else would he be given nothing but 'lost and found' cases? A runaway teenager pissed off about curfews, a philandering husband hiding out with the secretary up in the Poconos, an embezzler absconding with the company funds – it did not matter. It was his job to find them. Once they were found, however, another agent would take over and work on whatever juicy part of the story would lead to an even bigger case. He would find the thief, so another punk could come in and investigate the theft.

Connie Lulio had been coming to the office every week, like clockwork, about her missing husband. All Baker knew was that he had worked at Tuckner Wass and was involved in the Moreton scam. That was enough. He knew that in most cases like this, the guy would stay hidden for quite some time.

Eventually, he would turn up. Some irate investors would hire a private investigator who would find the guy swilling Tequila in Cabo San Lucas with some local tart. Some tabloid show would run a piece on it, and then, and only then, after the State Department lobbied for their extradition, failed, and left it to some bounty hunter to get him to El Paso, would the Bureau spring for economy fare to fly him down and both of them back. Since this would take, under the best of conditions, years, and he had only weeks, it would not be an exaggeration to say that the fate of Ray Lulio did not figure prominently in his work.

"Aw, damnit…Where is she?"

"Out in the lobby," answered the agent at the door. "Whaddya want me to tell her?"

"Tell her I'm busy, and that we still don't have anything on her husband. She'll get a call when…"

"When what?" came a woman's voice from around the

corner.

"When we have some information, Missus Lulio," said Baker, putting on a quick saccharine smile, and rising from his desk to greet Connie. "It's hard to find someone who doesn't want to be found."

"Then, maybe I should call CNN," she said matter-of-factly.

"Look, I know that the gut tells you to call the reporters in, but all you are going to do is make our job harder."

"No, Agent Baker, I think I should call CNN because Ray has been plastered all over my television this morning."

"Whaddya mean?" he asked before he turned to the other agent and asked him whether he had seen the coverage himself.

"Not yet. All they've been running is some story about a Cuban diplomat washing up on shore in Miami – wants to defect."

"That's Ray!" interrupted Connie.

"Your husband is a Cuban diplomat? I thought you said he was a trader?" asked Baker.

"He is a trader, or at least he was until he disappeared."

"Did you say 'trader', or 'traitor'," the other agent laughed.

Connie turned around and said, "Don't you have some coffee and donuts to fetch?"

"Shut the door on your way out, Thomas," growled Baker.

"Okay," he continued, as he gestured for Connie to take a seat. "I'm a little confused here. The news is running a story about a guy from Cuba who washed up on shore in Florida, looking for political asylum, and you say that he is your missing husband."

"Yes," she said. "Yes, I am."

"Look, Missus Lulio," he said, leaning forward and clasping his hands together on the desk, "think about what you're saying. I know that you're eager to find your husband – come to think about it, so are a few others – but don't you think that it's highly unlikely?"

"Yes," admitted Connie. "It sounds crazy. But I know my husband, and that's who I saw on TV."

"Missus Lulio, we get dozens of cases every year where someone thinks they know what the suspect looks like, and they'll swear on it, but it's not the same person."

"Agent Baker, it's my husband, not some guy who stole my purse! You don't think I know my own husband!"

"Now, now…calm down. I'm not saying that…"

"The hell you aren't!" snapped Connie. "Ray's my husband, and ever since the day he went missing, I've thought about him nonstop. He's a file to you, but he's someone important to me."

"Well, that may be true, but the guy in Florida says he's Cuban."

"It's him," she insisted. "I don't know why he says that. Maybe he took a shot to the head and had his brains scrambled."

"Well, that would be kinda convenient, wouldn't it?"

"Now, get me straight. I'm not here to help you arrest my husband. See? I want you to help me find him and bring him home. I know you wanna throw him in jail, and that's your business. Rest assured, I'll fight you tooth and nail on it, but right now he's missing, and that should be the priority!"

Baker sighed and pulled back from his desk. "Missus Lulio, I don't think you're understanding me. This man washed up on shore from Cuba. How does a guy from New York do that? Cuba – a country that none of us can set foot in. Okay, so he looks like your husband. You know him better than I do, so I'm not going to argue with you over that. But in this line of work we come across people who look like someone else all the time. Get up real close and you notice a small scar that shouldn't be there, or that the nose is slightly bent to one side. May look as close as a twin from a distance, but they're not the same."

"You just don't want to help me," replied Connie.

"I would love to help you but chasing some Cuban guy who floated in from Havana is not going to get me close to finding a Wall Street trader. Until I'm convinced otherwise, it's just wishful thinking. I wish you could see that."

Connie got up from the chair. "I see that if I'm going to get Ray back, it'll be no thanks to you…I'm sorry for wasting your time!"

With that, she turned and stormed out into the hallway.

Baker was tempted to shout out some words of consolation – or a warning not to be rash - but it was no use. Of course, she was upset that her husband was missing. He did not need to be married – still – to appreciate the sentiment.

Chapter 22

It was around eleven the next morning when a news van pulled up in front of the Lulio house.

"How's my makeup?" asked Rebecca Symes.

The driver, a rotund man named Roland, but who everyone called Rollo, shrugged as if to say, 'I dunno – fine I guess.'

"For chrissakes, Rollo, we broadcast in HD. I don't want to look like a goddamn circus clown," she said, as she pulled down the passenger side sun visor, and looked for herself in the attached mirror. "Gotta make this count."

'Gotta make this count' was a mantra she repeated often before the cameras were turned on. Whether it made any difference in the cosmic order of things was a topic for dispute, but it was a talisman that served to calm her nerves and hone her focus.

Earlier that morning, when the call came into the newsroom that someone needed to cover a missing person's story, she flatly refused. After all, she had been working the story concerning the near collapse of Tuckner Wass, and the downfall of its CEO, Harold Raphaelson. *Boy, was he ever a piece of work!*

Nevertheless, it was the biggest story in the city for some time, and it earned her network face time. After a couple of weeks, she had it all mapped out. She would write a book about it – after all, she did have a degree in English from Brown. She had the wherewithal to craft a story, and now all the raw material to source it.

To do a missing person's story was down with covering a quilting display at a local parish hall, or some art gallery show. Fluff pieces did not get you book deals, and it would not get a correspondent's job in Washington.

Of course, it was only after she had turned the story down that the reporter assigned had asked who was missing.

"Some guy named Lulio," said the assignments desk editor. "Was a trader on Wall Street."

Lulio...Lulio...Tuckner Wass! Shit!

"I'm taking it!" she yelled, as she sprinted to the desk.

"You already turned it down," said the editor.

"He's Tuckner Wass, and that's my story!" she protested.

"Fine...fine...take it," he sighed, giving a conciliatory look to the other reporter whose eyes were shooting daggers at the back of Rebecca's head.

And so, she did. She remembered the name from the list of subpoenas that the grand jury had issued. His was the only one that had not been served. Not that it mattered much. Raphaelson was going down for sure. Nevertheless, Lulio was a no show, and his wife was looking for him.

Poor woman. The sonofabitch was probably hiding in Mexico and banging a secretary. This is exactly what the narrative needed! The loyal spouse who, despite being a victim of her husband's greed and avarice, still loved him enough to want him back. The perfect ingredient to spice up a boring story of accounting fraud.

Confident that she was ready for the camera, she and Rollo exited the van. While he went around to the back of the vehicle to gather his equipment, she made her way up the front walk to the door. Within moments she was greeted by a woman who, despite her outward comportment, still looked as if she were on the verge of a major upset.

"Missus Lulio?" asked Rebecca.

"Which one? My mother-in-law is here too," came the reply.

The bastard! This poor woman left penniless and abandoned on the doorstep of her in-laws. Probably took her in to help cope with their own shame.

"Connie Lulio," she replied. "I'm Rebecca Symes from Channel Eight News. You called our station about your missing husband?"

165

"Uh...yes...Please, come in."

Rebecca and Rollo, who, by this time, had caught up with her, entered the front door and the living room where Connie formally greeted them. "Thank you for coming," she said. "I'm kind of surprised that you're even here. We're not, you know, famous or anything like that."

"Missus Lulio...Connie – can I call you Connie? Connie, your story is important regardless of who you are. These days, with everything that's going on in the world, even the rich and famous aren't what they used to be. We don't worship people anymore, but we still want to understand."

"I suppose," said Connie, who had not had the luxury of contemplating the larger world while her smaller version of it was so disheveled. "Anyway, where do you want to do this?"

"In here is just fine," replied Rebecca. "You can sit over there on the couch, and I'll get Rollo to set up over in that corner. You don't mind if he plugs in there?"

"No, that's fine. Just try not to disturb things too much. I don't want my in-laws walking into a mess."

Poor girl - they take her in after her dirtbag husband abandons her, but they have her on pins and needles the whole time. They're probably just trying to save face in the neighborhood by taking her in.

"No problem," she replied. "We certainly don't want things to be difficult for you when we leave."

Connie was confused. "Uhh...no. I just know that Bertie spent the morning cleaning, and I don't want to make a mess, that's all," she said.

"Anyhow, whenever you're ready, Rollo," she said, fixing her skirt and blouse, and taking a seat on the couch beside Connie.

"Give me a sound check," instructed Rollo, as he maneuvered his head behind the camera, now fastened upon a tripod.

"One, two...one, two...Peabody, Pulitzer," sounded off Rebecca with a deathly seriousness that betrayed her outward pleasant smile. That was not lost on Connie, and the knowledge of same did little to ease her mind.

"Good," replied the cameraman. "Roll on three."

The count, and then.

"...The accounting scandal that has shaken Wall Street and brought the venerable firm of Tuckner Wass to the brink of collapse has created hundreds of victims across the country and around the globe. One of those victims is Connie Lulio. Her story is even more tragic as it was more than just a loss of trust in a financial firm – it has also meant the betrayal by the man she loves..."

Connie sat open-jawed. *What the hell was all of this?*

"...Connie, your husband worked at Tuckner Wass?"

"Uh, yes. He was a salesman there. He hoped to become a trader...I know that because I worked there myself."

The last bit of information elicited a slight grimace from Rebecca. She gave a knowing look to Rollo, and then resumed the interview.

"...Am I correct in saying that you haven't seen him since the day that the SEC had the offices of Tuckner Wass and its shell company, Moreton Securities, raided?"

"Yes, that is correct."

"And exactly where was your husband, Ray, heading to when he left?"

"Well, he worked some evenings at Moreton..."

"He was involved at Moreton?"

"He was trying to earn a little extra cash...We've been living with his parents and we wanted to get a place of our own, and..."

"I see," interrupted Rebecca. "And now he's gone, and you haven't heard from him since?"

"No, although I am pretty sure he's in Miami right now."

"Miami is a very nice place. A person could easily sail to anywhere in the world from there."

"I suppose they could," muttered Connie.

"Especially if they were being sought by law enforcement agents?"

"Look, Ray has screwed up. I know that. But he's not a thief! I don't know how he got there. Or why he won't come home. I'm trying to find out, but the FBI is blowing me off, and it's been almost two months. I'm tired and I'm frustrated..."

I'm going to lose her. I've got to calm things down.

"Connie, why don't we take a break, okay? Maybe I can get you a glass of water?"

"I'll go get it," sighed Connie, as she got up from the couch.

"No, no...I'll do it," she insisted, and gestured for Connie to sit back down. "The kitchen's in there, right?"

"Yes," answered Connie. "Glasses are to the right of the sink." She was in no mood to argue. In fact, she was in no mood to do anything – fight, argue, protest. Truth be told, she was not really in the mood for doing this interview. She did not want an interview anyway. Ray had been missing for weeks, and he's in Florida. If the police were not going to follow up, then they needed an incentive, and a public one at that. End of story.

She wanted two things and two things only – to have her husband home, and to know exactly where he had been all this time.

It did not bother her that Rebecca was trying to make this into something bigger. That was her agenda, and welcome to it. Work on Wall Street and you learn that things only happen if people see those things fulfilling a greater objective of their own. In agreeing to this, she knew that there was an implicit tradeoff. Rebecca got a Tuckner Wass tie-in, while she got one step closer to getting Ray home. Somehow, though, it was not feeling like it was a straight-across trade, and she knew that she was not getting the better end of the bargain.

Rebecca returned with the glass of water and resumed her position. "Anytime you're ready to go on," she said sweetly.

Connie gulped down almost all the contents of the glass in one hearty swig, then, after catching her breath, she indicated that she was ready to proceed.

"Missus Lulio, do you know that your husband is the only person associated in the investigation that has an outstanding subpoena from the grand jury?"

Connie bolted up onto her feet. "I've had it!" she yelled. "This interview is over! Get out!"

Rebecca calmly gestured for Rollo to cut the recording and gather up his equipment. She turned to Connie and said "Missus Lulio, I am sorry about your husband – truly, I am – but your story is part of a bigger narrative."

"My life is not a narrative! My life is my own!" Connie spat back.

"Well, I'm sure you wouldn't want to see it that way," defended Rebecca. "Your husband was in the Moreton office when it was raided, and he hasn't been seen since. You're not going to tell me that it's a coincidence?"

"Actually, I'm not going to tell you anything more than I have! Like I said, this interview is over!" she growled.

Rebecca smiled, and then she and Rollo headed toward the front door. Rollo headed outside toward the van, but she stopped in the open entranceway and turned back to Connie.

"You know, if I were you, I would be asking why my husband had not tried to contact me – even ask me to meet him somewhere…Then again, you know him better than I do…Good luck."

She said nothing in reply, but simply stood and watched the reporter walk back to the van. Once it pulled away, she slowly closed the door. As she went back into the living room and sat down, those last words echoing in her ear.

How do you reconcile what you know with what others think that they understand? It is easy when you love, and you trust. Trust. That was the hard one.

If Ray had his reasons, they were not obvious to her. She certainly had spent enough time trying to wrap her head around every conceivable scenario that would explain everything nicely. Unfortunately, the only explanation that fit that way was the one that Rebecca had intimated. Was that why she was so upset? Either she was the only person in the world who knew the truth, or she was the only one who was blind to the lie. Whatever it ended up being, it was a lonely place to be.

For the rest of the afternoon, until Max and Bertie had returned from their outing, she contemplated whether it was possible to have love without trust, and whether the emotion she was feeling was that of having been played for a fool.

Chapter 23

"Raul, how are you, my friend?"

The Minister had found Raul Rodriguez in the back yard of his modest home, tending to a garden of assorted vegetables and flowers.

"So, I am your friend, am I?" he replied, continuing with his work, not even looking up at his boss – or former boss, for that matter. "I am doing very well, thank you. Things could not be better."

"Don't count on it. We have a problem, and your leave is terminated."

Of course, Rodriguez knew all of this. While he had been suspended from his duties, he had not dropped off the face of the earth. People came to visit, and they came to talk. He dropped the hoe on the ground, and in a manner that seemed to be purposefully nonchalant, he removed an old handkerchief from one of his back pockets and wiped the perspiration from his brow. "You had me escorted out of your office at gunpoint and held in a cell for interrogation for a week. I would consider that slightly more than a leave of absence."

"It was an overreaction, Raul, and I am sorry for it, but you were never fired, just given leave," said the Minister.

"At the end of a pistol, of course. I can only imagine what would have happened if you had fired me," he observed wryly. "I never wanted leave – never asked for it. That was your idea. I was perfectly happy to deal with whatever matters would arise from my activities."

"I know, but I need you back at the Ministry now. That American fellow you brought back. We need to do something."

"The one who snuck back to Florida, and has all of the Yanqui news channels following him like dogs? Yes, it looks very bad," he observed, still maintaining a sense of calm and poise.

"Bad!? They are more trigger happy up there than they have been in years. It's only a matter of time before they find out we kidnapped…"

"Now, hold on," argued Rodriguez. "We did not kidnap him. It was an agreement so that we could keep Vasquez in place. If you had let me handle this, Mister Lulio would have been returned to the United States, and your little mess in Florida would never have happened." Politics was politics the world over, and he knew that the Minister was placing his own spin on the situation.

"I doubt that those subtleties will be noticed by the White House," said the Minister. "We do not need another 'Bay of Pigs' – either one of us."

"They deported him. They were the ones who assumed that he was Vasquez. They took away his rights as a US citizen. How will that go over in an election year? Besides, has he told anyone who he really is?"

"He insists that his name is Antonio Vasquez, and that he is a defector. That is fine, but now his wife is giving interviews. Sooner or later this situation is going to find its way back to us – and when I say 'us', I mean you."

And so, there it is. Deny me the opportunity to see this through, to make good on the simple promises made to Lulio and end up creating a crisis of which you will end up pinning on me in the end. No, sir, I am not going to make it that easy for you – not in the least.

"Mr. Lulio does not appear to be in a hurry to let anyone know his real identity. That buys us some time," he observed, still managing to maintain a poker face.

"For what?"

"Well, first you need to promise me that I have a free hand. I get to deal with this as I see fit. Otherwise, I will stay here pruning my orchids."

That was exactly what he expected of his protégé – and the last thing that he really wanted to allow. No one did well at the political game by making mistakes, and no one was certain to survive by repeating them. Unfortunately, that logic assumed that options were available, which they were not. In this case, he was forced to find a fix from the very person who had broken things to begin with. What made it even worse was that Rodriguez knew it too.

"Fine," sighed the Minister, "but you better get results."

"Don't worry about that. Just get me the details on Lulio's activities while he was here – where he went, where he stayed, who he dealt with."

"You think we had the time to follow around some penniless American without a passport?" asked the Minister.

Rodriguez raised his eyebrow, cocking his head to one side.

"We've kept a healthy distance," admitted the Minister. "The only time we did anything was when we had him fired at a resort. Too much of a risk having him in close contact with *turistas*."

"As opposed to him sailing back to the U.S.?" questioned Rodriguez.

"Raul, you know full well what constraints I'm under! We haven't the resources to follow him around the clock! Besides, if I asked Public Security to do it, they would want to know why. That's the reason why I didn't have Mister Lulio sent to jail. They would want to have a talk with me, and I don't think you would want me to have that conversation, would you?!"

Rodriguez sighed and gave a reluctant nod. One week in prison, with the subsequent parole, was exceedingly generous compared to what another ministry would have doled out to him. He would never admit it to his boss, but his hurt pride had recovered by the time the car had dropped him off at his front door.

The Minister looked Rodriguez in the eyes for a moment, and then held out his hand. "Look, you'll have what you need to do the job."

Rodriguez paused, then turned in the direction of his patio. "I also expect that I will be able to pick up my letter as well?"

"Letter? What letter?" asked the Minister, clearly not in the mood for any surprises.

"The one that states that my arrest was a misunderstanding, and that my record of service is unblemished."

"You have some nerve making that kind of demand, after everything that has happened."

"And you are fresh out of options. You wouldn't have come to me otherwise."

The Minister lowered his eyes and took out a linen handkerchief to dab his forehead. "You are the one who created this mess to begin with," he argued. "I have no doubt that I would pay a heavy price for all of this, but I'll be damned if I would go down alone! Raul, if I go to prison, I wouldn't stop until you were in the next cell!"

Rodriguez maintained his best poker face, and after a pause for dramatic effect, he turned back to the Minister "So you will have that letter for me by this afternoon?" he asked.

"You'll have your goddamn letter!" barked the Minister. "Just get the job done, and don't get clever! You could ruin more than just the two of us!"

Chapter 24

Playa Gomez was finally settling down for a well-earned rest from the day's flurry of activity. The resort's nightclub had been closed for almost an hour, and most of the stragglers had already bobbed and weaved their way back to their guest rooms. A couple of resilient Liverpudlians, propping one another up at forty-five-degree angles, were belting out their own unique rendition of "You'll Never Walk Alone," much to the amusement of the cleaning ladies who would comment and giggle at the display.

Sofia was conflicted about it all. She knew that her date was English, and would likely pay handsomely, but she shuddered at the thought of knocking on the door and finding one of those two on the other side.

One date. That was all he got for her. After all that time helping him, giving him a place to stay and lining up a job, this was all she had to show for it. That was bad enough, but why did he have to hurt Orlando? He took his hospitality, his trust and friendship, and then stole him blind! "*El cabrón*...," she muttered under her breath. What he did was unforgivable.

She made her way down the concrete path, past the mass of palm fronds, to the door of the bungalow. It was one of the luxury villas on the resort grounds bordering the beach. It meant money, and it was the reason that she never negotiated price in advance. It was a very eclectic crowd that came to the Playa – everyone from European celebrities to young couples on their honeymoons, to single people who had bought their trip a couple of days before departure for a significant discount.

This accommodation, however, was not double occupancy auctioned off on a website. The man was a player. *If Raimundo was going to get her only one date, at least it was one that was going to pay well.*

She knocked on the door six times – two groups of three – as had been agreed. Within a moment, the door opened to reveal the presence of Robin St. John Roberts, clad in an ornately patterned silk robe.

"Are you Sofia?" he purred lecherously.

"Honey, I'm whoever you want me to be," she said as she brushed past him and into the anteroom.

"Well…," Roberts said, "I want to do something different."

"Ahh, that's not what we agreed on," answered Sofia, as she turned to face him with a finger pointed a couple of inches from his nose. She had learned early on that you had to be firm with them from the start. On the other hand, she was annoyed that Ray had not made it clear to this guy from the beginning. It was just another thing to hate the *Yanqui* for.

"No, no, no," Roberts laughed. "I see what you're thinking. You've got me all wrong. I don't expect anything from you – nothing at all."

Sofia was puzzled.

"You paid for a sleepover, so it's going to get kind of boring after a while."

Roberts laughed. "Good," he said. "Sense of humour – I like that."

"No," he added, "I know you must work very hard, always putting the other first. You see, I want to change that. I want to put you first this time."

"Mister, you don't make any sense," she said.

"Don't I, Sofia? Don't I?" he asked rhetorically. "You've lived your life in service to others – your family, your clients, and your country. At any time, has anyone ever asked you what you wanted?"

"No, but I don't need anything…"

"Stop it. Stop it right there. I said 'want' – not 'need', but 'want'."

"Well," she answered, "nobody, but I don't care…"

"You should care, you should," he said gently, as he took her by the hand and led her to the bed.

Sofia complied and sat down, still not sure what to make of the situation. "Nothing kinky, and I still get paid, right?"

"Of course," Roberts intoned in a sickly, syrupy voice, as he reached for the play button on the portable stereo.

What took place next was, to Sofia's mind, very much like experiencing a car crash – a split second of flurry stretched out as though it were minutes and hours.

First came the music – a lecherous voice groaning 'I like the way you move…' to a suggestive guitar grind. Then came Roberts' sad attempt at a seductive dance, highlighted by the dropping of the silk robe, revealing all except what lay mercifully hidden behind a black thong and a spastic grimace – one that changed to a horrified gasp when a half-dozen members of *la policia* burst through the door and put a quick end to the evening's festivities.

Sofia had been through this before, but not quite to this extent. Usually, one or two officers casually going through the motions, but not half the Playa Gomez constabulary. "What did you do?!" she shouted at Roberts. "You pervert! What did you do?!"

Roberts said nothing, the shock and surprise of the interruption having knocked him into some sort of a catatonic stupor. The policemen grabbed him, put on a pair of handcuffs, and unceremoniously pushed him along to the door like a ragdoll being tossed into a toybox. It was only when he had been led out into the night, and down along the cement path, that his brain had pulled out of neutral, and he started to consider the full weight of his predicament.

As he was being led away, Roberts took some consolation that he was in the one country in the world where this mess would not make it onto the evening news. Alas, it would take two weeks to shatter this false sense of security. This was when the first glimpses of grainy cellphone video made their way onto the celebrity tabloid shows.

As Roberts was busy preserving his dignity before the massed group of resort workers and patrons drawn to the commotion, he was too preoccupied to notice the presence of one Philip Burley of Sherburn, Yorkshire. Burley was more than familiar with Roberts, who he had sent five hundred pounds to purchase the acclaimed 'Acceleration' DVD and workbook. Alas, for him, the only things it seemed to accelerate were the breakdown of his marriage, and the downward spiral of his career.

Like his former mentor, however, he 'saw the opportunity' and sold the footage for ten times what he had originally paid Roberts. Surely Roberts would have been proud of his former student's acumen, had he not been more fixated on the feel of the cold holding cell bench on his buttocks, not to mention the strange expressions on the faces of his cellmates when they arrived at the station.

His partner, however, was spared much of the commotion, and a great deal of the indignity. She had been invited to ride in another car, without handcuffs, and a modicum of courteous chivalry that she would not have expected even under the best of circumstances. Once there, Sofia sat in the interview room for an hour before she was joined by a man who did not appear to be *policia*.

"Senorita Avecado. My name is Rodriguez, and I am here from the Ministry of Foreign Affairs."

"I didn't know I broke some treaty," she said sarcastically, as she crossed her arms.

"You are a prostitute, and you were in the company of a rather high-profile citizen of the United Kingdom. It is customary for us to be involved with sensitive matters pertaining to foreign guests."

"You didn't catch me doing anything. No money changed hands. Give me a fine for trespassing and let me go. I won't say anything."

"That's fine. I'm prepared to let the whole matter drop…but under one condition."

"What do you want?"

Rodriguez slid a photograph of Ray in front of her. "Tell me about your friend," he said.

"He's not my friend," she replied curtly, reaching out and pushing the picture back to him.

"You're saying you don't know him?"

"I said he is not my friend," she said matter-of-factly.

"Since I already know the answer to my question," he continued, "let's move on to the nature of your relationship. And I would ask you to answer my questions, and not the ones you make up for yourself."

Sofia paused for a moment, and then sighed. "We had a business arrangement," she explained.

"He was one of your boyfriends?"

"No, no. Not like that! We helped each other. I got him a job and a place to live, and he helped me work on my English."

"That is very generous payment for English lessons," observed Rodriguez. "What kind of job was it?"

"He worked in and around the pool at Playa Gomez," she replied.

"So, Mister Lulio – yes, I know who he is, and so do you – you get him a job around the pool at Playa Gomez. You and Roberts were detained at Playa Gomez, and Roberts tells me he found out about you from a pool attendant. Now, you tell me what else he did for you besides English lessons."

Sofia sat silently, partly out of fear of what might be in store for her, but mostly because she could not think of anything to say. She could deny everything, but what would be the point? Roberts had clearly been talking, and by her guess, he was a talker. This man obviously was not going to ask pointless questions – he had already said as much.

"What is Mister Lulio to you?" demanded Rodriguez.

Sofia began to smile. She leaned back in the chair; her arms still folded. "Well, what is he to you?" she countered with a newfound confidence. "Or is your job at the Foreign Ministry to track down horny *turistas?*"

"Look," he said in a far softer tone, "I really could care less what you do, or who you do it with." Sitting down across the table from her, he clasped his hands together and continued. "We know you broke the law, and because this is not your first time, it could become rather unpleasant for you. I am prepared to offer you a full amnesty, for this and the past charges, but you need to explain to me how you came to meet Ray Lulio, and how well did you get to know him."

Sofia smiled. "I'll be happy to tell you everything, once you sign something that backs up what you just said."

With that, Rodriguez withdrew a piece of paper and a pen from one of the inside breast pockets of his jacket. Unfolding the paper onto the table, he slid it, and the pen, in front of Sofia. She gave him an icy stare and made no attempt to read it, let alone affix her signature.

"You bastard!" she growled. "You had no intention of showing me this if I hadn't demanded it!"

"Sign it, don't sign it," he snapped "I don't give a shit! You can go to prison…"

As he reached over to pull the paper back towards him, she quickly slammed her hand down on the other side of it to stop him. "I didn't say I wouldn't sign it," she muttered. "Now, what do you want from me?"

*   *   *

Early the next morning, several news cameras were assembled in the media briefing room at the Foreign Ministry where Rodriguez had brought Sofia. As they stepped onto the platform behind the podium, he placed his hand over the microphone and whispered in her ear. "You understand what you need to do, right?"

Sofia said nothing but nodded accordingly.

Rodriguez leaned into the microphone and began to speak.

"Good morning, everyone," he said to the reporters present. "As you are aware, one of our colleagues, Antonio Vasquez, has recently made his way to the United States and declared his intention to seek political asylum.

"As you can appreciate, this situation has been distressing to Senor Vasquez's colleagues here in the Ministry, and among his family. I am joined today by his wife, Marta, who will be giving a brief statement. Senora Vasquez?"

Sofia gingerly took her place behind the microphone. She placed some papers on the podium and attempting to avoid eye contact with the audience, she began to read her statement.

"Thank you, Senor Rodriguez, and my thanks to all of you.

"It has been two weeks since my husband, Antonio, left our home. All of us who love him have been shocked and saddened by his decision to leave our land. My fear is that his decision was based on his desire to give me something he thought I desired.

"I would like to say to all of you, and hopefully to him, that I love him dearly, and want him to know that everything I could ever hope to want in life, I had here with him…Please come home to me, my love."

With that, she stepped aside and allowed Rodriguez to assume the podium. "Thank you, Marta. All of us admire your patriotism and your courage in doing this. We hope that your husband gets your message, and that you will be reunited once again."

Sofia smiled demurely.

Yes - and soon, so I can wring his neck!

Chapter 25

Baker gently tapped on the door that was already half-open. "You wanted to see me?" he asked.

"Come in, Frank," replied the man at the desk – Phil Cantor, the head of the FBI's New York office. "I've got a problem," he continued in a forcibly calm voice.

"Problem, Phil?" asked Baker, in a manner almost expecting some bad news.

"Yes, a problem," replied Cantor. "You see, I have two active cases on my desk here. One tells the story of a guy named Vasquez who defected from the Cuban Foreign Ministry and is being celebrated like some folk hero in Miami. The other is about a missing persons' case, a trader at Tuckner Wass named Ray Lulio who nobody has seen since his boss got arrested on live television a couple of months ago.

"This really shouldn't be a big deal, but I turn on the news channels and hear Vasquez's wife pleading for him to come back to Havana, and I hear Lulio's wife pleading for his return."

Baker sat silently in the chair across from Cantor, waiting for what he knew would come next.

"It's the same fucking guy, isn't it, Frank?"

"Now, Phil, we don't know..." began Baker.

"It's the same fucking guy, Frank!" snapped Cantor. "We don't know how he ended up in Cuba with a wife and a job as a diplomat eight weeks after he was helping screw over senior citizens in Nebraska, but it's the same fucking guy!"

"So, we bring him in," replied Baker.

Cantor smirked. "Bring him in. It's all that simple?" he snarled. "The government of Cuba, and half the city of Miami thinks he's Vasquez, and they're not blinking! In the meantime, I've got this Connie Lulio on every local station in the tristate area claiming he's really her husband. The State Department wants to sort out Vasquez, while the Director is calling me asking why we haven't done anything about the Lulio case!

"It's an election year, and the President is getting one line from the Secretary of State, and another from Homeland Security! Nobody can get to Vasquez, and Mrs. Lulio is telling anybody who'll listen that this office is not being cooperative!"

"Now hold on, Phil. We handled it like any other case. Besides, if he was working at Tuckner Wass, maybe he didn't want to be found."

Cantor looked at Baker without expression. "You're going to Miami, Frank, and you are going to sort this mess out. I am getting it in the neck, and it's going to stop! I want to know how this guy got to Cuba, and why they want him back so much."

"What about the Tuckner Wass stuff?"

"It'll wait. If we nail him on an espionage charge, that other stuff won't matter."

"Fine," sighed Baker, as he turned toward the door. "I'll fly out this afternoon."

The knot in Cantor's face loosened as he resumed reading the file.

"Nothing fancy, Frank," he said in a much calmer tone. "Just get him into custody and try to do it without pissing off half of southern Florida."

Baker nodded and headed out into the hallway. He did not make it ten feet before Thomas stopped him.

"Gotta look at this, Frank," he said.

"No time, "replied Baker, still walking down the hall with Thomas trying to keep up. "I've gotta fly out to Miami today."

"Not before you look at this," insisted Thomas, opening up a folder to reveal two photographs.

"That's our friend in Florida," said Baker. "Who's the other one?"

"Antonio Vasquez. That was taken at the airport when he

arrived in the country."

"Okay," said Baker. "Makes my life a lot easier. Our friend Mister Lulio escaped to Cuba to avoid arrest…"

"He didn't escape to Cuba."

"Then he made it look like he floated in from Cuba."

"No, he came from Cuba all right."

"Okay, he came from Cuba, but he didn't escape to Cuba…How the hell did he get there then?"

"You really want to know?" asked Thomas.

Baker frowned "You're going to say something to piss me off, aren't you…Okay…How did Ray Lulio end up in Cuba?"

"We sent him there."

Baker's eyes glazed over. "We sent him there," he muttered.

"The picture of Lulio, identifying him as Vasquez," explained Thomas, "was taken at Teterboro by INS. The other three people we sent back to Cuba match their entry photos."

Baker was still attempting to get his head around all of this. "You mean that INS didn't check the photos to see if it was the same guy?"

"Well, not this picture."

"Then what picture?" growled Baker. "The one from Lulio's fucking prom night?"

"No, they referenced the picture given to Homeland Security, from when the expulsion order was served, when they were outside their diplomatic compound. Homeland Security uses our agents for that kind of thing."

Baker knew that already, and it irked him a little bit to be given an orientation by a junior agent, but that was small beer compared to everything else. "And who was responsible for that?" he asked, becoming more annoyed at the prospect of this case becoming more convoluted than it already was.

"Fletcher and Ragusa," said Thomas.

Baker moved to sit down on the bench along the wall.

"Please tell me," he said, in an almost forced whisper, "that 'Fletcher and Ragusa' is the name of some law firm I've never heard of, and not the two morons whose desks are ten feet away from yours."

Thomas said nothing. He just stared at Baker with a meek smile.

"Sonofabitch!" yelled Baker. "We sent him to Cuba! We sent an American citizen to Cuba! Jesus, Mary and Joseph…"

"He said he was Vasquez. He lied about who he was," argued Thomas.

"You don't get it, do you?" snarled Baker. "We grabbed a US citizen off the street and deported him to a Communist dictatorship!"

"Obviously, he wanted to go," said Thomas. "He was on the run."

"Sure," said Baker sarcastically, "and that's why he escaped in a giant goddamn hotdog – because he wanted to stay in Cuba…You know, Thomas, it doesn't matter why he lied, or why he went. Shit, it doesn't even matter why he came back! We sent him, and that's all they're going to report on the evening news…You follow me?!"

Thomas left Baker, and the file, in the hall. The agent sat there, asking himself why this could not have happened six months from now, when he was in a boat on Saranac Lake and did not give a damn if the walls of this office caved in on everyone.

Chapter 26

At about ten thirty that night, Baker had finally arrived on the scene, which had all the makings of a side-show carnival. The combination of klieg lights from the camera crews, as well as the spotlights from the helicopters overhead made the street outside the Diaz house as bright as day. *Don't these bastards have a high-speed car chase to cover?*

He saw the Bureau's mobile command trailer parked along a side street around the corner, and dutifully pulled his car in behind. Before he had even had the chance to put the vehicle in park, an agent hurried over to his window, likely to tell him to move off. He pushed the button to lower it with one hand, while holding his badge and identification with the other.

"Frank Baker, with the New York office," he said before the other man had a chance to open his mouth. "Who's the agent in charge here?"

"Bill Corvin. He's in the command center," the agent said matter-of-factly. "We were told that New York had jurisdiction…"

"Is that a problem?" asked Baker, sensing an obvious undercurrent.

"We might not have the resources you have up there, but we can still…"

Baker grimaced. *Of course, they were going to have an attitude. Wouldn't he if another office were horning in on their turf? But that was not his problem. Lulio, or Vasquez, that was his problem, and - professional sympathies aside - he would step on anyone who made his life more complicated than it already was.*

"Okay, now let's get this straight. This guy is either one of two men. If he is Vasquez, then he was deported from New York. If, on the other hand, he's Ray Lulio, he's a missing person from New York, and likely a state's witness for a crime being prosecuted in New York. Are you seeing a pattern here?"

"I'm just saying that we have capable people here," defended the agent.

"Yeah, and if it were up to me, I'd hop on the next plane to JFK and let you guys clean this up…Let's play pretend. I'll pretend I want to be here, and you pretend that you're glad to see me…Okay, now where's Corvin?"

"Over here," the agent frowned, as he led Baker over and up into the trailer.

The command center was housed in a trailer that was larger than the ones they transported horses in, but much smaller than what a full-fledged semi would haul.   The inside was split into two rooms. One functioned as a makeshift control room, with rows of display monitors, telephones, and radio equipment mounted on walls and a desk that could accommodate a dozen people, if need be. Four agents had been assigned to operate this mass of electronics, which allowed real time communications with local law enforcement, first responders, local utilities, and, of course, the New York office - and Washington. The other room was a simple workspace where the main piece of furniture was a large backlit table, where maps, blueprints, and other diagrams could be laid out and painstakingly studied.

It was here that he met Bill Corvin, the senior agent in the Bureau's Miami office.

Baker saw a man in the prime of his career, much where he had been a decade ago. What he did not see was a man who had spent his entire career in south Florida, and everything that had entailed - drug cartels, organized crime, smuggling, and even Medicare fraud. Had Baker taken the time to contemplate what this man had seen - and done - he may have had a better appreciation for how much of an insult it was not to be trusted with a case, like this, right in his own back yard. Then again, as Baker had rationalized, if Corvin had known fully all the ins and outs of the situation, he might have been grateful for having been snubbed.

"Agent Baker," he intoned with the drawn-out cadence of a scolding teacher. "It's good of you to join us."

Oh, no - I'm not letting you take a piss to mark your territory!

"More effort on crowd control and less on sarcasm, and I might have gotten here sooner," he said.

Corvin grimaced. "Well, now that we've got introductions out of the way, can I fill you in on where we're at?"

Baker nodded, and proceeded to listen as Corvin outlined their surveillance, and what had gone on to that point. Privately, Baker was impressed by the work, and wondered why he had to be here, since Corvin had done such a thorough job. That was when he remembered that everything stemmed from a mistake in New York, and Cantor needed his ass covered, and that meant that he had no choice but to put his mark on it all. "Sounds good," he offered. "How soon before we can make an approach?"

"Depends on what you mean by 'approach'?" said Corvin. "Everything we've done is standard. We were told to 'wait for New York' so we did the best we could with the details we had."

"Nothing fancy," assured Baker. "I assume none of them are armed. Just a couple of us, and maybe an escort or two."

"Fifteen minutes soon enough?" asked Corvin.

Baker nodded. "Let's do it then," he said.

On the hour, at eleven o'clock exactly, a squad of SWAT officers from the Miami Dade authorities accompanied Baker and Corvin to the front gate outside the Diaz home. Corvin held back with the men, while Baker walked up the front step and approached the door.

"Mister Diaz, my name is Special Agent Frank Baker. I'm with the FBI. I would like to speak with Senor Vasquez."

"Fuck you, pig!" Diaz yelled through the door. "He's a political refugee."

"Mister Diaz," sighed Baker, "sooner or later, we are going to have to talk to him. Just please open the door and let me in. I'm unarmed and no one else will come in. You have my word."

"Nothin' doin'," came the reply. "This man is a hero in the struggle, and you wanna send him back!"

"Nobody wants to do anything…Look, I've got a warrant to enter your house whether you like it or not. I would prefer that we do this in a cool and calm fashion. I'm sure you would too."

No response.

"Mister Diaz, I said…," continued Baker.

"Go to hell!"

Baker banged his fist on the door furiously. "Now, look," he barked, "I've had less than four hours sleep and my blood sugar's pretty low! If you think I'm going to stand here all goddamn night, you are seriously mistaken!"

A moment of silence passed, and then Diaz yelled back "Then go home and eat a fuckin' chocolate bar!"

Baker felt the rage building up inside. He did not want to be here. Nobody wanted him there, either. And now, this guy was just going to prolong the agony. "All right, you sawed off little prick!" he screamed. "We'll do it my way!" With that, he stormed off down the walkway, almost knocking the front gate off its hinges as he went past.

"So, what's the plan, New York?" asked Corvin slyly, as he flew past. *A little thing like that sets you off, and you're in charge?*

"We're takin' him," he snapped, not stopping for a second. "Call somebody at Public Works. I want his water and his electricity cut."

"Anything else we can do for you?" Corvin asked sarcastically, as he turned and followed Baker to the command center.

"Yeah, call the Mayor and the Police Chief, and get them to do something about the crowd."

"Forget it. Nothing doing. It's an election year, and they're not about to piss off the Cuban community," came the reply.

"Great…just great. And if those people want to tear us apart?" asked Baker.

"Oh, they'll make sure we get out in one piece…no doubt about that," assured Corvin.

"All right," sighed Baker. "My pension was screwed the minute I got off the plane, so let's just get this done."

The two men headed back to the command center. By this time, it had become some dysfunctional beehive, with personnel darting back and forth, sometimes tripping over one another.

"Bill, I have Joe Gutierrez from FPL on the line," the agent said to Corvin, as he held out the telephone receiver.

"Put him on speaker," ordered Baker.

Corvin nodded to the agent, who did just that.

"Hello, Mister Gutierrez? This is Special Agent Frank Baker of the FBI. I'm sure someone has already filled you in on what's going on."

"Yeah, we've heard," said the voice on the other end of the line. "You want the power cut to that house."

"How soon can you do it?"

"That all depends," said Gutierrez.

"Depends?" asked Baker impatiently. "Depends on what? Just cut the power. You'd be able to do it if he was behind a couple of months on his bill!"

Gutierrez chose to ignore the obvious sarcasm. He was a utility grid engineer, and not a cop. His concern was how to do something, and not why it needed to be done. "Well," he explained with a remarkable degree of patience, "I can't get my crews anywhere near that house without a whole lot of trouble. The ones I've already talked to are refusing the call."

"So, you can't do it?" said Baker, making more of an observation than posing a question.

"No, we can cut the power to the house. We just need to throw the breakers at the nearest substation."

"Joe, it's Bill Corvin here. Exactly what are we looking at if we go that way?"

"Uh...Hi, Bill...Yeah, we're probably looking at a mile radius, assuming nothing goes wrong."

"Worst case scenario, Joe. What is it?" continued Corvin.

"Worst case? Well, it creates a power surge elsewhere in the grid. We end up with rolling blackouts as far north as Broward, and west out to Monroe."

"What's the likelihood of that?" interrupted Baker.

"Fairly low," replied Gutierrez, "but I can't rule it out. Of course, after we shut down, it'll take us about an hour to restore power to that part of the grid, or we'll definitely have a power surge. No matter what, some people are going to have some electronics and appliances fried – the ones that down have a surge protector. Normally, that wouldn't be an issue this late at night. Then again, who the hell is sleeping in that neighborhood? So, what do you want me to do?"

Baker bowed his head and began to rub his eyes.

"Hold tight, Joe," said Corvin. "We'll let you know in five, okay?"

He turned to Baker and said, "The Mayor and the Chief need to know what we're planning, and they need time to get their people in place."

Baker felt as though he had been kicked in the stomach. Rather than piloting this case in for a smooth landing, it felt like it was lurching into a death spiral. "Do what you have to," he said to Corvin, in a resigned tone. "I need a coffee."

Corvin turned to one of the junior agents nearby and asked him to escort Baker to where he could get some coffee and a bite to eat. He then resumed the conversation with Gutierrez on how best to cut the power without plunging half of Miami-Dade into a blackout.

Chapter 27

Baker grabbed the Styrofoam cup of black coffee and took a hearty gulp. He thought he would try it that way, thinking that 'straight up' would increase its potency. All it did, though, was to resurrect a gag reflex that had largely lain dormant since his freshman year at college.

He decided that going back to his rental and putting on the air conditioning was preferable to standing around and waiting for two or three levels of bureaucracy to figure out how best to extract one man from one house. The opinions surrounding the delaying this decision were made even more apparent by the members of the SWAT team who, upon the sight of Baker, stopped laughing at whatever it was that they had found so amusing.

Once he had settled his mind and allowed the car's cooling system to overtake the effects of humidity on him, he shut off the ignition and got out. *It's time to see what Corvin's got.* He returned to the command trailer to see a grim-faced Corvin standing with a man who was holding some sort of paper.

"So, are we good to go?" asked Baker, somehow sensing that the answer was going to be no.

"Special Agent Baker, this is Sammy Calderon, the head of a local group called the 'Sons of Jose Marti.' He says he has an injunction stopping any action to detain our friend."

"Agent Baker, I have this," said the man, as he handed the paper to him. "It's a court order issued by Justice Margeson of the 11th Circuit Court..."

"I can see what it is!" snapped Baker. "Do you realize that your friend in there is harboring a fugitive?"

"Yes, of course, but only from a brutal dictator who..."

"Mister Calderon, is it? Well, I don't know who you think you have in there, but he's not Cuban, and he's no refugee."

"Really?" asked Calderon. "And you know who he is?"

"In fact, I do. His name is Ray Lulio, and he's a former stockbroker on Wall Street. The SEC would like to have a chat with him."

Calderon looked at him for a moment, and then began to laugh. "Agent Baker, our people were there the night he came ashore. They checked everything on him - Cuban identification, Cuban clothes, Cuban money, and Cuban rum. I've also spent a lot of time with him. You are clearly confused and mistaken."

"You know, this isn't going to stop us, only slow us down," said Baker.

"I am sorry you feel that way," said Calderon, as he turned to walk away. He then stopped at the door, and said "You know, if I were you, I would view this as an opportunity to save yourself from an enormous mistake."

When Calderon left, Baker turned around to the sight of Corvin and three other agents staring at him.

"So?" asked Corvin. "What the hell are we supposed to do now? Do you know how much overtime we're racking up here? And for what?"

Baker gave a look that seemed to go clear past them and drill into the wall behind. He said nothing for what seemed like an eternity, then he focused back on Corvin's face.

"I came here to get that sonofabitch, and until I have him, we're not done." he said defiantly.

Corvin, though, was equally defiant in his belief that it was all a fool's errand. "I was told to cooperate with you, and I am, but goddamn it, I'm not going to stick my neck out over this...Geez, Baker, I've got to live in this friggin' city!"

Baker knew that he could not push any harder than he had without everything unravelling. He decided that he better take a more conciliatory tone if this was not going to blow up square in his face.

"Bill, look, I'm sorry...Give me twenty-four hours, and we'll have the whole thing wrapped up. I promise…I need some sleep…I can't think right now. In the morning, I'll have a game plan, and I'll guarantee it won't cause you any more grief."

Corvin looked at him, and then sighed "Okay, but I'm pulling out at one minute after midnight. If it doesn't get done by then, that's your problem."

Baker agreed, and the men shook hands to seal the deal.

It was about three o'clock when he left to get some rest, but not before leaving instructions that all positions were to be maintained. By this time, the crowds had died off considerably. Word had gone through the crowd that Calderon had got the courts to shut them down, so many of the loyal following had decided to use the break to go home and get some sleep themselves. This, of course, gave Gutierrez a chance to position a couple of FPL crews in closer proximity to the Diaz house, hopefully avoiding the kind of widespread shutdown he had anticipated.

Baker found a hotel a dozen or so blocks away and checked himself in. He was tired, and it was becoming increasingly impossible to think. The best thing he could possibly do, he concluded, was sleep, shower, and eat. As a peremptory move, he had called and left a message for cantor to explain the situation thus far, but that the delay was all *pro forma*, and that he would get it sorted out before the end of the day.

After a three-hour power nap, a lukewarm shower, and what remained of the continental breakfast being served in the lobby, he got in his car and headed back to the Diaz house.

What am I going to tell Phil when he calls, he asked himself? Cantor would be in the office within the hour and would hear his last update. He would then get a call where his bass would likely round off on him for not having Lulio bound up in a neat little package. *If it weren't for that damn court order…*

It took a couple of more minutes, and three more stop lights, before Baker had his epiphany. He knew what he needed to do to make this work. Just as well, as when Cantor called, he would be ready for him.

Sure enough, at five minutes after nine, his cell phone rang. It was New York. He took a deep breath. *Okay, he here we go.*

"Baker," he answered.

"Frank? It's Phil," came the reply. "Can we talk?"

"Yeah. I'm out of the staging area," he said as he pulled the car over to the side of the street.

"Okay, then…What the fuck is going on?! Why don't you have Lulio?!"

"You got the reports, Phil. Some Cuban group got a district court judge to slap an order on us. We're not even allowed to enter the front yard of the house."

The voice on the other end went quiet for a moment, and then, a sigh.

"Okay, Frank, I got Washington crawling up my asshole, and the only option we have right now is to pack it up…but that's not going to happen, is it."

It was not a question, but a clear statement of intent.

"Well…"

"Is it?!" snapped Cantor.

"No. No, Phil, it isn't… I have a plan, and if it works, I'll have Mister Lulio in custody within twenty-four hours."

"What is it?"

Baker knew he had become the proud owner of this mess, whether he wanted to admit it or not. Nothing to lose, except a pension, but even then, he would not lose it all, and he did squirrel away some money over the years. No, there was nothing to lose. A warm feeling came over him.

"You know, Phil, before I get into that, I just wanted to tell you something."

"Yeah…what's that?"

"You have to be, beyond a doubt, the sorriest sack of shit I have ever had the misfortune to work for."

"What?!"

"You heard me! Now, you little snots made this mess, and I'm the poor bastard that gets to clean it up. Well, the way I see it, you clowns have years in the Bureau to think about, but I'm out the door in four months. If there's any shitstorm from this, it's fallin' on you, you sawed off little prick!"

"Pretty brave talk, Frank, considering how badly I can fuck up your pension!" growled Cantor.

"And I can ask for immunity and testify before the Senate Judiciary Committee, so you're not going to do shit – understand -

because I have you by the balls…Correction…I think you are going to promote me to a higher pay grade, one that's gonna give me the pension that I deserve for babysitting you little ingrates all these years! But, then again, I could just let this whole thing blow up. I'll be sitting in a cabin upstate while all of you are ducking for cover…It's your call."

Dead silence. Cantor knew he was telling the truth.

"Frank," he began slowly, but with purpose, "you better make it right, because if you don't, I'll rip you a new one, and good! I won't go down alone!"

Baker chose to ignore the last comment. "Look," he explained, "the judge issued the order to protect Antonio Vasquez, right?"

"Go on."

"Ray Lulio is not Vasquez. That order is based on a false identity. We prove to the judge that he isn't who he says he is, and the order gets overturned…"

"And we get our man. That's fine, but we need to prove it first."

"Yeah, yeah, I know. It won't be easy, but it can be done."

"Whaddya mean? I'll bring Connie Lulio in to swear an affidavit. Simple enough."

"Phil, then it's just her word against his – and half of southern Florida. It's not enough to prove that he's Lulio. We also have to prove he's not Vasquez."

"How do you propose we do that?"

"Well," explained Baker, "We have a photo of the real Vasquez we got from DHS on his arrival, right. We knew that they sent Lulio in his place, which means…"

"Vasquez is still in New York," answered Cantor.

"Exactly. If you put some surveillance of the Cuban mission, and wait long enough, he'll show himself."

"What makes you think he'll step outside the gates?"

"Come on, Phil – he's a spy. No fucking good to them stuck in there."

"Let me rephrase that, Frank. What makes you think he's going to step outside those gates today?"

Frank remembered the deadline. Past midnight was as good as nothing. "Nothing," he sighed. "I'm rolling the dice on that one."

Cantor's tone changed, having sensed that, once again, he was in control of matters. "I'll put a team on the place this morning," he said.

"Good. That, and Connie Lulio's affidavit should be enough."

"Anything else I can do for you?" asked Cantor, with a hint of sarcasm.

"Yeah, fax everything you get to the Miami office the minute you have it. I'll pay a visit to Judge Margeson."

Baker knew that he would have Connie Lulio's paperwork immediately, but that getting anything on the real Antonio Vasquez would take all day, if even that quick. The odds were that it would come too late. What he did not count on was the fact that fate, having been fickle and aloof to this point, had decided on a change of heart.

The real Vasquez had, in fact, been sneaking in and out of the mission on a regular basis, although he had the good sense to go nowhere near the UN building where he was known well enough. Contrary to Rodriguez's belief that his remaining in New York would prove to be an asset, the Foreign Ministry now saw Vasquez as *persona non grata*. Beyond reading and analyzing the work of others in the mission, he had nothing to do. Just as the Minister had predicted, the government would be subsidizing him to do work there that easily could have been done back in Havana.

The tedium had been getting to him, but not as much as the situation back home. He had received a letter from his wife via the diplomatic pouch demanding to know who these people were – one pretending to be him, and one on television with her boss claiming to be Senora Vasquez. Although Vasquez had attempted to do his best to smooth over the situation without directly referring to either Rodriguez's original plan, or the damage control currently in play, it was not going as he had hoped. Between the self-censorship he exercised, and the redactions made by the Ministry, all she would receive was a letter that said "Trust me... I love you."

Initially, he had been cautioned to keep a low profile until he left. Then, with only a couple of days left before his return, the American washes up on shore, and his trip to Havana becomes postponed indefinitely. Sensing that he would never be able to return, and that if he did, he may be coming home to an empty apartment, Vasquez became rather depressed and maudlin. In the spy business, unfortunately, depression often equals recklessness.

Throughout history, foreign agents have been apprehended for a variety of transgressions – stealing microfilm, hacking government computer networks, or pilfering classified documents. Such is the stuff that feeds Hollywood scriptwriters and best-selling novelists. Antonio Vasquez's 'Achilles' Heel,' however, was another part of his body, and it had given him grief for more years than he could remember. He knew that the only thing that gave him any semblance of relief was almost impossible to obtain back home but was in plentiful supply in America. Whether it was a regular flare up of his condition, or it had been induced by the added stress of the situation, was hard to say. Nevertheless, he was left agonizing, literally, over an itch that he could not scratch. Baker's best hope, and, ultimately, his saving grace, occurred outside a Walgreens, where Antonio Vasquez was caught holding the bag – one full of toilet paper, dandruff shampoo, and several tubes of hemorrhoidal ointment. And so, shortly before noon, Antonio Vasquez – and his assorted toiletries – had been remanded into FBI custody.

Within two hours, he had been brought to the New York office, positively identified, and held under the charge that he had failed to leave the country under the original order. There was the obligatory phone call to the Mission, where the staff, mindful of the need to maintain support for Rodriguez's efforts, promptly declared that Vasquez was in Miami, and that this gentleman they had in their midst was an impostor. It would be one more hour before Connie Lulio would arrive, as she was among those who toiled at what remained of Tuckner Wass, now an over-glorified clerical project for federal regulators building their case against Harold Raphaelson. All she could do was to deny that the man was her husband, but that was enough.

By five that afternoon, the fax machine at the FBI's Miami office began to whirr and spit the pages of documentation that would, hopefully, save the day, and Baker along with it.

While Baker had been keeping vigil at the machine, Corvin and the others were maintaining their position around the Diaz house. While some of the people who had been there the previous day did return, the crowd was noticeably smaller. He had used the intervening time wisely, though. Joe Gutierrez had succeeded in getting a crew in long enough to have installed a remote breaker. Now, if it was necessary, the power could be cut to the house without affecting anyone else. The best part of it was that it could be done by simply throwing a switch from the command trailer.

This, of course, assumed that Baker would be successful in having the order overturned, which was not something he necessarily had faith in.

Justice Howard Margeson was on a break, or rather, recess from an appeals case that he was presiding over. It had been a long day, and he still had to review the day's transcript and measure it against his own notes. They were not his favorite cases to begin with. They were never about right or wrong, but some arcane detail or technicality. Yes, they might be as guilty as sin, but forget to dot an 'i' or cross a 't'. The job of an appeals judge was not to dispense justice, but to determine whether it had been done right the first time.

This was the frame of mind he was in when Baker finally showed up to the office. At first, it seemed as though it was a fool's errand, which was an easy assumption, given the honorable gentleman's disposition. Impatience, however, can often be an ally – especially when it manifests itself in a desire to quickly dispense with the pedantic and the trivial. Also, as Baker did not fully appreciate, an appointed judge does not have the vulnerabilities of one whose current and main preoccupation is re-election. Some have even overcompensated for the overtly political nature of their colleagues by heavily bending the other way. In the end, Baker did not realize how reluctant Margeson had been to issue what he deemed to be a 'partisan' order, and how eager he was to be given an excuse – any excuse – to rescind it.

For thirty minutes, Baker sat in Margeson's chambers, while the judge quietly studied the various documents, and Connie Lulio's affidavit. He looked through them once, then twice, and then placed the photographs of Lulio and the man claiming to be Vasquez side by side. He then placed the picture of Vasquez taken by INS on his entry into the US beside that of the man currently being held by the FBI. Finally, he looked up at Baker.

"You know," he said, taking off his glasses and rubbing the lenses with the end of his necktie, "I hate being made to look like an ass."

Baker did not know Margeson, but he had been in front of judges back in New York, and that kind of open admission never bode well. "I'm sorry, your honor. That wasn't my intention," he apologized.

"Not you...Calderon. He's behind all of this, isn't he?"

So, there's a back story here.

"Actually, sir, it's only my opinion, but I think that he's been played for a fool as well...Not to say that applies to you."

Margeson smiled. "I know what you mean...Agent Baker, I'm a judge. I like to deal with the law. If I wanted to get involved in politics, I would have tried a run for Congress years ago."

"I understand completely, your honor," concurred Baker. "This may be my very last big case, and it certainly not the one I wanted to go out on."

The judge nodded. "Well," he said, "I'm prepared to make it easy for you. I'll rescind the order...You know, if it hadn't been for the proof on Vasquez, I would have had to refuse you."

"I kinda thought so."

"I've had younger cops and agents walk away empty handed over the smallest of details," observed Margeson.

Baker rose from the chair opposite and reached out to shake his hand. "Well, judge," he said, "that's sort of how this whole mess started to begin with."

Margeson gave a knowing grin as he stood, shook Baker's hand, and led him to the door.

"Do you want me to tell Calderon about this?" asked Baker.

"No...leave it with me. He got me out of bed to issue it to begin with. I want the pleasure all for myself,"

Chapter 28

As a child, Ray had often imagined what it would be like to live in the country. When he was ten years old, his parents had enrolled him in a weeklong summer camp in Connecticut. Although he was, at times, terribly homesick, he loved to sleep in the tranquil setting of wooded rural New England. When he had returned, he found it difficult to sleep amid the noise on the street, and the lamps that replicated daytime on the sidewalks below. The move to the house in Queens was a marginal improvement, but insomnia was certainly no stranger to him.

The last couple of days, however, had to have been the worst in his entire life in terms of getting rest. If it was not the steady stream of well-wishers that seemed to come at all hours of the day, it was the cacophony of the crowd out on the street, including the police, who would occasionally bark orders through their bullhorns. The glare of the outside lights had been partially compensated for by the placement of heavy wool blankets over most of the windows of the house. All in all, it still added to his general feeling of disorientation.

Life in the Diaz household was not an easy thing either. As eagerly committed as Manny was to care for, and protect him, his wife was equally committed to seeing Ray dropkicked to the curb like a bag of kitchen scraps. Once the various visitors would leave the house, the fireworks would begin. It reached an imperfect resolution with Missus Diaz calling her husband an insensitive prick, then heading north to Davenport to live with her mother.

For a moment, Ray believed that her absence might improve matters, at least in the respect that she would not be shooting daggers at him every time they made eye contact. Unfortunately, Manny was one of those men who, despite what he told the world, needed someone to keep him firmly on the straight and narrow. Removing her from the equation was like removing the brakes from a speeding car. With no voice of sober moderation, and Manny's better angels on an indefinite sabbatical, Ray could feel the tension building up to the point where his stomach was forming itself into one big and painful gordian knot.

He grabbed a couple of pillows, a blanket, and crawled onto the floor of the closet in the guest room. *Cramped, yes, but pitch black and relatively quiet. If only he could stay in here, undisturbed and unmolested.*

At eleven o'clock, Frank Baker gathered the SWAT team, as well as Corvin's people together for the final brief. "Okay," he said, as he rolled out a blueprint of the Diaz house earlier secured from the city's planning department. "Here's how it's going to go down. Bill, you are going to run communications and handle the power cut."

Corvin nodded, as if only to humor him, while Baker directed his attention to the SWAT team.

"Captain, I need you and your men in position near the gate in the back fence. Have your night vision gear ready."

Baker then took his index finger and drew it across to the area of the diagram that indicated the front of the house. "I am going to go to the front door with a couple of agents – make it look routine. Of course, Diaz is going to stall, but that's fine. At eleven-thirty on the nose, Bill, you're going to cut the electricity to the house, and these gentlemen are going to enter from the back and get inside, locate our man, and get him out, as well as Diaz."

"Where are you going to go when this happens?" asked Corvin.

"Nowhere," answered Baker. "I'm going to keep banging on the door and yelling for him to open up. Once you patch through the 'all clear' signal, I'll make some scene, then leave like I'm pissed."

"Won't the crowd know we took him?" asked one of the agents.

"We turn the lights back on ten minutes after the signal, and we maintain a cordon of the house for another ten. By that time, we have Diaz on his way downtown to a holding cell, and Lulio well on his way to the helipad. Once we get out of Florida, we can release Diaz on account of a lack of evidence, and that's about it."

"And that's it," said Corvin, clearly not impressed by the level of confidence Baker had invested in this latest scheme.

"Yes, that's it," insisted Baker, not exactly sure what point he was trying to make, other than that of a general displeasure of the whole affair thus far. "Why? Do you have something you wanna add?"

"Well," began Corvin, doing his best to keep a lid on his baser emotions, "if you insist. First, you come down here and act like you're running the local office, you have every law enforcement agency in south Florida tied up. We've been sitting here two goddamn days, and if you're plan is off by so much as a minute in timing, we'll have a neighborhood riot on our hands. Now, you say in less than half an hour that will be it."

"Your point being?" asked Baker, determined not to let Corvin get to him – not here, and certainly not now.

"My point is this. Washington gave you the rope, but rest assured, if things go wrong, I'll happily be the one to hang you with it."

Baker shot a glare at him, then managed to recover his voice. "Do it right, and I'll be outta your hair within the hour. What's more, you'll save weeks of paperwork and having to testify at my disciplinary hearing too!"

Ray was half-asleep when he heard the banging at the front door. He struggled to make out what the voice outside was saying. It was nothing more than a muffled drone that oscillated up and down with whatever words were being used. The only thing he could make out with any clarity was the string of profanity spewing from Manny's mouth. Although he could hardly have thought it, it seemed to have become even more vulgar than the night before. For a moment, he wondered what he might do if Manny became completely unhinged.

He tried to tune it out and get some rest, but it was no use. What was the point of all this anyway, he wondered? Calderon had come by that morning to tell them that he had got the courts to block the police from the premises. Didn't he say that they were not even allowed on the property? Why were they at the door? It did not feel right.

Within moments, he heard Manny yell "What the fuck!" He tried to scramble to his feet but fell amid a pile of clothes he had knocked off their wire hangers, some of which fell on his head. He tried to find the doorknob, but the inside of the closet was black, with not even a sliver of light from under the door to give him some frame of reference. His hand pushed on the door and crept up the side, blindly searching once again for the latch. Suddenly, the door swung open, causing Ray, with all his weight leaning forward, to topple out onto the bedroom floor.

As disoriented as someone coming off a weekend bender, he was grabbed and dragged up onto his feet by a couple pairs of mysterious hands. Amid the dark, all he could make out were three sets of glowing green orb-like eyes, and a gruff, guttural voice yelling to "Get up! Move, move, move!"

Throwing what felt like a coat over his head, there was a person on either side of him, running so fast that he struggled to keep up. More than once, he felt his feet give way and his legs buckle. Fear and disorientation had seized his brain. He struggled just to comprehend what was going on, let alone his feelings about it.

Carpet underfoot turned to tile, turned to rough concrete, turned to wet grass. The air had changed, as did the level of noise. There was the swing of a gate with a rusty hinge, and a "hurry, hurry" being barked out. Then, a car door. No, a truck or a van of some sort. Up, and in, and then slam it went.

As he felt the vehicle lurch forward, the shroud was removed from his head. Dazed slightly, he took a moment to focus his eyes on the scene. Three men in military style uniforms – one on either side of him, with another sitting directly across.

"Wha ees going on?" asked Ray, still maintaining his faux accent.

"We know who you are, Mister Lulio," said the one sitting across from him. "The FBI has a lot of questions to ask you."

His heart sank. Finally. There it was. Everything comes to a head eventually. It is always a matter of time. The only question was what would it be? Tuckner Wass? Cuba? Both? Even one was worth at least twenty years or more. He slumped back against the wall of the van. No opportunities to be seen here.

Ray shivered in his t-shirt and trackpants. His travelling companions, bulked down in thick military fatigues and assault equipment, had decided among themselves to turn the vehicle's air conditioning system down as low as it would go. He suspected, though, that this was meant as much as a punishment for him as it was a relief for them. As much as he tried to focus his mind on his current predicament, the cold air distracted him back to the subject of his own personal comforts, and how he would be willing to sell his freedom, such as it was, for a single wool blanket.

The trip seemed to last for hours, not minutes, and the lack of windows deprived him of the ability to visually discern his situation. It made his stomach queasy, and he fought to suppress the bile that was attempting to build in his throat. Before long, however, the van came to a complete stop, and the rear doors were opened onto what looked like a small airport.

To his left, a couple of hundred yards away, he could see a helicopter, a Bell 429, cycling its rotors, its dual Pratt and Whitney engines emitting a high-pitched whine in anticipation of flight. A man was heading toward them from the direction of the aircraft. Ray was able to assume that he was to be placed on the aircraft, and that this person would be his travelling companion. It was made the more obvious to him when he heard the man tell the SWAT officers that he was taking over. It was the voice that was yelling at Diaz from the other side of the front door. It was the FBI.

"You're coming with me," he said to Ray, and taking him by the arm, led him to the helicopter.

Once Ray and his companion were in place, and buckled in the back of the craft, the agent leaned forward to the pilot and his navigator and gave them the word to lift off.

The helicopter raised itself from the ground in a shaky jerk, and turned in place ever so slightly, owing to the torque of the rotor blades. Ray had only been in the air once before, and that was the plane to Havana. The unique characteristics – or idiosyncrasies – of this craft, unnerved him even more, and left him feeling quite vulnerable to the physical forces of velocity and gravity.

No one aboard the craft, including his minder, had acknowledged his presence. They wore large earphone headsets that were connected to some internal communications setup. Ray was the only one who did not have a set to wear. Above the whirr of the jet engine, he could hear the agent shouting questions about the flight, such as arrival time and the weather, as well as his answers to whatever the other two had said, but that was it. No friendly banter, no harsh rejoinders. Nothing at all. The only conversation that Ray was party to happened to be the one going on in his head.

Baker, for his part, was exhausted, and just wanted to get to his destination. He had only been in Ray Lulio's presence for a matter of mere minutes, but this man had been a pain in his ass for the several weeks since his wife had walked into the New York office and declared that her loving husband had disappeared.

Forty minutes into the flight, the pilot's voice came over the radio. "Agent Baker...we're going to need to refuel before we go any further...I am going to route to Homestead."

"How long will it take for us to get it done?" he asked, somewhat frustrated by yet another in a series of delays and annoyances.

"About an hour, sir," replied the pilot, with the typical deference and precision of a military officer.

"Fine," sighed Baker. "Is there a place where we can get out and stretch our legs?"

"There's a pilot's lounge near the helipad. The mess won't be open at this hour, but you'll be able to go in anyway."

"Thanks," muttered Baker.

Within moments, the helicopter swooped lower toward what looked like an airport. Ray could see a large fluorescent yellow circle with a large letter 'H' just a few yards from a high mesh fence topped with razor wire. Once over the spot, the craft hovered just long enough to be almost still in the air, suspended like a hummingbird, then gently descended to the tarmac below. The whine of the engines reverberated off the ground and became a high-pitched squeal that would have deafened Ray if it had not been for the bulky earphones he was wearing.

The spotlights on the surrounding buildings created a shadow of the spinning rotors, which eventually went from an indiscernible blur to thick bands of black. The agent tapped Ray on his shoulder to get his attention, then motioned for him to follow him to the one-story brick building that lie to their left by about thirty yards. Ray nodded, removing his headset and seatbelt.

Without a word, both men climbed out of the helicopter and made their way to the building just as the ground crew was readying the craft for fueling – fastening the ground cable and dragging what looked like a fire hose from a large tank off in the corner.

Once inside, the two men stood alone, along a battery of vending machines. The only noise Ray could hear was the droning buzz of the fluorescent light ballasts in the arrival hall, and the screeching of jet engines, muffled by the thick reinforced glass doors that led out to the tarmac.

"Quiet place, huh?" he observed aloud, trying to break an increasingly awkward silence.

Baker said nothing. He had a passive gaze fixed on Ray but made no attempt to speak.

This situation continued for at least a couple of minutes more, until the obvious tension was becoming too much for Ray. "Aren't you going to say something? Anything?" he snapped.

Baker sneered for a moment. "I would," he sighed, "but I don't speak Spanish, and we don't have a translator."

Ray was not sure what to say next, but Baker's unwavering stare was as much incentive to speak as it was one to remain silent. "I don't suppose you could tell me how my wife is doing," he said.

"Depends on which one, Mister Lulio Vasquez," came the reply, now clearly infused with sarcasm.

"My name's Lulio, not Vasquez," sighed Ray.

"Maybe you should wait for your lawyer before you say that" observed Baker. "I mean, I certainly wouldn't want to deprive you of your rights."

"You know," began Ray, "this hasn't been easy for me either."

"My condolences," Baker muttered.

Both men remained tensely silent for the remaining time, until the co-pilot popped his head in the door and announced that it was time to go.

Now, above the ground, and looking out his window, Ray caught glimpses of the Interstate, the small towns and villages, the gas stations and restaurants that greeted the countless travelers to the south. As familiar as they were to him, on some level they felt as foreign as anything he had seen in Havana or Matanzas. In the dark, all he could see were the things that the moon and the streetlights would reveal. Maybe everything looked a little foreign from a thousand feet in the air. He wondered if God felt the same way when he looked down on it all.

He looked across to Baker, and tried to get his attention, but it was to no avail. Unfortunately, the agent had not interpreted their exchange at Homestead as anything approximating an 'icebreaker.'

Chapter 29

Despite the spartan, antiseptic conditions of the room, it was, by far, the most comfortable and inviting place he had been in for a long time. Ray instinctively knew this was because it was his and his alone. He had only spent the night at Homestead before being transferred to a military facility near Washington.

Although his movements were somewhat restricted to the barracks and its immediate grounds, he could roam anywhere beyond the floor where his quarters lie – provided he had an escort. Even that slight encumbrance was not much of an issue. The guards were, for the most part, relaxed and good natured. Ray reasoned that guarding him in a setting such as this was probably preferable to other places they could have been sent. A few times, he had been able to sit down with them for a game of Texas Hold 'Em – the only variation of poker that he knew how to play. On one occasion, he sat with them in the lounge and caught one of the college basketball games that comprise the 'March Madness' tournament. He had impressed his entourage by winning a friendly wager on the game, although he had only picked the winning squad – Villanova – because it happened to be the maiden name of one of his grandmothers.

Seven days had passed from the time of his arrival at the base to his first official meeting with Baker. During those days, Ray had been blissfully ignorant of the world around him, due mostly to the blocking of access to news channels, newspapers, and the Internet.

The reverse, however, could not be said, and it was the main reason why Baker ordered this cordon sanitaire.

The President, particularly concerned about the direction in which Florida's 29 Electoral College votes would be heading in roughly six months' time, was busy making the circuit throughout the southern part of the state.

While the 'Vasquez Affair,' as it had become known, would have had a relatively short shelf life outside of an election year, it had a growing resonance with voters of all stripes. In some polling, in fact, it was within striking distance of healthcare reform and the economy on the public consciousness.

This was very much to the consternation of political strategists in Washington who had reasoned, and not without merit, that keeping the 'Vasquez' out of the 'Vasquez Affair' would deprive the controversy of the very oxygen it needed to thrive. After a few days of silence and trusting the fates to throw up some new *cause celebre* – like an earthquake, or another grainy video from some terrorist group – would make the whole nonsense a non-starter. Unfortunately, their calculus had omitted an important variable, in the guise of a man with an axe to grind.

Manny Diaz had, because of the raid, become almost as big a deal as his former house guest. Everywhere, people were busying themselves interpreting the import of the action that put the "poor and humble Cuban refugee" into federal custody. Not only was it a breaking of faith with the denizens of Little Havana, but it also marked a threat to the freedom and liberty of all Americans, or so the pundits declared.

Such was the peculiar nature of this situation that Diaz could be standing on a podium with ACLU lawyers on a Tuesday and be feted at a meeting of the NRA on a Thursday. Republican ads spoke of Diaz's "enduring fight against godless Cuban Communism," while Democrats championed him as a compassionate humanitarian who "offered shelter and protection in the proudest traditions of the Republic."

Independents and Libertarians, eager not to be left out in the cold, railed against Washington powerbrokers who "violated the sanctity of the Diaz home, and their basic rights under the Constitution." A few conspiracy-minded individuals surmised that the whole situation did not smell right, and that the handling of the whole Diaz – Vasquez affair was being driven by some ubiquitous conspiracy at the highest levels of the US and Cuban governments, and that all was not as it appeared. Of course, these views were treated with the requisite humiliation and disdain that they deserved. On top of all of that, were the endless newspaper editorials and talk show personalities who waxed on about eminent domain, the rights of asylum seekers, *posse commitatus*, and every other pent-up grievance against Beltway insiders – real or imagined.

Diaz was, however, a simple man of the people, who had no desire for politics or public scrutiny. The only offer that he did take, however, was that of a lifetime supply of meat products, including frankfurters, from a major concern that had wished to feature him, and the Wienermobile, in a series of advertisements, and had booked the participation of both for the following year's Orange Bowl parade.

By far, however, it could be argued that the most satisfied person by all this attention was one Miles Foster, of the New York law firm of Birney, Standish, Fischer, and Stein. Foster had been given a rather high-profile client to defend, the former Chairman of investment bank Tuckner Wass, Hal Raphaelson. Up until the firestorm over the Diaz raid began to dominate the news cycle, the exploits of his client had been front and center in the public's attention. The grand jury had not gone well, and the federal prosecutor's office was playing up the controversy to such an extent that Foster despaired of finding an impartial jury. Now, with Diaz, and that hapless Cuban fellow, Vasquez, supplanting the attention on his client, he had high hopes going into the jury selection process.

The same, however, could not be said of Frank Baker, who knew that every column written, or sound bite recorded on this situation dug his hole a shovelful deeper. He threw down a pile of papers that sat on the table in front of him, and said aloud to himself, "These are the times that try men's souls – the New York Times, the LA Times, the London Times."

A few seconds later, Thomas came into the room. Cantor had insisted on sending another agent once they had arrived at the base, but Baker was offered his pick. Thomas was more than just the best of a bad lot, though. Baker genuinely liked him, and found the young agent perceptive of his likes, dislikes, and general mood.

"Everybody's here, Frank," he said. "Whenever you're ready."

"Cuban guy, too?"

"Yep, he got in this morning," answered Thomas. "He flew into Andrews, and rode down with some of our people, so nobody knows he's here."

"Good," sighed Baker, "everything's else is in the goddamn papers...I want this thing wrapped up today, and right now, I don't give a shit how it happens."

"Well, Phil's going to want..."

"Fuck Phil!" barked Baker. "He sits in his goddamn office yelling this and that, and I'm the one who has to clean up this mess. I'm six months away from retirement, and nothing – and I mean, nothing – is going to screw things up for me. Understand?"

Baker reached inside his jacket pocket and extracted a lighter and a pack of Marlboros. As he placed a cigarette in his mouth and produced a flame, Thomas frowned.

"You know you can't do that in here, Frank. They've got rules," he cautioned.

"Why is it that the world gets worse the more busybodies try to fix it?" growled Baker. "I mean there were fewer assholes around before they banned lead paint and made everybody wear a seatbelt. Well, I'm not giving this one up. I was raised in Virginia and went to Duke. This makes me a friggin' patriot!"

Thomas knew his mentor well enough to change tack. "Okay, okay, Frank...So do you want me to bring in Rodriguez a few minutes before?"

"Who's Rodriguez?"

"The Cuban guy," said Thomas.

"Ahh...no... Don't want to tip our hand," he said. "We know enough of the back story to figure out what happened. I don't need this guy to confuse things any more than they already are."

Thomas looked at Baker with a puzzled expression. "If we know the back story – or think we do – then what's the confusing part?"

Baker walked over to him and placed his hand on Thomas' shoulder. "Getting the genie back into the bottle," he said.

Thomas nodded knowingly and then said, "I'll meet you in the lounge in twenty minutes."

As he left the room, Baker went back to the stack of papers on the desk. *I can't put out this fire. The best I can hope for is a controlled burn.*

His mind turned, as it had a hundred times before, to how something like this could have happened to begin with. Dumb luck meets coincidence meets systemic failure – or stupidity. It would make for a very funny story if it didn't usher in the possibility of a war.

He looked at his watch. Ten more minutes. Ten more minutes and he did not have the slightest idea what he would say or do. Ten minutes to become completely wise and profound. Ten minutes to solve a crisis. Ten minutes to salvage a career that had been hit with a wrecking ball in a matter of days and hours.

*   *   *

Connie stood at the opposite end of the room, staring out the window onto the drifts of snow that blanketed the hard ground. She remembered a field trip she took to Washington in her senior year of high school, and how the cherry blossoms would be so beautiful in a few months.

"Connie," called the voice from the door.

She turned around to see her husband standing there, giving her a meek and tentative smile that was searching for some validation of feeling.

"Don't get me wrong," she said. "I really am glad to see you safe and sound, but I still think you're a bastard."

Ray's face turned to a black expression. "I know you're mad at me, and I'm sorry, but if you knew the whole story…"

"I know the story," she interrupted. "I told you about Hal. You told me not to worry…Well, worry is all I have done for two months."

Ray was about to respond, but Connie turned her attention back to the goings-on outside the window. "Please leave," she said, without any hint of emotion in her voice.

He apologized again, but no response was elicited. The one thing that he was craving more than anything else – absolution – was being withheld. It did not matter whether it was out of spite, or a desire not to indulge this dark mood of his. It wounded as much as a fierce punch to the solar plexus.

"I'm sorry, Connie," he repeated, not able to come up with

anything more compelling than this feeble *mea culpa*. "For what it's worth, I never betrayed you…Maybe I was stupid – and scared - but I wasn't dishonest, or disloyal…You can believe whatever you want, but I'm telling you the truth."

She said nothing, nor did she turn around to face him, for fear of letting him see her holding back her tears.

"I guess I'll see you with the others," he said in a muted tone, as he turned and walked back out into the corridor.

Within a few minutes everyone was gathered in a large lounge area. Ray thought it looked like the recreation room in a psychiatric hospital, like in the movies. At one end stood a large wooden table surrounded by a dozen vinyl clad chrome chairs.

Agent Baker gestured for everyone to take a seat.

"Ladies and gentlemen," he began, as he sat down, "I think that all of us can agree on two things."

"What would they be?" asked Rodriguez.

"None of us want to be here, and none of us want to deal with the consequences of getting this wrong."

Everyone muttered their agreement, until Connie fired back, "It's a little too late for that. Our family's gone through hell…"

"You tell them, honey…," said Ray.

"Oh, shut up," she hissed as she turned to her husband. "You're as bad as they are. Even worse – parading around with your little whore!"

"Who are you calling a whore?!" demanded Sofia. "I didn't ask for any of this! Do you think I invited him into my home?!"

"Well, actually you did," corrected Ray.

"Oh, shut up!" yelled Sofia.

"All of you can shut up!" yelled Baker. "You can sort out Mister Lulio's sex life on your own time – after we figure out how to resolve this situation."

"Agreed," said Rodriguez, to this point able to conceal his own irritation.

"Thank you," replied Baker. "After all, we are losing sight of the main issue, that of the kidnapping of a US citizen by Cuban authorities…"

"You mean the illegal deportation of a US citizen to Cuba by your authorities," corrected Rodriguez.

Baker shook his head. "I beg to differ, Senor Rodriguez. The

government of the United States does not simply grab people off
the street and ship them off to Cuba!"

Everyone at the table stared at Baker in complete silence.

"You all know very well what I am talking about!" he argued.
"Mister Lulio still hasn't explained why he was found with Cuban
nationals and did not try to identify himself."

"Because I didn't want to go back to my office," explained
Ray.

"Back to your office," sighed Baker "And for the record, why
would that be?"

"Because the NYPD was raiding it, and I didn't want to stick
around."

Connie leaned into Baker. "We have extra chairs if you want
to invite the SEC," she smirked.

Baker slowly lurched back, and with a heavy sigh, slumped in
his chair.

"Mister Lulio," he said, "this is, by far, the biggest mess I
have ever had to deal with – and that includes people trying to sell
nuclear secrets to tinpot dictatorships…No offense, Senor
Rodriguez."

"None taken," smiled Rodriguez, clearly enjoying Baker's
agitated state.

"There are three things that are holding me back from taking
you out behind and shooting you – the media hounds at the front
gate, the politicians pimping for votes, and my goddamn pension!"

Ray finally could not bear to be silent.

"Agent Baker," he interjected, "you were the people who sent
me to Havana." Then turning to Rodriguez, he said, "And you, you
were the people who didn't give me any choice."

"That is a bit simplistic, Mr. Lulio," defended Rodriguez.

"Is it?" asked Ray. "Is it, really? I mean are you people mad at
me, or the fact that neither of you can lay the blame on me without
taking it on the chin yourself. Now, I don't pretend to be an
innocent man. My crime was selling those penny stocks to some
granny in Tulsa. I accept that. But you committed a crime in
coercing me to go to Cuba, and you people committed one by
letting them do it.

"Agent Baker, you and Senor Rodriguez can keep blaming
each other, and blaming me, but that's not going to make all those

news crews at the gate pack up and go home."

"By the way," he added, turning to his wife, "I never had sex with Sofia. I may have committed fraud, and I may have acted like a pimp, but I never broke my vows to you."

Connie sat expressionless, only for the fact that she could not believe that this was her husband's justification for his behavior.

"Very touching," Baker said sardonically. "I think I saw that on a rerun of 'The Waltons.'. But let me rain on your parade a little bit. When our agents asked you to identify yourself, you let them believe you were Vasquez. You were outside the Mission, so Senor Rodriguez here had no power to detain you. You could have told the truth, but you didn't. Now, I'm not a legal expert, but I've been in the Bureau long enough to know that pulling the wool over the eyes of a cop doesn't make you innocent."

"Well," sighed Ray, with more than a hint of defiance in his voice, "we could play it that way – that is, if you're prepared for the fallout."

"You sound like a man who has everything to gain and nothing to lose," observed Rodriguez.

"No," said Ray, "I could lose my freedom. Then again, I lost it the day I met you, so the worst you can do to me is more of the same crap.

"But this isn't about me – or any of us – anymore. It's about everybody in the US and in Cuba who have been following this. It's about elections, and careers…Yes, I've had a lot of time to think, and read. I know what cards I'm holding, and I'm pretty sure I know what both of you have too."

"You, on the other hand, could become responsible for a war that makes the Bay of Pigs look like a beach party. And you, Agent Baker, will be an interesting footnote in the biggest political scandal since Watergate. How much will your pension be then?"

"You're not in a position to make threats," said Baker. "And you're not quite an innocent in all of this."

"And neither are you. None of you are," replied Ray. "Besides, I'm not interested in threats."

"What are you interested in?" asked Rodriguez.

Ray paused for a moment; all eyes focused on him.

Now, it seemed all so obvious.

"An opportunity," he said with a broad grin. "I see the

opportunity, and I intend to be the opportunity."

Baker and Rodriguez found themselves looking to each other for some sign of validation or help. "What the fuck is that supposed to mean?!" asked Baker.

"An opportunity for all three of us to walk away from this," said Ray. "I'll tell you if you give me a chance."

Baker stared at Ray for a moment. He began to squint and frown, before turning to Sofia and Connie. "Ladies," he said, "could you please wait for us in the other room?"

Sofia looked at Rodriguez, who nodded his approval at the suggestion. The military police that had been standing by the entrance had come forward to escort the women out of the room.

Once the door closed behind them, Baker directed his attention back to Ray and said tersely "Talk."

"We three are tied at the hips," continued Ray. "One goes down, and we all go. Nobody beyond this base gives a shit whether any of us walks away. I suspect they'd prefer we didn't so their asses are covered. Now, I have no desire to drown, or to pull either of you with me. So, I have a modest proposal that will be good for all of us…You know all about those - don't you, Senor."

Rodriguez smiled with a begrudging admiration. "We are waiting, Senor Lulio," he said. "Let's hear it."

Ray then proceeded to explain his grand strategy – one where, with some luck, no one would walk away chewed up by the whole affair. Yes, it was possible that each of them could come out of this whole mess with nary a scratch.

He knew that when he talked about consequences for Cuba and the United States, he was really talking about Rodriguez and Baker. They were both clearly identified as their nation's respective scapegoats should things take a turn for the worse. Ray also understood that given the past couple of months, neither one of these men was feeling particularly selfless and patriotic. Neither one seemed prepared to take a bullet for the team – at least, not any longer.

The plan had its roots in the time Ray had spent in seclusion on the base, walking the barrack halls, reading, and watching sports with his minders. He had discovered a word – a concept – even more powerful than opportunity. It was called strategy. Order from the randomness of chaos. Military bases served military personnel for military purposes. The only books, therefore, that were available to read, had clear martial overtones. After first devouring Sun Tzu's "The Art of War", he burned voraciously through Machiavelli's "Prince." By the day of the big tete-a-tete, he had already gone a couple of chapters into Von Clausewitz. Whether Baker and Rodriguez realized it or not, they did not have much of a chance.

It had only taken twenty minutes or so for the three men to sort out what Baker euphemistically referred to as their 'game plan.' Connie and Sofia had been sitting in the hallway, waiting patiently for this side conference to break. It was not a comfortable situation for either woman. As the only seating was a long wooden bench, they were forced by circumstance to sit beside one another.

No eye contact was ever made, no acknowledgement of either one's presence was put forth. Both sat silently, if not, nervously.

It was only when the men had left the room and ventured out into the hallway that Sofia said to Connie, still without turning her head, "You know, he still loves you."

Connie displayed a kind of grimaced smile and answered, "I know – but he's still a jackass."

Sofia smiled. "Yes – yes he is," she nodded.

Within a few minutes, the hallway had cleared. Everyone had gone – except for Ray and Connie. Nothing was said until Connie finally remarked "We need to set some things straight."

Whether it was a sense that he had finally achieved the upper hand in this whole mess, or that he finally felt empowered by what had just transpired, Ray's demeanor was noticeably different. "I agree," he replied, with as much dispassion as she had ever heard in his voice about anything.

"I think that you need to level with me about everything, and I mean everything. You have no idea what I went through."

"Funny. I could say the same thing," he said.

This display of aloof disconnect was not helping to smooth over the apparent roughness, and Connie was doing her best not to repeat the more emotional rejoinders of the day. "Regardless," she observed purposefully, "I think you'll agree that this whole situation was largely of your own doing."

Ray looked her in the eyes with dispassion. "To be quite honest, I don't really care what people think anymore. I've heard it all – I'm a hero, I'm a bum. You know something? I'm none of those things. I'm done listening to what all of you think of me. None of you have ever got it right anyway."

Connie felt stung. "You don't even care what I think?" she asked, more surprised than hurt.

Ray paused briefly to consider his words – a practice to which he had concluded was missing thus far in his life. "Honestly, I don't know. For what it's worth, though, I do care what you feel – that hasn't changed."

"So…what do you know?" she asked, hoping for some glimpse into the workings of his mind.

"I think…I think that everybody is looking out for themselves, and I'm making a big mistake if I don't do the same."

Chapter 30

Together they walked down the driveway to the front gate of the base – all except Connie. The throng of reporters rushed up to the makeshift podium where Agent Baker approached to speak.

"Ladies and gentlemen, I would like to introduce Senor Raul Rodriguez, representing the Foreign Ministry of the Republic of Cuba, who will be giving a prepared statement. We will not be taking any questions. Senor Rodriguez…"

"Thank you, Mister Baker. People of Cuba, and of America, on behalf of my colleague, Senor Antonio Vasquez, we wish to thank you for your patience and your concern.

"Throughout this situation, there have been several media reports surrounding Senor Vasquez, namely that he is - in fact - an American. I would point out that Senor Vasquez has never, himself, asserted such an identity, and that given the current situation between our two nations, it would be highly unlikely that a US citizen – documented or otherwise – would have been allowed entry to Cuba to begin with.

"After meeting with Missus Lulio, the matter of Senor Vasquez' identity has been resolved to everyone's full satisfaction. Senor Vasquez bears some resemblance to her missing husband, and after weeks of frantically searching for him, she believes that this hope had clouded her judgment. On behalf of my government, I wish to offer our deepest regrets at her disappointment, and we hope for her husband's safe return. It is for these reasons that she has declined to join us here, and we hope that you will respect her request for privacy as she deals with this disappointment.

"After some time for rest and personal reflection – and in no way encouraged by either government – Senor Vasquez has decided to return to Cuba..."

The crowd was overcome with a cacophony of gasps, groans, and whispers.

"Senor Vasquez made his journey to Florida in the hope that he might be able to establish a home for his wife, who has admitted to wanting to come to this country.

"Over the past week, it has become clear that his actions were done out of love and loyalty to Senora Vasquez, rather than any desire on his part to leave his homeland. For this, he was prepared to sacrifice his career and status in the Foreign Ministry. Senor Vasquez has appreciated the kindness and generosity of the American people, but now realizes that the place he is happiest is home in Cuba.

"Given the popular support for the Vasquezes, as well as in the interest of fostering a dialogue between our peoples, I have been instructed by the Office of the President to offer Senor Vasquez his prior office and status in the Cuban Foreign Ministry without condition. I am also instructed to offer Senora Vasquez the choice to either return with her husband, or to remain in the United States.

"Despite the outstanding differences between our two countries, this situation is about people, and matters of the heart. It is in that spirit that the Governments of the United States and of Cuba have put politics aside for the sake of these people. Thank you."

At that moment, the throng of reporters began to shout questions at Ray.

"Mister Vasquez, Mister Vasquez...Is it true? Is it true what he said?"

Ray gingerly stepped up to the microphone, leaned in, and in his thickest Spanish accent, uttered his first, last, and only word of the press conference.

"*Sí*."

*   *   *

The arrangements had been set for late in the afternoon. As an added precaution, Ray was accompanied by his 'wife' to the base's airstrip for a final heartfelt farewell. Unrequited love, sacrifice, duty – such were the overtones of the coverage of his departure. Not wanting any other narrative to encroach on the event, all involved had agreed to make the whole scene public – very public. The people of two nations demanded closure, and that is what they were going to get.

Ray and Sofia walked out of the terminal doors and out toward the Gulfstream parked a dozen yards away. As they walked toward the plane, the crowds lined up along the fences began to yell and shout. Some began to wave homemade signs and placards in both English and Spanish.

"You know, I don't know how I would have made it there without you," said Ray, as he waved toward the crowd. "I'm sorry about all the trouble I caused your uncle…"

"Just shut up and give me a hug. There are cameras over there," replied Sofia, giving him an affectionate embrace. "Orlando will be better than fine. Now, I can send him money every month, which should take care of him fine. Besides, something tells me that you make your own luck. We all do – him, and me. You just have to be smart enough to see your chance."

"Well," he answered, giving her a gentle kiss on the cheek," that may be, but I'd be lying if I said I didn't have my doubts."

"Shame on you," she chided. "You're the one who convinced me. I wouldn't have done half the things I did these past few weeks had it not been for you!"

"You sound like somebody who's seen Robin St. John Roberts in action," he said.

"Oh, I've seen your Mr. Roberts," she giggled. "I didn't find him half as motivational as you did! Now quit wasting time and get on that plane!"

Ray dutifully picked up his travel bag and headed to the jet, but not before stopping one last time and turning around.

"So, what are you going to do?" he asked. "It's a big country, and we do things differently here."

"More people, and more money, but not so different," she remarked. "Don't worry about me. Sofia Avecado always lands on her feet."

Ray smiled and turned back toward the plane again. He knew

she was right, and that after years of fending for herself under all those constraints, she would have a field day making it three. After one last glance, he climbed the steps into the fuselage of the jet. Once inside he set his bag in the storage area, and then sat down in one of the plush leather bucket seats, breathing a heavy sigh of relief.

"So, I hope you're going to show me around. You were down there long enough," the voice came from the back.

"We're only there for two weeks, Connie. I doubt they'll even let us go into the city. We do have to keep a low profile, you know," he said, turning to his wife who had boarded the plane from Andrews – away from the prying eyes of the press and onlookers.

"Like anyone down there will know who we are," she answered. "Are you sure they transferred the money?"

Ray pulled out an ATM card. "I checked it before I got here - $500,000 like the man promised."

"They should have paid interest, for the hell they put us through," protested Connie.

"Well, the feds pulled the charges, the vacation is free, and the Cubans are paying ten times what he Rodriguez originally offered," argued Ray. "The very least we can do is pay for the rum and cigars."

Connie leaned over and gave Ray a tender kiss. "I'm sorry I ever doubted you," she purred. "It hasn't been easy for me either."

"I know. You've been through a lot, and I know I've been the cause. Hopefully, this money will get us started in a new life. Anyway, when we get down there, I'm going to show you something Sofia taught me in Cuba," said Ray.

Connie's face flushed. "What could you possibly learn from her?!"

Ray laughed. "How to make a killer Piña Colada!"

Chapter 31

"And so, we flew to Cuba, then to Canada, rented a car, and drove back here. Took the money and set up a nice office for me and Connie. The Cubans send me money to invest, and I make a good cut. I handle other clients, like the ones Moreton used to go after, but I only invest them in blue chips, and I don't charge much of a commission. I still make a decent amount, but I leave them better off. Got this car and a nice apartment on the Upper East Side. Nobody gets in my way. In a couple of years, I might start up my own hedge fund.

"And the best thing about it is that I don't have to worry about the SEC or anything. The government doesn't want to talk about what happened.

"I suppose I could have tried to get a deal to pay taxes, but I want to do my share, you know, support the schools and stuff – give back to the community."

It took a few moments after Ray stopped talking before the newspaper vendor reacted. "So, that's your story?" he asked.

"Yes -that's pretty much it."

Portillo grinned for a moment, and then he began to laugh and point at Ray.

"Ahhh…That's a good one! You had me going for a while. You should write those things down. Somebody'll pay you good money for them!"

"It's true…honest," replied Ray. "I didn't make up a word of it."

Portillo raised his one eyebrow and cast a slightly jaundiced look toward him. "You sound like a guy I once read – Descartes. He said, 'I think, therefore I am'."

"Sounds like a pretty smart guy," observed Ray.

"Not really. Thinking that I'm a bird ain't gonna make me sprout feathers and fly around, is it?"

"Well, no…"

"So, thinking something ain't gonna make it so."

"Well, not all of the time," defended Ray.

"Right," said Portillo, as he picked up a dog-eared paperback that was the current focus of his reading. "Do ya see this one? This guy, Hume, he lived in Scotland a couple of hundred years ago. Do ya know what he said?"

"Not a clue," intoned Ray, pretty sure that whatever it was, it was not going to run in his favor.

"He said that if you can't prove it – ya know, like see it, measure it, count it – then it's probably bullshit. I like him much better than the French guy."

Ray grinned as he shook his head. "Believe what you want," he said, "but that's my story straight up."

"If that's true – and I'm not sayin' I believe you – then everything you've got is nothin' but a con."

"No," corrected Ray, "not a con. Not at all. You don't get it. It's about believing in yourself. No matter what happened to me, I always believed two things – that I could be a success, and that I deserved that success."

Portillo shook his head dismissively. "Yeah, yeah – nobody earns, but everybody deserves," he quipped. "Well, I believe I deserve to get paid for that paper you're holdin'."

Ray nodded, pulled out a fifty-dollar bill and smiled.

"Keep the change."